MUSKEG
A NOVEL

CALUMET EDITIONS

Minneapolis

First Edition July 2022
Muskeg. Copyright © 2022 by Carla J. Hagen.
All rights reserved.

No parts of this book may be used or reproduced by any means, graphic, electronic, or mechanical, including photocopying, recording, taping or by any information storage retrieval system, without the written permission of the publisher except in the case of brief quotations embodied in critical articles and reviews.

This is a work of fiction. All of the characters, names, incidents, organizations, and dialogue are either the products of the author's imagination or are used fictitiously.

Printed in the United States of America.
10 9 8 7 6 5 4 3 2 1

ISBN: 978-1-950743-85-8

Map drawn by John and LuAnn Hagen
Cover design by Kelly Grady
Book design by Gary Lindberg

MUSKEG
A NOVEL

CARLA J. HAGEN

CALUMET EDITIONS
Minneapolis

Muskeg (from Cree *maskek* and Ojibwe *mashkiig*, meaning "grassy bog") is a type of northern landscape characterized by a wet environment, vegetation and peat deposits. Chiefly used in North America, the term muskeg escapes precise scientific definition. It encompasses various types of wetlands found in the boreal zone, including bogs, fens, swamps and mires. In Canada, muskeg and other peatlands cover up to 1.2 million km2 or 12 percent of the country's surface.

    J. Terasmae, *The Canadian Encyclopedia*, February 7, 2006

Also by Carla J. Hagen

Hand Me Down My Walking Cane

For my brothers, John Hagen and Greg Hagen

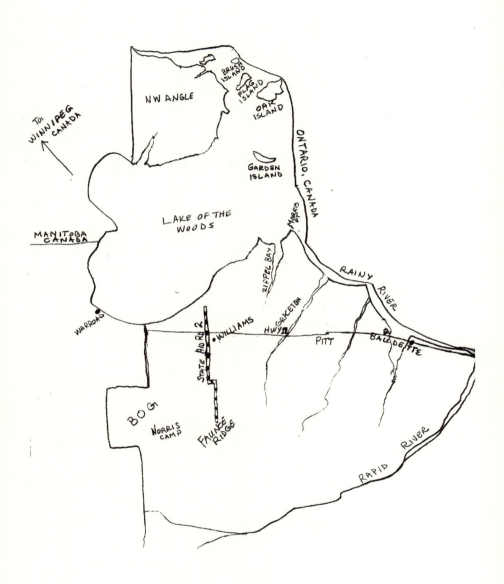

Chapter One

Hazel: Savannah, July 1922

Late night on the Fourth of July. Theda led Hazel through back streets to an alley thick with bamboo and trees draped in Spanish moss. Facing a vine-covered wall, Theda pushed her finger through the leaves, and Hazel heard a bell ring somewhere inside.

A deep female voice said, "Who goes there?"

"Two travelers in need of food and drink," Theda replied.

"Why then, come on in," said the voice, and a door swung open. Like magic, even though Hazel knew there were plenty of speakeasies in Savannah. The town had always been wet. People might put on airs about being descended straight from the Brits, but they lived to have a good time like the Spanish and French they pretended had nothing to do with them.

The place could have been a boxcar or an old shed, some building no one paid much attention to. The perfect spot for a hidden club. A tiny stage at one end where two Negro musicians played "The Saint Louis Blues" on clarinet and piano. God knows how they got it in there. At the other end, a kitchen with one stove and a cook frying shrimp. In between, about a dozen round tables around a tiny dance floor with a few couples, at first glance, men and women. She noticed a man in a tuxedo with the prettiest face she'd ever seen dancing close with a girl in a floaty, short flapper dress. When the song ended and the couple returned to their seats, Hazel could see that breasts curved the top of the jacket.

She nudged Theda. "Look."

Theda laughed. "So?"

"You been here before?" Hazel asked.

"This and some other ones. Only places girls like us can really have fun." She smiled. "'Cept your diner, maybe, after all the customers leave."

Hazel's face got hot. She admired how free Theda was in talking about these things but couldn't imagine doing it herself. She'd spent too many years trying to blend in.

A waitress with bobbed hair came up to their table. "What's your pleasure, ladies?"

"Why whiskey, of course, the house special," Theda said with a smile.

"Sure thing." The waitress winked at her.

"She's flirting with you," Hazel whispered after she left.

"Are you jealous?" Theda said. "No need. My heart is yours, Miss Hazel."

The whiskey arrived, and Theda raised her glass. "Here's to us, darlin'."

Hazel toasted but felt a catch in her throat. She wanted to feel relaxed and happy, but she didn't.

She took another sip and glanced around to make sure people weren't looking at them. Hard to break old habits. But nobody was paying attention. So she took in the room. Clinking glasses, murmur of voices, notes from the piano and clarinet, smell of seafood and perfume. The soft chair she would have sunk into if she hadn't been so antsy. She realized that the dancers, the people sitting at the tables, everyone in the kitchen and the bar were women. Some dressed as men, with hair cropped or pulled back. Others in short dresses that clung to their bodies and left their legs free. The musicians were the only men. And pretty much everyone smoked. Between the steam from frying shrimp and the cigarette haze, you could barely see. At the next table, one woman sat on another woman's lap, arms wrapped around each other, kissing passionately.

"See?" Theda said. "We're not the only ones."

But instead of relief, Hazel felt fear trickle down her spine. All her life she'd hidden who she was. Now in this nightclub of women, she felt naked, like the things that kept her safe had flown away: the diner, the creek, Milt, the daily specials, all her brothers and sisters. She was just an odd girl, as the papers called them, and the only one who knew her was Theda.

"Let's go somewhere else," she said. "Place makes me nervous."

"We just got here!" Theda placed her hand over Hazel's. "There are spots like this all over. New York, Paris, San Francisco."

Hazel marveled at her young, shining face. "Yes, but we're in Savannah."

"We could run away!" Theda said. "Live together where no one knows us."

"How about the diner? And Milt?"

Theda looked at her through thick lashes. "Milt's a swell guy. Maybe he'd let you get divorced."

Hazel didn't even know anyone who was divorced. Rich people did it, or so she heard, but they lived in a different world. Besides, she didn't want to divorce Milt. He was her best friend, the only one in the world who understood all the parts of her. "Why on earth would I do that?" She had no desire to plunge into a world she didn't know. "I never been to those places. I never been anywhere but here."

Couldn't they stay in Savannah? Couldn't Theda keep coming to the diner? Milt wasn't around that much, and she never asked him why, just as he never asked her what she did when he wasn't there. The H&M was a haven, and she loved it even more now that Theda was part of it. She'd never felt so warm and safe. And loved. She didn't want to think of changing anything right now.

She took Theda's hand. "Let's dance."

They got to their feet, and Theda giggled. "All right, who's going to lead?"

"You," Hazel said. "I'll follow."

I can't eat a thing, the piano player sang, as the clarinet wove a melody over and under him, *got those crazy blues...*

Hazel lay her head on Theda's shoulder, breathing in clean dress and warm skin. "Let's dance all night," she whispered. "Let's not sit down." Theda turned up Hazel's face, and they kissed right in front of all those people. Who weren't watching anyway. Four, five, six, who knows how many songs they danced to, swaying together, Hazel's eyes closed, Theda's body pressed against hers. Notes vibrated through her to the ends of her fingers, the dance floor just big enough for the two of them. No, not the dance floor, the little bubble that held them. Which she wanted to stay in forever.

Sometime later, maybe hours, maybe less, Hazel heard a sound, like the beat of the music, but louder. Like a drum. Against the door. *Go away,* she thought. But the beat turned into pounding, and it would not stop. She opened her eyes. Theda still held her, but the noise grew louder and louder, and then people started to scream *raid, raid!* The door bent inward like rubber, although she was sure it was made of wood. Then a foot in a black boot kicked through it and hung there, like a magic trick in a theater. She laughed, but Theda hushed her.

"We've got to get out of here. Now."

Hazel's belly turned to ice. "How?"

"Has to be a back way."

Hazel grabbed her hand. "I spotted one when we came in. Beside the kitchen."

They could barely move through the mass of women, all trying to escape.

Then the door with the boot crashed onto the dance floor, and the place filled with policemen. Earsplitting whistles. "Nobody leaves!"

The cops in front went straight for the two Negro musicians, grabbed the clarinet and threw it across the room. Others took their clubs to the piano while their companions grabbed the two men and started beating them.

"Here's our chance," Hazel said, pulling Theda toward the other door.

But the cops were bashing their way through the room, and they were going fast. Tables overturned. Glass shattered. Wood splintered. Screams. By the time Hazel and Theda elbowed their way to the back door, billy clubs blocked their way.

"Come on, let's go back," Theda said. "Maybe there's a chance…"

But they froze, smack up against the table of the woman in the tuxedo with cops surrounding her. They'd yanked her up by the shirt, had her dangling in the air, face bright red.

"You're choking her!" Hazel yelled.

"She wants to be a man, she can take it," the cop said.

Another turned to them. "What we got here? One with a big mouth—and a *pretty* one." He took his nightstick, ran it across Theda's chest, then put out his hand and stroked her face. "I can tell you just ain't found the right man yet," he said. His fingers grazed her mouth, just long enough for Theda to sink her teeth into them.

He jumped back. "Whore!" he yelled. His long arm and fist knocked Theda to the floor. Blood ran from her nose onto her dress.

Flames of rage climbed in Hazel's body. Any minute she'd catch fire. But first, she would punish him, kill him if she could. She jumped on the cop, jammed her thumbs into his eyes. "You miserable son of a bitch!"

He screamed, and for a minute, maybe a second, she felt pure joy. Then a crack on her head that reverberated through her body and a pain so big it swallowed everything.

* * *

Something moved and bumped under her, and every time it did, her head hurt worse. It was dark, her lips were dry and she was thirsty. Moaning all around. Her head rested on something soft. A lap. A sound came out of her mouth.

Then two hands on her head. "Hazel."

"Theda?" she whispered.

"Yes," said the voice. "I've got you."

"Are we in purgatory?"

"No, darlin'. In the paddy wagon on our way downtown."

Then the world went dark again.

She had snatches of memory, like bits of a dream. Stumbling out of the wagon. Camera flashes. *Look this way!* Someone grabbing her arm and walking her down a long hall that stunk of old cigarettes and urine and feces and vomit all mixed together in a big cloud that made her choke. Then some kind of room with no place to sit down. Theda's voice saying, "Give her the bench. The coppers knocked her out, and she's bleeding." Then she was lying on something hard and must've blacked out again.

*　*　*

The next day, maybe the day after, the cell door opened, and she and the other women moved together like a long, slow centipede down a hallway. Hazel heard their feet, *shshsh,* as they lurched up to another hallway she prayed was the last. No one talked except the guards, who nudged them along. *C'mon now. Don't be draggin' your feet. Ain't got all day.* The words blurred with the shuffling feet. Where was Theda? Had they taken her away?

People lined the hall, but she couldn't tell who they were and didn't care to look. Cameras like giant eyes pointed at them.

"Got something to say?"

"Over here!"

"*Vultures*!" someone behind her hissed.

Hazel turned to see Theda, dress torn, nose swollen, eye purple and black. They squeezed hands and moved with the others toward wide doors that swung open into a large courtroom. Every seat was full, but it didn't matter because they were not going to be sitting down. The guards pushed them to the front, where a judge with white hair and a dusty black robe sat up on a dais. Like a preacher, Hazel thought, with a very large pulpit.

"Bailiff, read the charges," he said.

A man in what looked like another police uniform stepped forward with a big sheet of paper. "Imbibing in an illegal establishment, disturbing the peace..."

"Anything else?" the judge asked.

"Battery of a policeman, two counts."

He frowned. "Let's hear those first. Read the names of the accused."

"Theda Alexander and Hazel Goodwin."

"Step to the front," the judge said, scowling down at them. "Those are serious crimes. What kind of girls are you?" Laughter rippled through the room. He banged his gavel. "Bail in the amount of three hundred apiece."

Hazel gasped. She and Milt could never come up with that kind of money.

He leaned over the bench. "You're lucky. If you were men, I'd be holding you without bond."

"All right," he continued. "Everyone else up here. You heard the charges: disturbing the peace. Imbibing in an illegal house. Guess real ladies are a thing of the past. You're coming back to this courtroom a week from today. Fifty dollars on each of you."

He turned to Hazel and Theda. "That means seven hundred for you two, three hundred fifty each. And you better have a lawyer when you come back. You're going to need one."

The guards marched them back the way they came but took her and Theda to a cell by themselves. One pulled out a newspaper. "See?" he leered. "You girls made the headlines." PERVERTED SPEAKEASY BUSTED UP ON NATIONAL HOLIDAY! WOMEN DRESSED LIKE MEN!

Hazel sank down on the bench, closed her eyes and leaned her head against the cool wall. She wondered if her family had seen the papers. Her customers. Milt. "What am I going to do?" she muttered. "What the hell am I going to do?"

"Hazel," Theda said, "I got us into this, and I intend to get us out."

Hazel opened her eyes. "Too late for that, baby. The H&M—it's over. I'll never be able to make a living in this town again. And God knows what that judge will do to us. Send us to the big house, maybe."

"No." Theda's voice was hard and decided, even though the black and purple eye made her look like a clown. "We're not going to the big house or the cooler or the hoosegow or anyplace else. Look, one thing I know—money can buy you out of a lot of trouble. And my family's got more than they know what to do with. They're going to put up our bail and give us a lawyer, and we're getting the hell out of here."

Hazel sighed. Theda lived in a different world, even now when they were sitting together in the county jail. "I got to sleep, honey," she said, curling up on the bench. Hard as hell, but she was so tired it seemed she could sleep on anything, anywhere now.

* * *

The next morning, she awoke to hear Theda whispering with someone. She started. "Who's this?" she said.

"Our lawyer, Robert John Williams," Theda said, "What'd I tell you?"

She sat up and saw a middle-aged man with receding reddish hair and brows so bushy she could barely see his eyes. He wore an expensive-looking black suit and shoes to match. She rubbed her eyes and shook her head to clear the cobwebs.

"The bail is paid," he said. "You'll be out in an hour or so. I changed the court date, got a special one for just you two. The family doesn't want Miss Alexander appearing with all the…others. No more newspaper stories."

"But what about our charges?" Hazel said. "Battery, all the rest?"

Williams waggled his eyebrows. "We'll see. The judge owes me a favor or two." He stood up. "I'll be waiting outside." He banged on the cell door. "Guard! I'm ready to go."

Once he'd left, Hazel glanced at Theda. "So we're out? Just like that?"

Theda's smile was grim, not really a smile. "Money," she said. "Good old family money."

"But we could still go to prison, couldn't we?"

Theda sat down and put her arms around Hazel. "No. But nothing's free."

"What do you mean?" Hazel said.

"I don't know yet, darlin'. Wish I did."

* * *

After a while, the guards came to lead them down the putrid hall and out a side door. Hazel took a deep breath. Air! She never knew how sweet it was. Wished it was water so she could take a big drink.

Williams stood outside a shiny black car with shades on the windows and a driver who got out and opened the back door so Theda and Hazel could get in. Williams climbed into the front, and Theda gave instructions to the driver. The seats were so soft that Hazel was tempted to lean back and sleep again. Instead, she peeked out around the shades to see buildings, houses and trees pass by. They looked strange, like part of a new city, not Savannah. Theda, as if she guessed Hazel's thoughts, took her hand and drew a heart in her palm.

When they pulled up in front of the H&M, a Closed sign hung in the window. Hazel's belly contracted. Had she been gone that long? Had Milt moved? What awaited her inside?

"My secretary will send you a note about our meeting," Williams said.

Hazel searched for her key in the purse the jail had returned to her and opened the door. The kitchen was clean, but there was no smell of food or even coffee. Was she in the right place? Had she dreamed the diner?

She looked through the cupboards and found a can of coffee. The smell of fresh grounds made her so happy she felt like crying, but she held off until she'd run fresh water into the pot and added the coffee. Then she sat at the table, put her head down and sobbed. Maybe she was crying loud. Maybe the billy clubs still crashed in her ears. But she didn't hear the door, didn't hear anyone's footsteps until Milt was right there.

"Hazel."

She looked up at him through blurry eyes. "They finally let me out," she said.

"Let's take a look at you." He examined her face, then ran large, warm fingers through her hair and over her scalp until he found the bump.

"Ouch!"

"Christ, it's big as my fist. Anyone look at it?"

She shook her head. "Just Theda. And a couple of the girls who were in with us. They said the coppers love to use their stick, especially when it's people…"

"Like us." Milt finished the sentence for her. They'd never really talked about how they were different. It was just something they understood that didn't need saying, like how Savannah got hot as hell in the summers. "If I had the flatfoot who done this to you, I'd…" Another surprise. Milt never talked that way, never said he was going to beat somebody up, though Hazel figured he knew how to protect himself. Men had to know, especially men like him. Good thing he was big and strong.

He patted her shoulder and stepped back. "You go get yourself a bath and come on back down. I'll finish making coffee and bring it up. Make some breakfast."

Milt had never cooked for her before. Or given orders. Tears welled up in her eyes again.

"You cry," he said. "Cry all you want. I'll be here."

When she came back from the bath—surely the best of her life—Milt had fixed scrambled eggs and toast and poured her more coffee. He sat down. "Tell me all about it."

"Me and Theda went to see the fireworks, and then we ended up at a speak, and then…"

Milt shook his head. "Theda's so young. And reckless."

"But I went right along with her. Started to get a bad feeling, but it was too late."

What if they'd just come back to the H&M? What if they'd never gone out? She shook her head. So many little things that ended up in the biggest mess she'd ever been in.

"I knew something was wrong when you weren't back on Wednesday," Milt said. "So I put out the Closed sign. Not too many people came by anyway—day after a holiday, I s'pose. Then on Thursday I went outside, and there was three papers, maybe more, that somebody left. Things written on them."

Hazel's head jerked to attention. "What things?"

"You don't want to know. I read 'em and threw them away. But there was your name. Your picture. And you looked so tough, so beat up. After that, I just kept the sign in the window and closed all the shades. Felt godawful I wasn't there to do something. They could of hit me 'stead of you. My hard head, maybe it wouldn't of hurt so much."

"Ah, Milt." She put her hand on his. "Guess you didn't know what you were in for when we got hitched."

"Sure I did. We've always looked out for each other. But we never talked about—somebody…coming along."

"I'm sorry," she whispered.

"Nothing to be sorry about. I like Theda. Everything was fine 'til now."

Hazel nodded, miserable. "I know, Miltie."

* * *

She got a note the next day on fancy white stationery. She was to go to Williams' office to meet with him and Theda and talk about court.

Hazel put on her best clothes for the meeting: a green cotton dress like she'd wear to Mass. Shoes with heels and a little strap. Lipstick. It was July and sizzling, or she might have worn a jacket, too. She even put on a dark gray cloche, the only one she had, because it made her look more like a regular woman, not an odd girl, and hid the bump, though her thick red hair pretty much took care of that. Never was very partial to hats and or paid much attention to the styles. But still, she supposed that in some ways, she did look pretty regular—average height, sturdy body that stayed trim because she was always moving. A few freckles—that came with the red hair. She was all right, not a beauty like Theda, but that was fine. When you were good-looking, people paid too much attention to you, and Hazel had always liked to stay invisible.

She took a streetcar downtown and walked past the courthouse, which also housed the jail. She shuddered and hoped no one would recognize her. But not a soul looked her way. Men in suits climbed up and down the courthouse steps like ants on a hill. She continued to the brick building with a big gold plaque: *Robert John Williams, Esquire, Attorney at Law,* letters carved into flourishes.

She went in and gave her name, as softly as she could, to the gray-haired receptionist with a crisp white blouse and glasses perched on her nose. "I'll tell Mr. Williams you're here," she said. "Miss Alexander should be arriving any minute."

Hazel felt a surge of hope at the prospect of seeing Theda. They'd get out of this one way or another. And then they'd see. Maybe Theda could work at the H&M. Maybe life would go on as it did before. But she remembered the headlines the jail guard showed them. The diner was never going to be the way it was. Not as long as she, Hazel, was there. Unless she set up another kitchen in the back and never showed her face. Her belly turned cold.

Theda walked in, wearing a black tailored suit with a narrow skirt and fitted jacket. She looked like a lawyer herself, or what Hazel imagined a woman lawyer would look like. She relaxed and smiled. Just seeing Theda made everything better.

But Theda wasn't smiling. Her black and purple eye was fading to yellow; she was pale, and there were purple smudges under her eyes like she hadn't been sleeping. She sat down next to Hazel and took her hand, fingers cold, not warm like they usually were. Bit her lip, like she was trying not to cry. Then she came in closer and cupped her hand around Hazel's ear. "I love you," she whispered.

Hazel's throat stung. "I love you, too, baby."

"Just remember that," Theda said. "No matter what happens."

Hazel could tell the receptionist was trying to hear what they were saying. Busybody. She'd just have to wonder. "Mr. Williams will see you, now that you're both here." She frowned over her glasses.

The lawyer's door had a gold plaque much like the one Hazel had seen outside. *Mr. Robert John Williams, Esquire, Attorney at Law.* She wanted to laugh. Was he worried people would forget who he was by the time they walked in? But she took a breath and sobered herself as the receptionist ushered them into the office. It was dim and paneled with dark wood. White shutters on the windows kept out the summer heat, and an overhead fan provided some breeze.

Williams, in a navy-blue suit, pointed at two plush red chairs in front of his oak desk. "Sit down. We've got a lot to talk about."

Theda took a seat and folded her arms. "Let's get this over with."

"Very well. I've got papers for you to sign. But before that, just let me say how lucky you are. *Both* of you." He looked first at Hazel, then at Theda. "You assaulted a police officer. You could go to prison for that. There are those who say you should." He cleared his throat. "Not to mention drinking in an establishment that caters to…"

"Girls like us?" Theda said.

"*You*," Williams said, glaring at her, "should be grateful your family is well off. And generous. Willing to help you *and* your friend."

Theda's laugh was brittle. "Yeah, they're the bee's knees all right."

Was this the carefree girl Hazel had fallen in love with? She sounded like she'd aged twenty years since the Fourth. The sadness that had fallen over her that night in the speakeasy returned and weighed down her shoulders. Happiness was a firefly, here for a second, then gone.

Williams opened a drawer and took out some papers he placed face down on the desk. "The charges will be dismissed," he said. "All of them. Drinking in a speakeasy, disturbing the peace and, most important of all, the two battery charges."

"Dismissed? For good?" Hazel said. "You mean we don't have to go back to court?"

Theda placed a hand on her arm. "Wait," she said.

Williams flipped over the pages, which had lots of typed words on them. "There's a contract I drew up. That the Alexander family paid a lot of money for," he said.

"How much?" Hazel asked.

"Never mind," Williams replied. "Like I said, a lot. But there are conditions."

"Just get to it," Theda said, sinking back in her chair so Hazel could barely see her.

Williams turned to Hazel. "The family knows you're older, that you run a business—that you're supposedly...*married*. They believe *you* influenced their daughter, drew her in and got her in trouble, and they're just relieved you got caught before something worse happened. They believe that Theodora—"

Theda made a face. "If you can't say my name, it's Miss Alexander."

He waved a hand as if to shoo away a fly. "As you wish," he said. "They believe Miss Alexander is a completely feminine healthy girl. That she never would have gone near such a place if she hadn't been with you."

Theda snorted. "Shows how much they know about *me*."

"They know enough," Williams snapped. "Enough to try to keep you from ruining your life."

The lawyer made Hazel sound evil, like in the nursery rhyme: *Won't you come into my parlor, said the spider to the fly...*

"So the first condition," he said to Hazel, "is that you're not to have any contact with Miss Alexander. Not in person, not by phone, not by letter or telegraph."

Hazel's head throbbed. The ceiling fan sounded like a train engine.

"And the second," he went on, "is very simple. You must leave town. Leave Savannah. For good."

Hazel watched his mouth open and close, saw his eyebrows move, smelled the cigar smoke in the room. Then she realized what he'd said. "What are you talking about? I've lived here all my life. My family is here. My diner is here. My *husband* is here."

"Nonetheless," said the lawyer. "That didn't keep you away from Miss Alexander in the past. And the family doesn't believe you'd stay away from her in the future, even with the agreement. So, in exchange for getting the charges dismissed, they've decided you must go."

"Go where?" She sat up straight. "I don't know anyone in Atlanta. A few relations in Macon."

Williams raised his brows far enough that she could see his cold blue eyes. "The family wants you as far away from Miss Alexander as possible. I've bought you a one-way train ticket to Minneapolis, Minnesota. In the North. About as far north as you can go."

"Minneapolis? Minnesota?" Hazel said. "I've never even heard—"

"I'm sure you can find it on a map," Williams interrupted her. "A sizable city. Bigger than Savannah. A bit colder, of course." He opened his desk drawer and withdrew an envelope. "Here's your ticket. The family even got you a sleeping berth."

His mouth formed a tight smile, which made Hazel want to slap him. "What if I don't want to go?"

He cleared his throat. "Well, to begin with, the charges will be reinstated. And there are certain things…the diner, for example. I submit you'll have a hard time attracting customers now, after all the news. But let's say you do. The Alexanders have friends in the newspapers. Who could write stories about what kind of woman runs the place."

"You can't just take away my livelihood," Hazel said. "Our livelihood, Milt's and mine."

"You're being given your freedom, Mrs. Goodwin. You won't be paraded through the courts again. You're not going to prison. Does that seem a small thing?"

"How dare you lecture her?" Theda said.

Williams kept staring at Hazel. "Besides, there are places—hospitals—for women like you. Where they cure you of your…*disease*. Would you rather end up in one of them?"

Hazel felt like he'd punched her in the belly.

"And by the way," the lawyer added, glancing at Theda. "That goes for both of you. If your family was just anyone, you might both end up there. Try to remember that, and maybe you'll be a little more appreciative."

Theda laughed. "I thought I was—what did you say? A healthy girl, completely feminine?"

"That's what your family believes," Williams said. "I have my own opinion." He cleared his throat. "In any event, you have a choice. You can sign this agreement—or take your chances and face the charges."

Theda turned to Hazel. "Now you see what my family's really like."

"Don't forget," Williams said, "This contract is only valid if both of you sign it. You must abide by the same conditions as Mrs. Goodwin. Not see her or write to her or call her. *And* obey your parents."

Theda took out a cigarette, lit it and blew smoke across the desk at him. "Well, maybe I'll just leave town with her. Then you'll be rid of the both of us. Can't say as I want to stay here."

But Hazel could see how things were. "Theda," she said. "We don't have a choice."

* * *

Milt listened intently when she came home and spilled it out in one long sentence with no pauses. "So they want to ride you out of town on a rail. Maybe they're just trying to scare you."

"Oh, they're serious," Hazel said. "They set the court date three weeks out. Once I leave, the lawyer cancels it, and it's all over. If I'm still here, the charges don't get dismissed and I'll have to go to court again. And so will Theda."

"How're they going to know you left?"

"Williams will be at the station."

Milt got up and started pacing. "This is no deal. This is blackmail."

"Yes," Hazel said. "I know." She felt numb. "But they got us. And you'll have to stay and run the diner. We're going to need the money, and we'll make more if I'm not here." She grabbed his hand. "Maybe it'll blow over, and I can come back before too long."

"I wonder," Milt said, looking off. "I got to think about this. You can't just get on a train to nowhere."

Hazel massaged her temples. "That's what it feels like all right."

He got up. "I'm going down to the docks. Talk to my buddies. Some of them done a lot of traveling. See what they know about Minneapolis."

* * *

By the next morning, Milt had a plan. "The boys told me about a fellow, Magnus—runs a speakeasy in Minneapolis called the Merry Widow. Everyone goes there, even the cops, 'cause they run a full kitchen, all three meals, and great food. So no raids. And they say he's always looking for a good cook."

"No time to write to him and get a letter back," Hazel mused.

"There's no address. 'Cause it's a speak, see? You just go there. Boys say it's close to the Milwaukee Depot, which is where you'd come in. Three, four blocks, maybe."

* * *

Two weeks later, Hazel boarded the train to Minneapolis. It was a sultry morning with a thread of cool air that would be gone before noon, but even so, she didn't want to leave. Milt carried her bags on and got her comfortable, fussing over her in a way that made her throat hurt. He hugged her and landed an awkward kiss on the top of her head. "Write me soon's you get a place," he said. "Even if it's General Delivery. And I'll write you back.."

"God, Miltie. I'm going to miss you something terrible."

She watched her big husband walk off the train, stop on the platform, wave to her, pushing hair out of his eyes like he always did. She'd never loved him more, even if not the same way she loved Theda. Whom she hadn't seen since the morning in the lawyer's office.

And there, just beyond Milt, Robert John Williams, Esquire, leaning up against the wall, in a dark suit and hat, cigar in his mouth, making sure she left town for that place called Minneapolis, Minnesota.

Chapter Two

Hazel: Oak Island, August 1937

Hazel sat on the dock swinging her legs, having a smoke and a cup of coffee, her favorite mid-morning ritual after the breakfast rush at Oak Island Fishing Resort. Fishermen were out on Lake of the Woods, lines in the water. Minnie McGregor, with whom she'd run the resort since fall of 1925, was back up at the lodge, going through the paperwork Hazel despised. Give her a kitchen, a garden and a well-stocked pantry, and she could create food that made folks cry with happiness. Men traveled miles of bad roads with their gear, loaded it into boats and crossed Lake of the Woods, hoping it was in a good mood and didn't swamp them, their destination a resort run by two women who might as well have been married to each other. But no one ever said anything, because they were far from town gossips, the food and fishing were good, the cabins snug pine and cedar and the waves lulled them to sleep at night.

Minnie didn't approve of Hazel's smoking, at least not in the lodge, although their guests filled the standing ashtrays to overflowing every day. But they were men. Occasionally a wife would tag along, usually a tomboy who liked to fish and drink and smoke with her husband and the other men, and Minnie would put up with her. But then Minnie was old-fashioned. Proper. Maybe the twelve years she had on Hazel, maybe just the way she was.

Two things Hazel had never told Minnie: The way Theda's absence still hurt, a dull ache like an old bruise that never quite went away, and how Hazel's passion for her still smoldered down deep. Hazel loved Minnie—a gentle, abiding love like church on Sunday. A mature love, she often thought, as befit her forty-one years. She felt grateful and lucky but still wondered what had become of her twenty-six-year-old self, the one she left in Savannah. Milt sent a letter every couple of months or so, but Theda had been silent for the eleven years since Hazel wrote her that she was moving from Minneapolis to Oak Island.

She blew smoke over the waves lapping at the wooden pilings of the dock, gazed out at the vast sparkling blue that was Lake of the Woods. An inland sea. In the distance, she spotted the mail boat approaching from the American mainland. Oak, largest of the islands nestled just inside the Minnesota Northwest Angle, northernmost point of the United States, had its own post office at the Bay Store west of the resort. So why was the boat headed straight for her dock? Some special delivery? She and Minnie weren't expecting anything. As the boat approached, Hazel could see there were three people in it. Not unusual in the summer for folks to hop a ride with the mail boat, spend a night or two somewhere, maybe more, with one of the few families who lived on the island, then go back to the mainland the same way they came. But Hal, the mailman, always dropped them at the Bay Store, not at the resort.

She squinted her eyes. She'd always been nearsighted but hated to wear glasses. One, she was vain. And two, they bothered her. They clung to her face, which she often touched, wiping off kitchen sweat or pushing back tendrils of still-red hair, thanks to regular henna rinses. Minnie teased her about it. Her own black hair was threaded with gray, but she didn't give a care, just wore it in a long braid or wound it into a bun, at least when the fishermen were there. After they tucked into their cabins for the night, she'd shake it down around her shoulders for special time with Hazel, when they'd drink coffee—sometimes spiked—pop popcorn, play checkers or just talk over the raspberry cordial Hazel put up every year.

She could now see that one of the people in the boat was a woman, who was waving at her. Hazel waved back. The boat got closer. Hazel still saw it like a distant painting, slightly blurred around the edges. Then the woman cupped hands around her mouth and yelled, "Hazel!" Hazel put down her cup and chucked the rest of her smoke into the water. What the Sam Hill…? Now she started to make out the woman. Dark hair on the short side. Behind her, a boy.

The funny thing about being nearsighted was that things were hazy only until they got to a certain point. So as the boat came in to dock, it was like it pushed through a cloud, and Hazel could see clear as anything.

"Sweet baby Jesus!" she yelled, jumping to her feet, heart racing.

The woman was Theda.

Fifteen long years since Hazel had seen her. Which suddenly collapsed into two minutes, one minute, then nothing, as the boat came in, and Theda, reckless as ever, stood up.

"Sit down! We'll tip!" Hal yelled.

But Theda leaped to the dock, one long leg out behind her like a ballet dancer, and the boat wobbled but stayed upright, and Hazel wasn't sure she'd make it or fall in the water, her crazy girl, but then they were hugging hard and crying, and Theda smelled of that perfume she always wore, and everything else pretty much fell away except for the two of them.

By the time Hazel pulled back and became aware of the rest of the world again, the boy was standing to one side looking none too happy, two suitcases sat on the dock and the mail boat was pulling away toward the Bay Store. "Thanks, Hal!" she yelled after him.

Finally, she took a good look at Theda. Hair tousled as usual. Even back in the 1920s, she never bothered with the marcel style that was all the rage, just cut it in a sort of bob and let it go. Same sapphire eyes, thick black lashes smudged around them. Dressed in wide-legged navy-blue pants and a white sailor shirt she probably designed and sewed herself.

"Holy blessed Virgin," Hazel said, because that was all that came to mind. "And who's this?" Although she wasn't sure why she asked, it had to be Theda's baby, now half-grown.

"My son," Theda said, nudging him forward. Same dark hair, but brown eyes. "Teddy, this is Hazel Goodwin."

"Hello, Teddy," Hazel said, putting out a hand. "You're a long way from home, I reckon." She had no idea what else to say, having not been around kids for quite a while, and especially this one, Theda's boy.

"Yes, ma'am." His tone was polite, but his eyes remained thoughtful and guarded.

"I bet y'all are starving," Hazel said. "That long ride across the lake and all. Come on up to the lodge and I'll make some breakfast."

"I could eat a horse," Theda said. "All I've had is black coffee, and anyway, I know yours is a whole lot better."

"I'm not hungry," Teddy said.

"Not even for gingersnaps and lemonade?" she said, bending down so she was eye to eye with him.

The boy shook his head and turned to his mother. "Can we go for a walk?"

"Not right now, darlin'. Me and Miss Hazel got a lot to talk about."

She turned to Hazel. "Is it—safe? For him to roam around by himself? He likes to do that." She smiled down at him. "Independent little cuss."

"Wonder where he got that from?" Hazel said. "Oh, he'll be just fine. Might run into a deer, maybe a fox, but that's about all." She pointed to the lodge and a path that wound past it. "See that trail, Teddy? It'll take you clear to the other side of the island."

Teddy stared at her, then Theda, and stalked off toward the path.

Little brat. But then Hazel remembered herself as a child and felt a flash of compassion. A long way from Savannah to Oak Island, and she'd wager he didn't know more than a thimbleful of the history that'd brought him here today.

And they were finally alone, standing on the resort dock. Hazel shook her head to make sure she wasn't imagining the whole thing. "Theda," she said, rolling the name around on her tongue. She wanted to say it over and over again. "What in God's green earth are you doing here?"

Theda's smile vanished. "I didn't know where else to go. Who else to turn to. I hated to just show up like this, no warning or anything, but…"

"What happened?" Hazel noticed the circles under Theda's eyes, how the skin on her face was drawn, making her cheekbones stick out.

"Look." Theda pulled down the collar of her blouse. There was no mistaking the finger mark bruises that ringed her neck. Hazel used to see them sometimes on the shop girls who took their lunch at the H&M. They'd try to cover them with scarves, but she could always tell. Something about the way they slunk in like they were trying to be invisible.

"Albert?"

Theda nodded. "I thought he was fine with our little arranged marriage, especially since I produced an heir for him. And for a long time, he left us alone. But now he's got all kinds of ideas. Wants Teddy to go to military school. Wants me to be a *real wife*." She shuddered. "There's a lot more—too much to tell you right this minute. But I ran away, and he's on my trail. Probably with detectives." Her eyes pleaded. "Teddy and I need a place to hide."

Minutes later, Hazel pushed open the door to the great room of the lodge, feeling guilty, excited and scared as hell to face Minnie. The long room with a sloping roof had once been the front porch. After the Crash eased a bit and Prohibition ended, she and Minnie had it enclosed and built a bigger porch on the west side where fishermen could sit, have a beer and watch the boats come in. The walls were birch paneling, pale and cool in the morning light, with a stone fireplace made of rocks gathered from the shore. Kerosene lamps hung from the ceiling. A counter of knotty pine enclosed a desk where Minnie was working, dark head bent over her task. Above her on the wall, a row of keys.

She looked up when the door opened. "Hey," she said. "I was thinking about a fish fry when the boats come in. Those boys can never get enough walleye."

"I know," Hazel said. The "boys" were veterans of the Great War who reunited every summer at the resort. "But I have to introduce you to someone." She took a deep breath and guided Theda through the door. "Minnie, this is Theda." Minnie stood up, face blank with shock. Small and compact, she wore her usual black trousers, white shirt and long black jacket. Hair pulled back in a tidy bun, no earrings.

"She and Teddy, her boy, they're in a…life and death situation, you could say, and—"

Theda walked right to her and offered a hand. "I'm so sorry. Believe me, I never wanted to put y'all out like this."

Minnie gave her a tight smile and shook her hand. "So you're Theda."

Hazel knew that Minnie would never be impolite to anyone. But it hurt to see the questions in her eyes.

"And you're Minnie. What a beautiful place you have here."

Minnie nodded. "You go ahead and make yourself comfortable," she said in her resort owner voice. She waved at the blue plush couch where the fishermen liked to gather. "Hazel, why don't you come with me?"

Hazel followed Minnie through the swinging door, turning her head to Theda. "Just give us a few minutes," she said, hoping it wouldn't be more than that.

Minnie stopped in the hall off the kitchen. "Did you have any idea she was coming?" Red splotched her neck, which Hazel always said was the most expressive part of her body.

"I swear I didn't. Hal brought her on the mail boat just now. She's running away from her husband. Who's a brute." The skin on her face felt tight enough to crack. And beneath that, Savannah was creeping into her body: soft air, smell of just-shucked oysters, fresh sliced tomatoes; how she'd take a break from cooking specials at the H&M to grab some fresh air, sit outside and have a smoke to the hum of cicadas.

"I swear," she repeated, and it came out, "Ah swear." Her voice was moving south, picking up Spanish moss, passing houses with balconies and shutters closed against the heat, like a train speeding into the station and not a thing she could do about it. "I wrote her twelve years ago when I moved to the island. She was in a tough spot with him then. I told her if things ever got really bad, to the point she was in danger, she could come here."

"Why didn't you tell me?"

Minnie's eyes looked like deep, distant wells.

"I never thought it would come to that. It was a goodbye letter. She'd had the baby—Teddy—and all she wanted was to raise him right. You and I were making our life here." A life of cold fresh air, thundering waves and stars hanging low in the sky. "We had the resort. And Rosie."

Rose McGregor, Minnie's orphaned great-niece, was just thirteen when Hazel first came to Oak Island on a fishing trip, fifteen when she returned in 1925 and stayed. Hazel loved Rose like a daughter and couldn't imagine life without her.

"But Hazel. What do you expect me to do?" Each word clear, slow and separate, like pebbles dropped in water. "Put her up? Stand aside so you can…get *acquainted* again?"

Hazel felt like the worst kind of traitor. "God, Min, I don't know. I haven't even had time to catch my breath…"

Minnie's voice rose. "She's beautiful. And young."

Hazel had never seen Minnie like this. She was usually the one who never got ruffled.

"Just six years younger than me—"

"Which makes me old enough to be her mother," Minnie snapped.

Hazel flinched. "Minnie. Please. I saw the bruises on her neck. We've got to help her." She corrected herself. "Help *them*." She and Minnie were standing close but not touching. She reached out for her hand. "I came here, didn't I? Never went back to Savannah."

Minnie sighed but didn't take her hand away. "Maybe it was the lake you stayed for. Or Rosie. I don't rightly know."

Hazel tugged on her hand. "Min. Look at me. I chose *you*. Nothing changes that."

"Not even Theda?" Minnie said.

Hazel shook her head, hoping to God she was telling the truth, not just trying to convince herself. "No. Not even Theda."

"I'm going for a walk," Minnie said. "Clear my head."

And she was gone.

Hazel exhaled hard, went into the kitchen and greeted the Conley girls who had just rowed over from Flag Island and were washing up the breakfast dishes. She prepared strong coffee the way Theda liked it, got a bunch of ginger snaps from the green glass jar on the counter, put everything on a tray and headed back toward the lobby.

Here we go.

Right now, with Theda sitting there, Hazel felt chopped in two, like the platinum-haired girl in a bright red dress on stage with the magician, still grinning after he sawed her in half and displayed her to the audience, upper body in a trunk, lower part from the waist down sticking out of another trunk.

What would it take for her, Hazel, to be one again?

Theda had curled up on the couch. "It's so cozy here. And cool. How divine, August without the heat!"

Hazel laughed. "This *is* our heat. Hot as it gets here, though July's probably a little warmer. By August, fall's already coming."

She set down the tray and poured coffee. Theda took a sip and let out a deep sigh. "Mmm, mmm. I haven't tasted anything this good since you left. Why can't everyone make good coffee?"

Hazel, suddenly shy, looked down and busied herself with the cookies and her chair. Anything not to look at Theda's shining face and fall in love all over again.

"I never thought I'd see you," Theda said.

"Me, neither. Did Milt tell you how to find me?"

Dear Milt. The only one back in Savannah who knew about her life now. Big, shambling Milt with his shy smile and overalls that made him look like a farmer. Her best friend since childhood. No more interested in girls than she was in boys.

Theda nodded. "I knew you were on an island by Canada, but I had no idea how to get here. Milt showed me on a map where I'd have to go. I drove. The car's back at Morris Point. I thought it was safer than taking trains—Albert could check passenger lists." She put her cup down. "Far as he's concerned, he owns me, and Teddy's his child, not mine. This January, when Teddy turned twelve, he started to come around again. Fine, I thought. After all, he's the father. But then he had to dress up so Albert could take him to the club. And Albert wouldn't stop talking about how his son will be a man soon and has to be ready to take over the family lumber business. That's when we started to go at it. Teddy will do whatever he wants to do, I said. He's not a little puppet made in your image." She paused. "Then it got worse. He started to want time with his *wife*. And if I wasn't interested, which of course I wasn't, he'd get rough. I fought him off, told him that was all over. He said, 'You're my legally wed wife, and either you start acting like it or I'll take Teddy away.' I got him out the door and then a few days later, I got this letter."

She pulled out an envelope and extracted paper with an elaborate gilt letterhead: *The McCallie School, Preparatory School for Boys, Chattanooga, Tennessee*:

> *It gives us great pleasure to inform you that your son, Theodore Albert Hawkins, has been accepted for Fall Term 1937 at The McCallie School. We are particularly gratified when the sons—and in your case, the grandsons as well—of alumni enroll in our institution. We assure them the best preparation for college and business as well as rigorous military training, in the best McCallie tradition. As you know, many of our graduates became officers who served with Distinction in the Great War. May your son also know the honor of serving his country…*

She looked up. "Albert was planning it all along. Press me for 'marital privileges.' Then get Teddy to the prep school that would mold him into a little image of his father."

"But you're his mother. You raised him—"

"That's not all." Theda snorted a bitter laugh and shook her head. "I have to hand it to Albert, he's thought of everything. He's suing for custody. So Teddy won't turn into…someone like me. If I don't agree—and maybe even if I do—he's promised to get me locked up someplace where they can cure my *problem*."

Hazel looked around the lobby. Paintings of waves breaking on the rocks, sunrise, fishing boats, Oak Island from the water with the resort in the distance. The comfort they once offered had disappeared. She turned back, rested her head in her hands. "Oh, my God, Theda. Is this what we started way back in Savannah?"

Chapter Three

Hazel: Savannah, April–July 1922

The long trip north and west to Minneapolis gave Hazel plenty of time to recall how things started with Theda. On a spring day already hot as midsummer, after the lunch rush when Hazel was cleaning up, whistling, not thinking much of anything, a young woman sauntered into the diner. She had dark, wavy hair cut in a bob, but the heat had turned it into an unruly halo that framed her face and accented her kohl-lined eyes. She wore a simple blue dress that ended just above the knee, much shorter than Hazel's. A flapper dress. Hazel preferred trousers, but that was out of the question for her. Customers expected skirts and an apron.

The girl sat down at the counter and leaned forward, voice low, although she was the only customer. "Have you got some coffee? And water?"

Hazel nodded, went to the kitchen and came back with a steaming cup of joe and a pitcher of water. She served the girl without looking at her directly. Something about her made Hazel feel off-balance, maybe the perfume, mixed with sweat and—wasn't that liquor? With Prohibition, speakeasies popped up all over, in basements, behind false doors. Hazel would have considered one for the H&M, except it was too tiny. Usually, it was men who came in with booze on their breath, not women, and certainly not women alone.

The girl drank coffee, chased it with water and studied Hazel through thick lashes. "You've saved my life."

Hazel laughed. "Don't be silly."

Her eyes were wide and dark blue. "Oh, I'm serious. I was up all night, you see; haven't slept, haven't eaten, haven't gotten out of my party clothes. I'm a mess. And I have to get sober." Her voice flowed but was husky. Water over rough stones, Hazel thought. A voice too old for her. "What's your name?" she asked.

"Hazel. What's yours?"

The girl clapped her hands. "Oh, that's so sweet and old-fashioned! I wish I had a name like that."

"So what *is* your name?" Hazel was curious by now.

"Theda. Like Theda Bara, except my given name is Theodora, but no one calls me that."

She drained her cup and Hazel refilled it. Theda Bara, The Vamp, who graced the movies Hazel and Milt saw on occasion. Well.

"Your coffee's nice and strong. At home, they make it weak. Or not at all. Mother goes through times when all she'll drink is tea. She shuts herself up in her room and does breathing exercises. She's very *spiritual*..." Theda rolled her eyes.

"Does she know you've been out all night?" Hazel asked. Her own ma would have taken a switch to her if she'd done that.

"Ha! She wouldn't even notice. The servants, maybe. But no one else."

The servants? "What about your pa?"

Theda waved a hand. "He's dead. At least that's what Mother says. Whatever happened to him, he left us a lot of money. Good thing, too, because Mother never worked a day in her life. Can't do anything. Alma—she's the cook—makes all the food."

"And what do *you* do?" Hazel asked.

Theda leaned her chin on her hand. "Well, I graduated from school," she said. "A girls' school, of course." She scrunched up her nose. "And now I go to parties and dinners, smoke cigarettes...pretty boring." Her smile dazzled Hazel. "It's fun to talk with you. No one ever asks me about myself."

Hazel shook her head to shrug off the comment, pretending that exotic creatures like Theda walked into her café every day.

"What about you?" said Theda. "You run this place?"

Hazel nodded. She felt shy.

"By yourself?"

"Sort of." Why was she saying it like that?

"You married?"

An electric current coursed through Hazel's body. Was she married, really? Not like other women she knew. "In a way."

Now Theda looked at her with curiosity. And laughed. "That's funny," she said. "How can you be married *in a way*?"

"Hard to explain," Hazel said. In fact, she'd never tried. What were she and Milt to each other? "Are you hungry?" she asked the girl. Anything to change the subject.

"Oh, God, yes!" She giggled. "I can't remember the last time I ate. Yesterday, maybe?"

Hazel pulled out a frying pan, grateful for something to do. "How about…" she said, over the clatter. "How about a fried oyster sandwich with fresh sliced tomato? And some peach cobbler?" She flashed a grin. So much easier to talk about food. "I made it this morning."

"That's perfect! I'm so glad I came here!"

"How did you find this place anyway?" Hazel said. Her usual clientele consisted of working men wanting breakfast or office girls grabbing the blue plate special. People who joked with her but were serious about getting some food and getting it fast. No one lingered except her and Milt.

"How *did* I get here?" Theda sounded genuinely puzzled. "Let's see. I left the party sometime this morning—or maybe around noon. I was so sick of those people. They were getting drunk again, and I'd had enough. So I started to walk—"

"In this sun?" Hazel said. The girl should have been drenched with sweat. No one with any sense walked in the heat of the day in Savannah.

"I stayed in the shade," Theda replied. "Stopped in parks, sat on benches, under trees. I wanted to get as far away as I could. So I just kept going until I saw the little creek and your café right beside it, and I thought, there's a place I can rest."

An odd creature, Hazel thought. Much too colorful to have landed at the H&M Diner.

It didn't take long for her to shuck the oysters, clean them, fry them in butter, slice up the tomatoes and the bread. As she worked, little tingles of excitement surged through her hands and out the ends of her fingers, a disturbing, delicious sensation. As much as possible, she kept her back to the young woman, who kept chattering. How good the food smelled, how no one but Alma ever cooked something specially for her, how jake the diner was, how bored she'd been until she stumbled in the door, because of course she did stumble, to look at her you might think she was still stewed, but really all she needed was a little food and a good night's sleep as long as her silly friends didn't find her and drag her out to another party, maybe she'd just hide here for a while...

Hazel arranged the sandwich with sliced tomatoes and some watercress, along with a big red and white checked napkin and set it before her.

Theda bit into it. "How delicious!" She made as if to swoon. "How can you make something so good so fast?"

"Practice," Hazel said, smiling. "But if you talk too much, it'll get cold."

"You're right."

She devoured the oyster sandwich, then the tomatoes on which she sprinkled lots of salt and pepper. Tomato juice ran down her mouth, and she dabbed it with the napkin. She pushed the plate away. "Oh, that was good. Did you say you had peach cobbler?"

Hazel cleared the dishes and served her a big helping with fresh whipped cream on top. She poured her another cup of coffee, then served herself one, too. She needed a cigarette. Should she get one now or wait? The diner closed at 4:00, and it was at least that, if not later. She went over to the door and turned the sign to CLOSED.

Theda watched her. "Am I keeping you here late?"

"Don't worry about that," Hazel said. "I live upstairs. Don't have anywhere else to go." She realized she didn't say, "*We* live upstairs." It wasn't like she was hiding anything; she'd already said she was married.

But she and Milt each had their own lives. He might be off buying supplies right now or looking for a shady spot to fish. Hazel didn't really know what he did when he wasn't around and didn't wonder. She was just glad he'd married her, which allowed her to live free of the usual demands women had to put up with.

Hazel pulled a pack of smokes from behind the counter, offered one to Theda, then struck a match and lit them both. Two things really cleared her head—well, maybe three: washing her hair and letting it dry in the sun. A good cup of coffee. And a cigarette. Of course, women weren't supposed to smoke, but Hazel didn't worry about that. And she had a feeling her visitor didn't either. With the food made, dishes cleared and her beloved smoke in her nostrils, she relaxed a little.

"So, how old are you?"

"Twenty. Alma says I'm getting old. Mother would love to marry me off to some fat old rich man." She shuddered. "I could go to school somewhere, I s'pose. But the truth is I don't care to settle down. I want to stow away on a boat. Or take a train somewhere. Get out of Savannah—maybe leave the country. And never come back."

She sat back and took a long drink of coffee.

"Whew!" Hazel shook her head.

She'd never even been out of Savannah except for a trip to Macon to spend time with cousins. But when the girl spoke, she imagined docks congested with trunks, people in traveling clothes, boat whistles, smell of salt. The big train station in downtown Savannah. Thought of herself in this little café, cooking up meals, her and Milt sharing a bed like brother and sister. What *did* she want to do in life? She wasn't that old, just twenty-six, or about to be, but she felt ancient next to Theda.

"Don't you want to get married?" she asked, amazed to hear the words coming out of her mouth. That was what people used to ask her, and it always made her laugh. Truth is, she didn't know why anyone would want to get hitched except to have children. Or, in her case, to blend in.

Theda's eyes were so dark, with shadows and kohl under them, that they looked bruised. She scrutinized Hazel's face. "Of course not," she said. "Did *you* want to get married, or was it something you had to do?"

Hazel flushed red. The girl, beneath her prattle, understood more than she let on.

"Well, I wasn't in trouble, if that's what you mean." How could she be talking this way to a stranger?

"No children?" Theda asked.

Hazel shook her head, blowing out smoke.

"Do you want them? Children?"

She choked and had to drink water. "Kids? Me? No, I got a passel of nieces and nephews. I don't need any of my own."

Theda seemed to listen carefully. Then that silvery laugh again. "I don't either. Want kids, I mean. Mother says pretty soon I'll be too old, but I don't care. I just want to do something interesting."

Hazel had never had a conversation like this, much less on such short acquaintance. "Aren't you having fun? With the parties and all?"

The girl rested her chin on her hands and frowned. "Not really. Like I said, I'm bored. I don't know what to do with myself."

Hazel nearly laughed at the furrowed brow. Theda was a spoiled child, of course, but she felt an odd mix of affection and compassion for her.

Theda looked up through the thick lashes. "What would you do if you were me?"

The girl kept her on her toes, that was for sure. "If I was you? With all the money I wanted and time on my hands?" She thought. "I'd buy a ticket on a ship and sail to Europe and keep going 'til I got good and sick of traveling. Then maybe move to one of those big cities. Paris, New York, London. I'd make sure I never got bored."

She and Theda were alike in that way. Boredom was the one thing Hazel couldn't abide. Right now, she kept it away by listening to stories from her customers, giving them advice and imagining things she might do someday. But she didn't know how long she could be content with just conjuring up adventures. Sometimes she felt like she was rowing in a back bay, close enough to the ocean she could hear the horns of ships, the cry of seagulls, but too far to see it.

What she'd done most of her life, Hazel reflected, was hide in plain sight. Be the tomboy she was, flaunt her red hair, say crazy things. *Oh, that Hazel,* people said. *She's a caution.* They laughed and shook their heads. They saw the Hazel she wanted them to see, not the one underneath. But this girl, not that much younger than she after all, understood.

"I've never been abroad," Theda said, looking into space. "Some of the people in my crowd have. But everyone's too busy drinking and dancing and cutting up." She poured another glass of water. Hazel couldn't tell if she was talking to her or thinking out loud.

"Would one of them go with you?" she asked.

Theda shook her head. "Oh, no. I wouldn't want that. I mean, they're fine. Some I've known since primary school. But it would be like taking Savannah to Europe. All the same people, the same things to talk about. I wouldn't learn a thing."

"You could go alone," Hazel offered. "Things are different now. Women can even vote."

"Alone?" Theda repeated. "That would be *miserable*." She laughed. "Besides, Mother wouldn't give me the money. I don't think it'd matter to her that much, but she cares about what people say. She'd make me get a chaperone." She wrinkled her nose.

Hazel felt a wave of gratitude that she hadn't grown up rich. In some ways, she had more freedom than Theda. But she was married. Sort of. With a business to run. "Someone from church?" she asked. "A friend of your mother's?"

"Oh, almost anyone would do. Older than me. Respectable. Probably married." She looked hard at Hazel. "How old are you?"

"Going on twenty-six." Hazel didn't usually discuss her age, but today she was opening her mouth about all kinds of things.

"And you're married. You could do it!"

"*Me*?" The girl was crazy. Maybe she had bad gin the night before. "I can't just up and leave. I got a job. And…a husband."

Theda looked around. "Well, I don't see a husband anyplace. Are you sure you're really married? Or do you just tell people that so they won't bother you?"

Hazel felt a flush climb her neck to the roots of her hair.

The girl—Hazel always referred to her that way, The Girl, as if there had been no other—looked at her with a serious face. "You're blushing," she said.

Blood rushed to Hazel's head and thrummed in her ears. She reached out to the counter for support. She'd never fainted, but she might be about to. When she woke up that morning, it never occurred to her that someone would enter her restaurant, her world, and light it up in such an unbearable way.

"Are you all right?" Theda asked.

Hazel heard her voice as if from a long way away. And couldn't answer.

"Do you want me to leave?"

Leave? She wanted Theda to take a seat in the diner and never go away. She wanted to throw up. She wanted to drink cool water. She wanted to pack a bag, lock the door, toss the keys back in through the window and never come back. So many things that it made her temples throb. All she could do was shake her head.

Theda stood up. "I'll come back tomorrow. About the same time. I won't be tight, I promise. You can rest. And we'll talk more."

She leaned across the counter and gave Hazel a soft kiss on her forehead, as her mother might have if she'd been that kind of mother. "I'll be back," she repeated in a soothing voice.

And before Hazel could recover herself, she'd slipped out the door, trailing perfume in her wake.

* * *

It seemed like in no time, Hazel could not conceive of the diner without Theda, food without Theda, anything without Theda. It occurred to her that she'd never had a real friend, someone she could say anything to and hide nothing from. It happened so fast and easy.

"So who's this Theda?" Milt asked.

"You two have to meet. Never seen anyone quite like her." Hazel would laugh and shake her head because she still couldn't quite believe it.

Then one afternoon, Milt came back from wherever he'd been when they were sitting in the kitchen drinking coffee and having a smoke. He smiled. "So this must be Theda."

Hazel searched his eyes. Maybe he wasn't happy about another person coming into their little world. But she saw nothing but his kind gaze, laced with curiosity.

Theda smiled back. "And you're the husband."

To Hazel's astonishment, quiet Milt poured himself a cup, sat down and chatted. "I'm gone a lot," he said to Theda. "Nice that Hazel has some company."

After Theda left, Hazel could hardly wait to ask him what he thought.

"She's a real nice girl," he said. "You've been perkier since she's been coming around."

Hazel took that as his blessing.

She had no idea what he did in the days and nights he was away from the diner and their apartment on the second floor. He tended the garden and the books, kept the kitchen supplied, repaired whatever needed fixing and cleaned up the kitchen and the diner, but after he met Theda, Hazel saw him less and less. As for her, she threw herself into cooking, tried new recipes, invented desserts. Theda came each day after the lunch rush. They would eat together since there was never time when the H&M was full. Then they cleaned up and talked for hours. Sometimes they walked, if it was cool enough, continuing their conversation. Every now and then, they went to the movies.

Hazel supposed that sooner or later, they'd run into someone who knew one of them, but she wasn't too worried. Even though she was six years older than Theda and of a different class, they were both young women. Which was a revelation. Even in her childhood, climbing trees, looking for adventure, Hazel never felt young if youth meant being carefree, lost in the moment. Maybe a few minutes here and there, contemplating her music teacher's beautiful hands and throat. But for the most part, Hazel was a girl in action, running to stay ahead of her family, her teachers and their expectations. She never really relaxed until Theda. She found herself spilling all kinds of secrets, some of them not nearly so horrible once they were out of her mouth.

And the diner prospered. Customers increased; her experiments with recipes acquired some fame in Savannah. Every now and then, there was a line out the door, especially on Thursdays, which Hazel named Surprise Day. She didn't post the menu anywhere, told people when they came in what she was serving, and they could stay or not. Almost no one left.

* * *

Milt noticed they were making more money. He smiled as they ate breakfast one day before dawn, their custom and the one intimacy they'd always shared. "I don't know what you're doing," he said. "But we're chopping in high cotton. I'm laying away money. Never know when it'll come in handy." The birds started their song as they sat across from each other at the small table, the smells of fresh coffee and bacon filling the kitchen.

"Theda's our good luck charm," Hazel said, laughing.

But it was no joke. Theda was a beam of light that lifted Hazel above the everyday worries and humdrum activities that had made up her life before. She loved this early hour with its peace and lack of complications. "How about you, Milt? I never see you anymore. Where do you go? What do you do?"

Milt shrugged. "Oh, this and that." The sky lightened behind him. "I like to go down to the port. I always thought maybe if I didn't farm, I'd be a sailor. But Mama and Papa had other ideas."

Hazel looked at him closely. "Milton Goodwin!" she exclaimed. "You never told me all this before. One day I'll wake up and find you shipped out to China or some such place."

He shrugged. "Who knows. Can't say I've ever been in love with this diner. It's something for you, more like."

"But it makes us a good living," Hazel said. Her voice sounded too bright, too chirpy. She loved the H&M more since Theda had become part of it.

Silence fell between them.

"I do worry some," Milt said. "Not about the diner. About you and Theda."

"Why?"

Milt sat back, a veil settling over his eyes. "If you're out and about, two women, and someone gets the wrong idea…who knows what could happen."

If he were a different kind of man, if they had a marriage like other folks did, Hazel might have taken that as a threat. But Milt was trying to warn her of something. Except that in her hazy state of bliss, she didn't want to know.

"I always look after myself, Milt. You know that."

"Well, keep an eye on her, too. She's just a young pup."

On his way out, he patted her shoulder. His hand was comforting—big, callused and warm. "Be careful. Over here, around the diner, everybody knows us. Out there in Savannah, it's not like that."

"Things are changing, Milt," Hazel said. "Even in Savannah."

"Maybe," Milt said. "But all I'm saying is don't count on it too much."

And he left out the back door.

* * *

If Milt was really worried about her, Hazel reasoned, wouldn't he stick around more? He wasn't mad at her, that she knew. Maybe giving her room. Trying to ensure that whatever she was up to would take place in the confines of the diner and the creek—not out in the city that wasn't really theirs and never would be. Savannah belonged to the old, moneyed classes who traced their roots back to the early settlements and saw everyone who didn't as inferior. For all its lush trees and gardens, its broad avenues, Savannah was as closed as a Southern Baptist church on a Monday morning. Hazel grew up Catholic—another thing that made her an outsider—and though she wasn't particularly religious, she loved the fact that you could wander into a Catholic church and talk to God any old time. Or go to Mass. You didn't have to wait until Sunday.

* * *

Fourth of July was coming. Lots of people would leave town. Businesses would close. It was a time when folks ate, drank, picnicked, danced, forgot the rest of their lives. Hazel and Theda planned to celebrate, too. There would be a parade and a band playing John Phillip Sousa marches. Fireworks over the Savannah River, picnics on the shore and in every park in the city. It would be hot, of course, but festivities would go on. Hazel wanted to get lost with Theda inside the holiday, feel it go to her head.

On the Fourth, Milt was nowhere to be seen. Hadn't come home the night before, but Hazel wasn't concerned. They'd always given each other plenty of elbow room, their marriage so different from those of her brothers and sisters. And what a relief that none of them had called for a family celebration! For one thing, she would have been stuck cooking.

And what about Theda? Hazel didn't want to answer questions and, even more, didn't want to share her with anyone else. These days she felt like a cork bobbing in warm water, safe in the shallows. A wonderful feeling unless the tide came in and swept you out to sea. Hazel liked it there, being with Theda, not worrying about anything except getting the food out every day at the diner.

On the morning of the Fourth, they packed a picnic lunch: fried chicken, peach cobbler, green beans, a hunk of bread. They drank coffee and nibbled on the cobbler that was too good to save. Theda had spent the night. Hazel gave her the bed and slept on the sofa, even though it would have been fine to share—after all, they were both girls—but something made her hold back.

It was cool in the kitchen, shades drawn against the heat. Theda always looked, Hazel observed, like she'd just gotten out of bed, short dark hair mussed around her face, blue eyes darkened with circles. Which only made her look more lovely. She set down her coffee cup. "Theda, I never asked you this before, but I keep wondering. Why do you like to go around with me? You're rich, you could do anything you want, meet anybody. So why you staying with me in my little diner, away from everything?"

Theda looked confused. Then her eyes sparkled. "Why Hazel Goodwin," she said. "I'm so crazy about you, I can hardly stand it." She leaned across the table and kissed her. Then teased open her lips and explored her mouth with a curious tongue. Like no one ever had before.

Hazel's center turned hot and liquid. Her head tilted back as Theda's lips explored her neck. So this was what it was like.

At some point, Theda took her hand and led her upstairs. Although Hazel didn't know who was leading who. She could barely wait to get to the bed. The one she shared with Milt.

The one where no one had ever made love before.

By the time she became aware of things again, Theda's hair had gotten even messier, and hers had come all the way down, making her want to cut it very short, so Theda wouldn't have to push it aside to search for her earlobe. They lay in the rumpled covers, robes on the floor, arched toward each other.

"Let's go out and see some fireworks," Theda said. "We can pretend they're for us."

"Why, ain't they?" said Hazel.

* * *

At some point later, they walked toward the harbor in the gathering dusk. A little breeze moved the air. Hazel could hear a brass band, marches, all of it drifting around them. People strolled, families, young men, sweethearts, no one going anywhere fast. And not a soul Hazel recognized. But then she knew so few people. Just her family, a few friends and the regulars at the diner.

Theda reached for her hand. It wasn't uncommon for women to walk hand in hand or arm in arm, but Hazel felt a little shiver. "No, sugar," she said.

"Why not?" said Theda. "Isn't this the Jazz Age?" She laughed.

"Maybe in New York," Hazel replied. She remembered Milt's warning. "But we're in Savannah."

They were almost at the harbor. Hazel could see the boats and sparklers, smell popcorn, hear laughter and more music.

"Let's sit right here, under this tree." Theda pointed out a magnolia draped in trailing moss.

Hazel wanted to stay there all night, pretend it was their kingdom, where no one else could enter. Theda lay on the ground, propping up her head with one hand, gazing out at the harbor, kicking her feet up in the air. Were they the only two girls in Savannah who shared this secret? Could people tell by looking at them? Could anyone even see them? Walkers passed, voices and laughs trailing into the warm night. Hazel leaned against the trunk, caressed Theda's soft curls. Her lover. Theda made little contented noises, like a kitten.

At some point, Hazel must have dropped off. She awoke to Theda's tickling her, laughed and opened her eyes. Darkness still hung thick over the magnolia, but the bands had ceased, and she could see only a few people walking, vague shapes in light-colored clothing. "What time do you s'pose it is?" she said.

Theda shrugged. "Who knows? But it's still night." She sat up. "And I've got an idea."

"You do, do you?"

Sometimes Hazel felt a decade older than Theda, not a mere six years.

"Yes. There's a place. I've only been once before, but it's swell. There's music and you can drink—"

"A speakeasy?"

"I suppose. Come on, let's go. You'll like it." She stood up and pulled Hazel's hand. "Who knows when we'll get away like this again?"

Why was Theda talking like that? Why wouldn't they get away soon? It felt easy, natural, like getting up in the morning and putting on coffee.

But Hazel got to her feet. Really, all she wanted was to be with Theda. So, she followed her down tiny streets and alleys until they squeezed through what was more like a crack than a path, damp walls touching them on either side.

Chapter Four

Hazel: Oak Island & Baudette, August 1937

After supper on the day Theda arrived, Hazel and Minnie went down to the wooden rockers beside the water, where they liked to talk until dark. They'd settled Theda and Teddy in the cabin farthest from the lodge. The big lake was calm, and waves lapped the rocks with a *shhh* sound. If only their conversation were as peaceful, Hazel thought.

"I know Theda can't stay here," she said. "But she's got to go someplace she'll be safe. Or at least hard to find."

She heard the frustration in Minnie's voice. "You don't owe her anything. If she managed to get all the way up here, then she can find a hiding place by herself. It's a big country."

Hazel turned to look straight at Minnie. "Don't you think you're being a little rough on her? Outside of Teddy, I'm all she's got. Her family's useless. Wouldn't help her anyway. I don't know if I'm her only friend, but after all we went through together, when we were so young.... That's something that doesn't go away."

Minnie jabbed the air with her finger. "You see? That's how she ropes you in. Theda, with all her money and her pretty eyes. Poor little rich girl. And only Hazel can save her." She shook her head. "I think she wants you back, and the more you get mixed up with her, the more—" She stopped, folded her arms across her chest and rocked back and forth.

"The more what? Don't you trust me?"

"You're different. Already. And I've seen the way she looks at you..."

Hazel knew what she meant. Of course, she loved Minnie. And seeing Theda, smelling her perfume, hearing her voice, embracing her, made her feel tickly inside, like she'd been drinking Champagne. But she could hardly tell Minnie that. "Look," she tried. "It's like this. Years go by, then something happens, and just like that, your past and present are smack together. But I'll tell you one thing. Of the two of us, I got the best deal. It didn't feel like it at first—leaving the only place I'd ever lived, the diner, Milt—but I got the chance to make my life over. I came here. I found you and Rosie and the island. She's got nothing but her boy."

Minnie sniffed. "And more money than we'll ever have in our lives."

They wouldn't resolve the Theda question that night, Hazel knew. "I've been thinking," she said. "I need to take her into Baudette to see Sadie. She'll know what to do."

"Well, then at least she won't be here," Minnie concluded.

*　*　*

Sadie Robinette, half-French, half-Indian—half and half, as she liked to say—ran the Hotel Pascal, along with François, who no one knew much about, except he was from Quebec and had been with Sadie since the 1920s in Winnipeg. Something happened there that neither of them would talk about, and then they moved down to Baudette and bought the hotel, which Sadie named for her father, Pascal Robinette.

Some people were afraid of her. Tall, with dark hair and café au lait skin, good looking in a rough kind of way and no problem saying what was on her mind. Folks said she was strong as a man and could shoot better than anyone in the county. She ran the hotel as a brothel and speakeasy until the Crash. Then, when no one had money to pay for girls, she made it into a real hotel, mainly for travelers to and from Canada, and kept the speakeasy going. Now with Prohibition over, Hotel Pascal had a legal bar and the best food in town, thanks to François, who cooked as good as Hazel. Maybe even better.

It had taken Hazel a while to warm up to Sadie, who first struck her as brisk and rude. "She should have been mayor," she'd tell Minnie. "She loves bossing people around." But in the end, she came to like Sadie, hard edges and all, after she helped out Rose and Emil and hosted their wedding at the hotel back in May the year before.

* * *

A few days later, she and Theda arrived at the Hotel Pascal. Teddy stayed on the back patio, examining plants and trees. "Look, Mama," he said to Theda. "See how this pine is different from the ones back home?"

"You show me later, darlin'. Me and Hazel are going inside."

With Sadie and François around the round oak table in the kitchen, Theda began. "I met Hazel back in 1922 when I was nothing but a spoiled little flapper," she began. "Never knew anyone like her. And then…" She looked at Hazel with such longing that Hazel felt exposed like she was sitting in her underwear.

"Then you got even closer," Sadie finished her sentence.

"Yes, that's it," Theda went on. "And on Fourth of July, we went to a speak I knew for just girls. But the cops busted in. Roughed us up and arrested everybody. I thought we'd get out right away, but Hazel and I got charges of attacking the police, so the judge set our bail sky high."

"Of course." Sadie's smile was grim.

"Anyway, my family helped us out," Theda said. "In a way. Paid our bail and hired a lawyer who got the charges dismissed. But there was a catch. They made Hazel leave town. We weren't even supposed to write each other. And my father said I had a choice—marry Albert Hawkins, some fellow I'd never even met, with lots of lumber money—or they'd stick me in a hospital to 'cure' me of liking women." Her eyes met Hazel's.

"I told Albert it was an arrangement, nothing more, and not to expect me to be a real wife to him. But he thought he could change me." She shuddered. "Finally, he got the idea and pretty much left me alone until he decided he needed an heir. I thought maybe then he'd lay off. So I had Teddy. 'All right,' I told him. 'You've got your son. Now we live our own lives.' And that worked until this last year. Teddy was getting bigger, and Albert started to come around again. Wanted him to go to military school and then take over the lumber company." She sighed. "And then he said it was time for me to be a real wife to him. I laughed, but he swore if I didn't do what he wanted, he'd take Teddy away and put me away in a hospital where they turn girls like me into *real women*. And he let me know he meant business." She pulled down her shirt collar and showed the bruises on her neck. "So I got all the money I could, took Teddy and left at night. Somehow we got all the way up here—farthest place I could run and not leave the country. And who else could I go to but Hazel?"

Hazel's belly contracted. She felt again the moist joy of being new lovers. And comrades. Hazel and Theda against the world. Something Minnie would never understand.

Theda let out a deep breath. "But that's not the end of it. Albert Hawkins can't stand to lose. He'll hire detectives—probably Pinkertons, he always used them to break strikes—and he'll find me. Or die trying. I need to go someplace even he won't think of."

"Albert Hawkins," Sadie said, as if trying out the name on her tongue to see how it felt. "De*tec*tives." She shook her head. "What some men won't do to try to break a woman. Like a goddamn horse." She straightened up. "We'll be ready for him and his dicks whenever they show up. But Theda can't stay in town. And she's a sitting duck out at Oak Island. All Albert has to do is get a boat and go across the lake."

"The baby bootleggers," François said, tilting his head. "Are they still out in the bog?" The baby bootleggers, Hazel knew, were farmers scattered throughout the bog area who ran small, remote stills, sometimes powered by car batteries.

"Who knows," Sadie said. "Only way to find out is drive those godforsaken roads and find them, wherever they're living. But they wouldn't have room for Theda. And then there's the boy."

Theda flushed. "Where I go, Teddy goes. That's what Albert's really after, anyway—his son."

Hazel remembered how she'd taken on Robert John Williams in his law office all those years ago. Like a mother bear with those she loved.

"Oh, don't count on it," Sadie said. "Men like him can't ever seem to get it into their heads that a woman's just not interested."

Hazel suspected that Sadie spoke from experience, although she knew little of her past. She heard François humming to himself, glanced at him and saw he was looking far away.

"He's thinking," Sadie said.

"Little Roy and Marie," François said finally. "They are still at Faunce Ridge when they do not play music here at the hotel, yes? And no one goes there because most of the people, they leave already, and besides, it is so hard to find with the wild roads."

Theda looked puzzled, and Sadie explained. "A little place in the woods. A ghost town really. The Government cleared most everyone out of there last summer. But some people stayed—except now there's no post office, and they stopped grading the roads, so driving is tough, especially after a rain."

François leaned forward. "And the ones who stay, they are singular people. Little Roy plays the fiddle, but he does not talk. Many years ago, his family died in the 1910 Fire." He sighed. "It took Baudette, many towns along the border. And ever since, Little Roy says not one word. But when he makes music, he speaks. Marie Niemi is there, too. She has cows, a horse, chickens and she knows ways to cure people."

"Really?" Theda said.

"Yup," Sadie answered. "But anyway, they started playing and singing together—Marie sings, Little Roy doesn't—and they play for dances at the hotel. Friday and Saturday night, then they go back to Faunce. In fact, they should be here any minute. If you and your boy could stay out there in the forest with them, Albert would have a hell of a time finding you."

Theda was silent for a few minutes. "Do they have a grocery store? What about school in the fall?"

Sadie pulled out a pack of Lucky Strikes, offered it before she lit one for herself and blew out a long plume of smoke. "No school anymore. Most of the kids are gone. And the store is closed. But Marie grows pretty much everything you could want to eat. The rest they buy in Williams. About twelve miles away."

Theda looked dazed. "Where would we stay?"

"Well," said Hazel, trying to envision the place. It'd been a while since she'd been there. "Plenty of houses still standing, I imagine. Our Rose lived there for a while. So did her husband, Emil, and his family. Now I guess it's just Little Roy and Marie." She tried to but could not imagine Theda there, among the hardscrabble homes, the evergreens, the bog.

"And the DuPrees," Sadie said. "Loggers. Crazy bastards. They swear they'll only come out feet first." She laughed. "I like that. Folks who fight back."

Hazel heard music from the lobby.

"Ah." François nodded. "Little Roy tuning his fiddle."

Hazel hadn't seen Little Roy since Rose and Emil's wedding when he and Marie played for hours. Hard to believe all those songs could come out of the head of one small man.

"Come on out and meet them," Sadie said.

Morning sun lit up the lobby, where a compact man with a battered gray felt hat pulled down over his face plucked at the strings of a fiddle. His pants and shirt were patched but looked clean. The dust on his boots made them look gray, not black. One foot tapped. He didn't look up as they came in, but the woman beside him did.

She was tall and straight, with dark hair and golden-brown eyes the color of maple syrup, in a pale blue dress washed many times. Which she wore, Hazel thought, with dignity worthy of a grand gown. She stepped forward. "H'lo, Hazel." She put out a strong hand to Theda. "Marie Niemi," she said. "This here's Little Roy, but don't expect him to say anything."

"Theda Alexander. And anyone who plays fiddle is all right by me."

Little Roy began to play a slow version of "Bye, Bye, Blackbird," still not looking up.

Theda clapped her hands. "Ohhhhh, I love that song!"

He raised his hat and smiled at her, face leathery and tanned by the sun with eyes clear and green as pools in a pine forest.

Theda clapped a hand over her mouth. "For a man, you sure have pretty eyes!"

Sadie laughed. "Damn, Little Roy. Can't say she's wrong."

Girl still says whatever comes into her head, Hazel thought. Little Roy quickly lowered his head before she could tell whether he was blushing. She stopped herself from smiling so as not to embarrass him more. "Theda's from Georgia, where I come from," she said. "And she always speaks her mind."

The front door opened, and Teddy came in. "Want to go walk by the river, Mama?" he said. "Canada's just across the way!"

"Later," Sadie said. "Right now, let's all sit down together." She waved at the battered leather chairs and couch in the lobby.

Hazel let Theda do the talking. "I certainly don't want to impose," she said. "Or put folks in danger. Because if Albert figures out where I'm at.... And Hazel's already suffered enough on account of me."

Her voice was so tender that Hazel quickly said, "Oh, I'm fine."

"Well," Marie said. "Faunce is a good place if you want to keep people away. Roads are terrible. They flood when it rains. Cars get stuck, trucks, too. And we're on a ridge, so we can see and hear the engines before they get there. And there's the bog, which most people are scared of—one thing we know is that it don't take kindly to strangers. Especially if they're up to no good." She looked at Little Roy. "Can't speak for Roy, of course, but I wouldn't mind having some company out there."

"But where'd we stay? Doesn't sound like you have a hotel out there."

"Tell you what," Marie said. "My house is too small to put you up, but I've got a barn. Animals downstairs, of course, but there's a real nice hayloft. The horse and the cows keep it warm. And I'll fix it up for you."

Theda turned to her son. "Teddy, what do you think?"

It looked to Hazel like Teddy was interested but trying not to show it. "Well…I don't know what a bog is. Being out in the woods sounds sort of fun. But where would we sleep? Are there beds?"

"Roy and me, we'll figure out beds, won't we?"

The fiddler nodded.

"And my horse, Butter," Marie said. "He loves to get his exercise. You like to ride horse?"

"I s'pose," Teddy said. "Are there any other boys out there?"

"Maybe the Dupree boys," Sadie said. "But just think—woods and a bog and horses and fiddle music. Don't you think that'll keep you occupied for a while?"

"Maybe." Teddy drew a circle on the floor with his foot.

Theda glanced at him. "He'll be fine."

Hazel wondered if that was just wishful thinking. But where else could they go?

"And I drove up here," Theda continued. "So I've got a car for whatever you need. I could go into town, get groceries. And when it comes to sewing, I can do pretty much anything, so if there's something you need fixed... I don't want to be a burden."

Little Roy smiled. He must like the plan.

He really did have pretty eyes, Hazel thought. Wasted on a man, of course, but that was another matter. "Well," she said, "now that everything's settled, I guess I better be off."

"Not yet!" Theda said. "Let's go for a walk."

Teddy frowned. Theda gave him a stern look. "Son, don't pout. You and I are going to be together a lot, but Hazel's going back to the island."

She and Hazel strolled down the hill to the bay, sat on the dock and dangled their feet over the edge, dipping them into the water.

"Do you still have the things I sewed for you?" Theda asked.

"Are you kidding? I wear the cotton dress all the time. And the robe every night. But not many places I can use the green silk tea dress—too bad, because I love it."

"I would have made you more this time, except we had to leave so fast." Theda sighed. "It's going to be nice not to run for a while. It was scary. I didn't even turn on the headlights 'til we got out of Savannah. Took back roads all the way up here. Milt's map helped. And thank God I have a pretty good sense of direction."

Hazel sighed. "Oh, baby." So easy to slip into the old words. She pictured Minnie and immediately felt guilty. But the sun shone down and sparkled the water and Hazel's worries lifted. *Can't we just stay here forever?* she thought. *Make time stand still for a change?*

As if guessing her thoughts, Theda said, "Hazel? Won't you stay a little longer? Come along when they take us out to this place Faunce Ridge? Sadie seems fine. I like her—but I feel so alone. Even with Teddy."

Hazel meant to say that she really had to get back to Oak, that the resort was busy this time of year, that Minnie was waiting. But when she looked at Theda and her dark blue water eyes, none of that came out.

"Of course I will," she said.

Chapter Five

Hazel: Minneapolis, August 1922–Christmas 1922

The Milwaukee Depot in Minneapolis was large and grand, with marble floors and high windows, but when Hazel stepped outside into the August afternoon, the air was not cool, as she had hoped, but steamy like Savannah. As she looked around, trying to figure out what to do next, a middle-aged woman in a blue suit that reminded her of a military uniform came up to her.

"Hello!" she said. "Just arrived in Minneapolis?"

Hazel nodded.

"Have a place to stay?"

She was taken aback at how forward the woman was, how rude the question. No one in Savannah would ever approach a stranger and ask such intimate things. She frowned, weighing whether to even reply.

"Oh! I've offended you!" the woman said. She dug in her pocketbook. "I didn't mean to. Look—here's my card. I'm from Travelers Aid. We help women get settled in the city, so they don't fall in with…bad people, if you know what I mean."

Hazel did know what she meant. The woman looked and sounded like a Sunday School teacher trying to herd wayward children. But sure enough, the card said *Travelers Aid* in glossy black letters, and down below in finer print, *A service for working women.*

"I'm not working," Hazel said, reluctant to say even that much. "I just got here." And she was tired and thirsty and in no mood to answer stupid questions.

"My name is Margaret." The woman put out a hand, which Hazel took out of courtesy. "And I can tell you some places—decent ones, where you'll be safe. With other working women."

"I told you—" Hazel began.

"Oh, I know you just stepped off the train. But I'm guessing you'll be looking for a job. That's what brings most girls to the city. There's the Woman's Hotel—the Woman's Christian Association runs it."

Milt had mentioned a hotel by that name, Hazel remembered. Maybe this Yankee woman was on the level after all. "The Woman's Christian Association?" she repeated.

"Yes," Margaret said. "They set it up so that young women would have a safe place to go where they wouldn't pay much money—fifty cents a night, I believe."

"Hmmm…is it far?" Hazel was desperate to put down her bags, wash up and drink water, lemonade, something cool.

"About three blocks away," Margaret said. "I can walk you there."

"All right." Three blocks wasn't much, fifty cents was a good price and the longer they stood in the heat, the more exhausted she felt.

They passed a sort of plaza with a half-circle of columns. "Gateway Park," Margaret said. "That's what they call this whole area—The Gateway." Beyond that, businesses selling soft drinks, candy, cigars and newspapers. And a few that advertised "A Dime a Dance!"

"Just ignore those places," Margaret told her. "There's a little bit of everything around the train station, but as long as you dress modestly, no one will bother you."

Modestly? What did that mean? Theda would get bothered a lot, even covered head to toe, but Hazel guessed that she wouldn't attract that kind of attention no matter what she wore.

The Woman's Hotel was a three-story building that looked to be made of sandstone. A fire escape zigzagged across the front. Inside,

Margaret greeted the clerk behind the desk by name and said, "This is—"

"Hazel Goodwin," Hazel said. "From Savannah, Georgia."

"My! You didn't tell me!" Margaret said. Then to the clerk, "She's looking for a room."

"For how long?"

Hazel hesitated. She wanted to say a week, a month, after which she'd be heading home to Savannah and the H&M and Milt and—one way or another—to Theda. After all, they'd just signed a piece of paper, nothing more. But as she stood in the lobby, with its polished wood floors, thick walls and feeling of solidity, it began to dawn on her that she was in a place so different from Savannah it might have been another country. And no endpoint in sight.

"I don't know," she said.

The clerk glanced at Margaret and back at her. "A few months? September's coming up. Should we say until the end of the year? You'll have a better idea then." Her face softened. "Plus it's a bit cheaper than by the night. Now there are rules, of course—no men, no liquor, no gambling. And you'll share a bathroom."

Hazel nodded. She just wanted her room. "How much?" she asked, although she'd already decided she'd stay here. It seemed safe and well kept, and it would do. Almost anything would. She filled out papers with her name and address back home, then put down money for the remaining months. It came out to forty-five cents a night, not bad.

"Here's your key," the clerk said. "Number 307. Third floor. A sweet little room. I'm sure you'll find it to your liking."

"Can someone take Miss Goodwin upstairs?" Margaret asked.

"*Mrs.* Goodwin," Hazel corrected her.

"Well, aren't you full of surprises? Mrs. Goodwin from Savannah, Georgia, then."

"I'm sure I can find my way." Hazel wondered if being married would give her any protection in this new city. Or would people just wonder why her husband wasn't with her?

"Would you like me to go up with you?" Margaret asked.

Hazel shook her head. "No thanks."

She picked up her suitcases and headed for the stairs at the end of the lobby. Finally, she got to the third floor and found 307: a narrow room with two windows, flowered wallpaper, a single bed, a washstand, a dresser and a closet. The bathroom was down the hall, and that was fine. Everything looked and smelled clean, and the windows let in a little breeze. Thank God for the extra money she and Milt had salted away. If not for that, she'd be in some boardinghouse with roommates, a curfew and a house mother watching her every move.

She poured water from the pitcher on the washstand and drank the whole glass. Then she lay down on the bed, not even bothering to take off her shoes and was asleep within minutes. The last thing she remembered was wishing that Theda was curled up beside her; and that Milt was somewhere nearby keeping watch.

* * *

The next day Hazel set off for the Merry Widow speakeasy. She knew better than to ask anyone at the hotel how to get there. She doubted they'd consider working there suitable for a woman. Milt had said it was near the Mississippi River, which she could scarcely believe was all the way up here in the North. She put on a dress, a hat and good walking shoes. First, she retraced her steps to the Milwaukee Depot on Washington Avenue, then walked north. There were very few buildings on the side of the street closest to the river—mainly trees, brush and a few ramshackle dwellings. She decided to explore a footpath that snaked just below, dipping and rising with the contour of the bank. She'd always liked to walk, and the breeze from the river ruffled her hair and helped distract her from all she had just left. She couldn't just curl up into a ball of misery. First she had to get a job, settle in, catch up on her sleep. There'd be plenty of time later to cry and be sad.

Up ahead, just at the edge of the riverbank, she noticed a building partly dug into the hillside. Like a cave, she thought. These northerners. No windows that she could see, and all covered with vines like the speakeasy in Savannah. She smelled frying food, approached the place and looked for a door. Nothing obvious, but footprints on one side of the structure, and when she got closer, she saw a peephole and knocked. No answer at first, then a male voice said, "Yeah?"

"I'm looking for Magnus," she said. "Is he here?"

"Who wants to know?"

"Hazel Goodwin," she replied, feeling silly, then pathetic. "From Savannah, Georgia. I'm looking for work as a cook."

A door swung open, and a tall, husky man with tousled dark hair and stubble on his chin stood in front of her. "Well, why didn't you say so right off the bat?" he said, in a voice that seemed to echo out of his barrel chest, covered in a half-open shirt with the sleeves rolled up. He swiped an arm across his ruddy face, shining with sweat. "Sorry," he said and stepped outside, letting the door close behind him.

"So hot in there," he said. "My cook up and left in July. Can't say I blame him. I probably would of quit, too. In the winter, it's cozy with the kitchen and no windows, but in the summer, it's pure hell. Nobody wants to cook in my place once summer comes." He put out a large hand. "Magnus Giles," he said. "Pleased to meet you, Hazel Goodwin from Savannah."

For the moment, Hazel couldn't think of anything to say.

"Sure you want to work in this hellhole? I mean the heat, not the place itself. But then again, you're from the South, you're probably used to it," Magnus went on. "None of my people could take it today. So I went down to the river and brought back a whole mess of catfish. Think you can cook 'em?"

Hazel couldn't help but laugh. "Mr. Giles—"

"Call me Magnus, for Christ's sake! Only the cops use my last name."

"I reckon I can cook pretty much anything," she said. "You just show me this catfish."

"Be my guest." Magnus opened the door for her.

"Can we leave it open?" she asked. "That's how we cool off our kitchens in Georgia."

Thus began Hazel's career at the Merry Widow.

August 15, 1922

Dear Milt,

Well, I found the Merry Widow—a spot overlooking the Mississippi, except the windows are all boarded up, because it's a speakeasy. Sort of an odd place— half of it's built right into the riverbank. Magnus, my new boss, says an old hermit dug it out to stay warm in the winter and keep people away. And I guess he kept digging because it stretches way back into the hillside and takes up almost half a block lengthwise. Kind of like a big cave, except with tables and a bar and a good-sized kitchen. I actually thought it was a lot cooler inside than out, all protected by the earth, but then I'm used to the heat, and folks up here aren't.

First thing Magnus had me do was cook up some catfish. He liked it, and so I'm hired! He pays a real fair wage, plus part of the tips at the end of the night. I'm staying at the Woman's Hotel not far from here. I've got my own room, it's comfy and quiet and the rate is good. I usually eat my meals at The Widow. In the morning, I pick up rolls at a bakery, go straight there and make a pot of real coffee—they brew it too weak up here. I'll see how the money is after the first of the year—boardinghouses are cheaper, but I'd have a roommate and not much privacy, so if I can stay where I am, I'm better off. I'll be making decent money at The Widow, and not much to spend it on. All I do is go to work, take walks along the river and come back to the hotel.

I miss you and Theda something awful. Also, the H&M and the creek. But I'm trying not to think about anything 'til I get set up here. Easier that way. Have you seen Theda? I know she'll find a way to sneak me a letter. Maybe give it to you. Are you eating OK? How's the new cook? Probably not as good as me, but I hope the customers like her food.

*Love,
Hazel*

But there was no word from Theda until just before Christmas, although Milt wrote Hazel regularly. He hadn't heard anything either. Hazel struggled each day not to despair. She kept herself busy. The changing weather helped. By late October, icy winds blew down the streets of Minneapolis, and she had to go out and buy wool skirts, a wool dress, coat and hat, gloves, boots and a long scarf to wrap around her. She'd never seen so much wool, never imagined air could be so cold. Inside the Merry Widow, as Magnus had promised, it was always cozy, what with the big cookstove and her cooking up soup and stews and the other things people ate in the winter in Minnesota. But the air outside! Hazel had never felt anything so cold and penetrating. She put on all her layers every time she went out, but still, she felt the wind. Although she had to admit that the snow, which started falling in November, was real pretty. The Mississippi had chunks of ice but never seemed to really freeze over, or if it did, only for a few days or a week. The current kept it open, Magnus said. With the leaves off the trees, she could see it better, the hardworking river that flowed all the way south to the Delta. Sometimes she wished it would take her along, float her like a log or a stray boat, but usually it was a comfort, plain and simple.

Then she got a big package from Milt. It had a letter from him, some newspaper clippings and—oh, joy!—finally a letter from Theda with her perfume drifting out of it. She set that aside and saved it for last. Milt wrote:

Dear Hazel,

Diner is going okay. We still have most of the regulars. Some of them miss you and ask about you. Others don't say anything, but we're making good money. I'm sending you some by Western Union so you can have a little extra for Christmas. I know you say you're earning okay at The Merry Widow, but I want to make sure you don't want for anything.

Well, I got some news, and it's not good, so brace yourself.

Theda's family married her off. Just like that. She snuck out to see me a couple weeks ago and told me. They really clamped down on her after the raid, hardly let her out of their sight. But the family cook's always been her friend and covers for her when she needs to get away. If she was from a regular family, it wouldn't be so hard, but they're old Savannah money, so she didn't have much choice. Either she got married and respectable, or they'd ship her off somewhere. I sent the clippings. If you ask me, it just ain't fair —you up there, Theda sold off to the highest bidder, like she says. Makes me glad we're not rich. We got our problems, but not like that.

Maybe the New Year will be better. I sure hope so.

Yours,
Milt

Hazel unfolded the clippings from the society page of the Savannah newspaper. A headline read: *Miss Alexander Becomes Bride of Albert Hawkins.* Below, a photograph of Theda, in white, unsmiling, alongside a compact, muscular man who looked older. Dark hair with some gray and a smile that looked forced. *Albert Hawkins, owner of lumber companies in Georgia and elsewhere, weds Miss Theodora Alexander in an elegant afternoon ceremony...*

Hazel had to stop reading. She closed her eyes. *Oh, my God, Theda,* she thought. *What have they done to you?* And how would the two of them ever be able to reunite? Her belly contracted as it had so many times during the days after the raid.

Finally, she opened Theda's letter:

My dearest, darling Hazel,

These past months have been the worst of my life. I've missed you every single day. I try to imagine you by my side, hear your voice, feel your touch. It's my only pleasure, because my family's kept me a prisoner. I never thought they were capable of this—no one seemed to give a care what I did until the raid and the newspapers. They actually hired a guard to make sure I couldn't sneak out of the house like I used to do. I've been sewing just to keep my hands busy and my mind off this hell.

But that's not even the worst. <u>They have married me off</u>. Like I was chattel, which in their eyes I am. Something to be bought and sold. I mean that. I'm sure they paid. They might call it a dowry, but it was a business deal. With Albert Hawkins, 30 but still single, rich as King Midas, according to my father, and wanting an heir. I think they had to sweeten the pot because of this "problem" I have with liking girls. (And not just any girl, but <u>you</u>!) Because you see, Hazel, for them, it's a sickness. A stain on the family name. So they have to try to cover it up. Which is where Albert comes in.

They said it was either marry him or go to a hospital for women with "delusions." I don't even want to think what that might be like, and so I figured anything was better. Maybe, I thought, just maybe, Albert would listen to reason. I told him I really don't like men in that way, never have, but I could tell he didn't understand. Said he could change me! Like he was a wizard! I just laughed. Told him I need a lot of independence, that I'm a loner. That part went better. He said he has to travel for business anyway. Which made me hope that he has other women—like all the rich men in this town, starting with dearest Father, who's not dead after all and has a second family in Atlanta (just found out about that). He magically appeared after I got out of jail.

So by the time you read this, I'll be a married woman. In name only, but still.... What's comforting me (aside from thoughts of you) is imagining myself as Houdini, locked up in a trunk with chains. Maybe even underwater. And like him, I will find a way out. I don't know when I'll see you or talk to you again, but I'll stay in touch through Milt. Such a good man. Thanks to Alma, I've been able to sneak out a few times to see him and get news about you. Glad you're safe up there, tho it's so far away it makes me want to cry. But I'm trying to keep my wits about me and stay strong.

Wish me luck. Maybe Albert's got a whole harem of women and will leave me alone. Or maybe I'll somehow produce a scion for him and be able to live my life. And please, above all, don't forget what I told you in Williams' office. My time with you—our time—has been the best of my life. I regret nothing.

Your Theda

Hazel's eyes burned. She wished she were back in Savannah to protect Theda, whisk her away to some place cramped minds and prejudices couldn't reach. If she'd known things were going to turn out like this, she would have just fed Theda and sent her away forever the day she came to the diner. But would she have been able to resist her? Who knows.

I regret nothing, she repeated, from the end of Theda's letter. But she, Hazel, did regret things. She'd created a disaster for herself, Theda and Milt. Not to mention her family, from whom she'd heard nothing since the newspapers ran the story with her name and picture. Had they disowned her? While they didn't have money like Theda's folks, Hazel knew they despised people who made a spectacle of themselves. Which she certainly had, even if that was never her plan. Her family had worked hard to buy their small houses, dress decently, do everything they could not to be seen as poor white trash. And then their daughter was arrested in an illegal bar for odd girls. They might never speak to her again.

* * *

She had a little Christmas dinner with Magnus, the barmaid and the rest of the crew at the Merry Widow. She roasted a ham and served it with baked potatoes, green beans and an apple cake. Magnus toasted with the house whiskey. "Here's to a good year!" Hazel could barely think of the coming 1923, which seemed empty and cold as a cave on the Mississippi. She got up to make coffee so the others wouldn't see her long face.

On Christmas Eve, she took a trolley over to the Minneapolis Basilica for midnight Mass. She wanted to get lost, be where no one knew her.

And as far as she could tell, no one did.

Chapter Six

Theda: Faunce Ridge, August 1937

In the early morning, Theda followed Sadie's car out of Baudette and south of town. Nothing but trees, fields, the occasional farm—the soil black unlike the red Georgia clay—and a white clapboard country schoolhouse. And Hazel, hair like a warming flame, riding shotgun beside her, with Teddy asleep in the back seat. She'd dreamed of the three of them together, and now she felt she was back in that dream, comforting and strange.

"Slow down and turn here," Hazel said, pointing at two narrow tracks of gravel and sand, a ridge of grass in the middle. It couldn't be a road.

"Are you sure?"

"This is what roads are like in this country. They look more like paths, but they all go somewhere. The bog, all the little towns people built are up ahead."

Trees began to appear. First straight, spindly saplings, then evergreens she'd never seen before and finally graceful white ones with peeling bark that looked like something out of a Japanese ink drawing. "What are these?" she asked Hazel.

"Birch. The straight ones are poplar."

The trees grew thicker and closer to the road as they drove further west, grass so high that it brushed the underside of her car. Theda struggled to keep going forward. "Why would anyone build a town here?"

Hazel shrugged. "Land was cheap and no one to get in their business. For a lot of folks, that was heaven."

Theda pondered this. "But groceries, a pharmacy, needles and thread...?"

"Oh, they had a general store that sold pretty much everything," Hazel said. "Ruby's. You'll see it or what's left of it."

Then, although the day was clear, something like fog began to drift through the open windows. It smelled bittersweet and tickled the back of Theda's throat. "Hazel, what is this? Are you sure we're going the right way? I can't take Teddy into a fire."

"Oh, it's fine," Hazel said. "Just another queer thing about this country. Muskeg smoke—that's what they call it here. The bog has layers of peat, and in late summer, early fall, when things dry out, it starts to smolder way down deep. The smell is odd. Took me a while to get accustomed, but now I kind of like it."

Theda didn't know whether she liked it or not. The trees, the lonely road, the odd smoke all made her feel sad and full of longing. She glanced at Hazel. "Any more coffee?"

Hazel reached for the thermos and poured her a cup.

The hot liquid soothed her throat. She'd barely slept the night before, wondering where they were going and for how long and if she could protect Teddy from his father. Now they'd escaped Savannah, she was less worried about Albert's threats to throw her into a hospital. It would be harder for him to take Teddy away from her, she reasoned, in this remote place where he wouldn't be able to control the legal system like he could in Georgia.

She slowed down. The road was getting even rougher. Deep holes, lots of bumps. She groaned, worrying about the car. She had absolutely no idea how it worked, much less how to fix it, and she hoped it didn't break down. Then she remembered what Teddy always said. *Smooth roads are boring, Mama.* She laughed.

"This child of mine," she said when Hazel looked at her. "He just loves bumpy roads. He thinks flying up and down in the car is the best thing in the world."

"Well, he should be real happy about now." Hazel looked around.

Muskeg

"We're getting close."

The road widened, and Theda could see evidence of a town or what had been a town. They were in a clearing, on a street of sorts. No people, although there were at least a dozen houses, maybe more, all deserted, and an empty building with a wide front porch, a tattered American flag and a life-sized tin sign of a man in a top hat and an elegant Chesterfield coat, holding a cigarette.

"That was Ruby's place," Hazel said. "General store and post office. Ruby was a pistol. Look at her the wrong way and she'd yell at you, but she made the best root beer…"

Sadie stopped up ahead, and so did Theda. Teddy stirred in the backseat. "Are we there?"

"We'll find out soon enough," Theda said. "Go back to sleep."

Sadie and François came over to the car. "This is it," Sadie said. "Let's go see Marie."

"What about Teddy?" He'd already dozed off again.

"He'll be fine," Sadie said. "Nice and quiet here."

Theda gave him a last look and climbed out of the car with Hazel. The air felt fresh, even with the mysterious smoke odor. *Muskeg*. Around the empty houses, more evergreens and the slender white birch.

Marie came down the road to meet them in another blue dress that came halfway down her calves. Theda guessed it was homemade and admired its simple lines, even though she guessed fashion was the last thing on Marie's mind.

In contrast to her golden-brown, dreamy eyes, Marie spoke in short, clipped sentences and seemed to know exactly what she was talking about. "You and your boy, Teddy, you're going to stay with me for a while. Until all this clears up. Let me show you."

"Show us what?" Teddy had gotten out of the car and was behind them.

Theda felt a rush of tenderness. "Thought you were asleep, darlin'."

"I didn't want to miss out." Teddy extended his hand like a full-grown man. "Pleased to see you, again, ma'am." Theda watched Marie smile, take in her boy, too grown-up for his twelve years. And much better behaved than he'd been in the past few days with Hazel and Sadie.

She smiled over his head at Hazel. She knew that her old love wasn't much for kids, but she hoped in time she'd get close to Teddy. She still dreamed of the three of them settling down somewhere once all this was over.

They followed Marie down a trail that opened onto a small cemetery with gravestones and rough wooden crosses. So different from the cemeteries in Savannah with their elaborately carved marble and granite angels. She stopped. She'd always been queasy about walking on the dead.

"Don't worry," Marie said. "It's the old settlers, the ones who homesteaded and passed on. They're peaceful down there. Maybe even lonely. Probably nice for them to hear voices every now and then."

Theda nodded but stepped carefully. The path on the other side of the cemetery circled around a thicket of evergreens that smelled spicy when she held a branch to her nose.

"Cedar," Marie said.

Finally another clearing with a small house, an equally small barn and a corral with a golden palomino who came up to the fence and whinnied. Marie stroked his head. "This is Butter. And Butter, this here is Theda and Teddy."

"A horse!" Teddy exclaimed. It was the first time since they arrived that Theda had heard anything like excitement in his voice.

Marie opened the door to the little house. "Come on in. You'll all get to know each other soon enough."

They walked into a room with a large iron cookstove. Warm and cozy, it smelled of dill and other plants Theda couldn't identify drying in upside-down bouquets on nails high up on the walls. A garden brought indoors. "It's like something in a fairy tale," she said.

Marie laughed. "Hope it's a good one, not one of those with witches and trolls." She pulled out benches and chairs, and soon they were all sitting around the table, eating some kind of bread with cranberries and nuts and drinking coffee with fresh cream.

Once they ate, Marie took them out to see the barn. Theda had never been inside a barn, although she'd seen them from the road on drives around Savannah, and she was struck by how warm it was. Butter stood in a stall munching hay. Nearby, two black and white cows switched their tails back and forth and mooed.

Teddy laughed. "I never heard a cow moo before."

"Why? What do cows in Savannah say?" Marie pointed to a ladder built flush against the wall at the far end of the barn. "Follow me."

Theda turned. "You coming, Hazel?"

"Sure." She grinned. "Always did love to climb when I was a girl."

Marie was already up the ladder and Teddy after her. Theda followed, then Hazel. Five or six wooden rungs led up through an opening in the ceiling to the second story of the barn, which had open arches on either end that let in the sun.

"The haymow," Marie said. "Hayloft, some people call it."

Large mounds of hay were piled up high, but in a corner swept clean to reveal a rough wooden floor stood two small beds made of logs. Each had a mattress of some sort, a quilt and a pillow. Between them, a small table with a kerosene lantern.

"This here is where you'll sleep," said Marie. "Not fancy, but you'll see that Butter and the two cows keep it nice and warm. Still August, but it's cool at night out here. If you get cold, I'll bring more quilts."

It reminded Theda of the drawings in the books she'd read to Teddy as a young child: cozy beds, moon peeking in through the window. Her bedroom in Savannah was spacious and comfortable, so big she could get lost in it. But now, as she beheld the two neat beds with their colorful quilts, a sensation of peace crept into her body, and she realized she hadn't felt so safe since her time back at the H&M diner. She bit her lip to keep from tearing up.

"Well, Teddy," she said. "What do you think of our new place?" She hoped he liked it or would at least tolerate it. You could never tell—he'd been raised with a lot of luxury, although she'd always taught him that fine things were the least important part of life.

He stood silent, looking around the hayloft bedroom, the large windows. Finally, he said, "Well, Mama, I guess I never thought about sleeping in a barn. Sort of like camping, I suppose."

At least he was trying to be polite. It was a start.

Before Sadie left with Hazel and François, she pulled out a map of Lake of the Woods County and spread it on the hood of her car. "Look, Theda. Albert and his boys can't hardly find their way out here unless they come to Baudette. Just one road from the south—Highway 72, see?—the one we were on before we turned off—and it ends at the border. Then they'll have to take 11 west to go into Baudette. With any luck, they'll land at my hotel. One way or another, I'll find out. Town ain't that big. Nobody knows you two are out here 'cept Hazel and Minnie and François and me."

Theda pointed to Oak Island at the top of the map "What if they go there and try to make Hazel talk?" The very thought of Albert and his goons at the resort made her feel sick inside.

Hazel put her hand on her arm. "We'll be ready. I promise."

Sadie shook her head. "They might just be fool enough to try that. But hopefully, we'd find out first. The only way they can get there that makes any sense is through Baudette. Then a boat. Albert might have detectives with him, but they won't be able to cross that lake by themselves. No one can unless they're used to it."

Theda wasn't convinced. "He's got enough money to buy off every cop and sheriff and judge for miles around. He could raise his own private army. What if he rents a plane? What then?"

Sadie nodded. "The thing with bullies is sooner or later, they get so cocksure, they don't look where they're going. Faunce Ridge ain't the only ghost town out here—there's half a dozen or so villages where nobody lives anymore in God knows how many thousand acres, trees and bog and so grown over, you can't see nothing." Her voice lowered, became soothing. "Besides, too much fear's not good for you or the boy."

She jabbed at the map. "Remember, no one's left here but Marie and Little Roy and you two. That's it. The Duprees, of course, but they're loggers with a place back in the woods, and they'd rather die than talk to outsiders about what happens or who they see around here. Plus it ain't hunting season yet. So no strangers coming around."

Theda nodded as if she actually understood. But she didn't. Nor was she reassured. The mention of roads and boats and detectives and strangers made her hands shake. She hid them behind her so it wouldn't show. And Hazel, bless her heart, grabbed them in her warm fingers. "Don't worry," she whispered in her ear.

"Besides," Sadie said. "He's just one man. With his weak place, like any man. Once we find that, don't matter how many people he hires."

Theda hoped she was right. What was Albert's weak spot? Not her. That she knew, despite his demands that she be a "real wife" to him. And not even Teddy. Maybe his pride. Or his need to control everyone and everything around him.

"I got to go now, honey," Hazel said.

Sadie and François moved away. They understood, Theda thought.

"Will you write?" she asked Hazel, trying not to sound pleading.

"Oh, darlin'. I'd have to send the letters to Hotel Pascal, so Sadie and François can bring them out. No post office here anymore."

"But you'll write at least one? Promise?"

Hazel nodded.

They had a long, quiet embrace. Theda tried to memorize the way Hazel smelled, the warmth of her body. She knew Minnie was waiting back on the island, but she wasn't going to think about that now. "I love you," she said.

"Love you, too," Hazel whispered.

But even that didn't comfort Theda. What did Hazel mean? That she loved her because of all they'd been through when they were young? Could Hazel love her and Minnie at the same time?

Finally, Theda let her pull away, but she didn't want to.

* * *

She and Teddy went to bed not long after supper, a tasty venison stew with potatoes and carrots and onions. In the twilight that Marie said lingered for hours, they climbed the ladder in the barn, warmed by animal vapor and fragrant with fresh hay. Theda lit the kerosene lantern just long enough for them to get into bed and cover up. They'd wash the next day at the pump or the flowing artesian well near the garden. The water was pure and very cold, with a slight reddish tinge. "Iron," Marie had said. "It's good for you."

She took off her outer clothes and slipped into bed, keeping her back turned to Teddy, who was becoming a man faster than she would have liked. The mattress was filled with soft cloth, maybe rags Marie had collected. She burrowed around to make a space for her body and lay back on the feather pillow. Her body began to relax in a way it hadn't since they left Savannah.

She looked across at Teddy. "Are you warm enough?"

"Yeah," he said, gazing up at the rafters that arced over their heads.

Theda blew out the lamp. Outside the haymow window, stars and a crescent moon glowed in the darkening sky.

"You know what? I might get to like it here, Mama. But..." Teddy trailed off, and she heard the even breathing that meant he'd fallen asleep.

Just before Theda slept, she saw a barn swallow. Marie had told her they made their nests in the rafters. It flitted in through the haymow window, silhouetted for a second against the dying light.

Chapter Seven

Hazel: Minneapolis, January 1923

Hazel brooded about Theda's forced marriage to Albert as she trudged the snowy sidewalks to the Merry Widow, dodging patches of ice, face wrapped in wool scarves to keep out the wind. Would she submit to him or put up a fight? Was it worth it to resist since he'd probably win? And how on earth could she escape? Albert had money to pay servants, even guards, to make sure she didn't get away. Theda might be smart and spirited, but she was no Houdini. Of course, there were other things she could do. Put a sleeping powder in his food, bribe the people he hired and make her getaway. If she had to, would Theda attack Albert? Kill him if she was forced to defend herself? Certain tabloid headlines began to jump out at her from sidewalk newsstands: HUSBAND MURDERED IN HIS BED! WIFE ARRESTED! Or in the more scandalous publications: KILLED HER HUSBAND! PERVERTED GIRL LOVE NEST! Hazel guessed there was more to these stories—a husband who cheated on the wife; a desperate woman who was tired of being beaten. Or someone who liked girls but wasn't lucky enough to have a husband like Milt.

But despite Hazel's ruminations, it was always a relief to jingle the doorbell of the Merry Widow and enter the smoky interior, half cave, half building. Hazel had never been much of a drinker. For her, the kitchen was the heart of the Widow, and she loved the fact that when she walked in, the first thing she picked up was the scent of onions, steak, bacon, fried eggs and potatoes, whatever she'd cooked the day before. Along with something sweet, because she insisted on making desserts for the customers. And, of course, coffee.

Magnus teased her. "What you trying to pull, Hazel? Keep on cooking and baking like you do, and you'll turn the damn place into a restaurant! We're running a speak, here, don't you know." He'd frown in mock anger, which made her laugh. She knew Magnus prized her cooking skills, which was a comfort and distracted her from worrying about Theda.

* * *

One night Magnus invited her out for a steak dinner. Once they were settled and the waiter took their order, he said, "You've been looking pretty down in the mouth lately, Hazel. I know this ain't your place, and the winters are godawful, but I got the feeling it's more than that. What the hell happened to make you come all the way up here? I know it wasn't for the snow and ice."

Hazel laughed and then teared up. She was grateful for a decent place to stay and a job she liked. And she knew she was lucky not to be behind bars or in some asylum. But still.

"Aw, didn't mean to make you cry." Magnus patted her hand with his big one. "You're part of my crew, and my crew's my family."

Maybe better than family, Hazel thought. She'd never be able to talk with her sister, Mavis, about these things. Or any of her brothers and sisters. Just Milt. But Magnus made everyone feel welcome. He always greeted the customers, exchanged a few words, shook hands, made sure they got their order. And all kinds of people came to The Merry Widow. Lots of men, of course, including cops and lawyers and judges from the nearby courthouse, but also women, sometimes with men, but often with other girls. And although Hazel couldn't tell for sure, it looked like some of them might be sweethearts. The way they sat close together and whispered. How one would touch the other's hand or arm, sometimes her hair. Girls like her.

"Well," Hazel said. "Truth is, I had to leave. Didn't have a choice."

Magnus's brow furrowed.

Muskeg

"There was a speakeasy in Savannah," Hazel began, but then stopped. Because that wasn't really when everything started. When was it? When Theda arrived at the H&M? When she married Milt? She tried again. "You see, when I was little, I knew I was different from the other girls. I liked to play with boys—climb trees, anything outdoors. My girlfriends had their dolls and then when they got older, all they could think about was boys and getting married. That was the farthest thing from my mind. I knew I didn't like boys that way, but I just kept my mouth shut and lay low."

And she told him the whole story.

Magnus ordered coffee, puffed on his cigar and listened, nodding at times. "Way I see it," he said, "Don't matter who's sweet on who. Who you bunk down with. Unless it's a kid." He told her about his childhood. "They took my poor ma and stuck her in the crazy hospital. My pa was long gone. So for me, it was the orphanage with the nuns or the streets. I didn't like rules, so I went to the streets. And I got used to pretty much everything. 'Cept the dirty old men who liked boys. Or little girls."

He'd come up way rougher than her, Hazel reflected. No wonder he understood things other people didn't.

"So they chased you out of town. Made you leave your place and your diner and Milt and married your girl off to some rich fellow," he said. "And now you have to hope she gets away from the husband. Maybe after a while, things calm down and you can go back down there. Or have her come up here."

She nodded. "That's about the size of it."

Magnus pushed the coffee cup toward her. "Have some 'fore it gets cold."

Hazel obeyed. Too weak, as usual.

He lit up another cigar, blew a cloud of smoke. Hazel had never liked cigars, but now that she'd been around Magnus, she'd not only gotten used to the odor but didn't even mind it anymore.

"But for now, here you are in a big city in the North."

"Yes."

Hazel thought of the cold waiting for her outside the restaurant.

"Way I see it, sometimes you just got to make your family. Even if it's not the one you started with. For better or worse, you got us—the crew at the Merry Widow. People to talk to, eat meals with, have a little fun."

Hazel looked through the cigar haze at Magnus's ruddy face, the laugh wrinkles around his eyes. He was right. If Milt and Theda were her second family, the ones who accepted her as her original family never could, then the bartenders and the other workers at The Merry Widow made up the third. She thought of their jokes, their camaraderie, small kindnesses. How one of the men would always insist on walking her back to the Woman's Hotel after dark. How often they praised her food, the new dishes, the good coffee. "Keeps us awake," Ike, one of the bartenders, told her.

A warm glow nestled into her stomach along with the food she'd just eaten. "Thank you, Magnus," she said.

"Don't get me wrong," he replied. "You've had some hard knocks. But—"

"It could be worse," Hazel finished his sentence. People in Minnesota said that a lot.

"Tell you what," Magnus said. "This July, I'm going way up north for a fishing trip. Two weeks. Take some of the fellows with me. You come, too. It's a beautiful place, an island. You'll feel better, even if you don't like to fish."

"So summer's going to come?" Hazel was only half-joking.

"Hell yes!" Magnus laughed his big laugh. "Just wait. Spring comes, people go crazy. They toss their winter clothes, they sit outside, they sing, say hi to everyone who goes by. It's a great time."

* * *

That night, Hazel started a letter to Milt. *I still miss you and everyone and everything something terrible. But I think I landed in a good spot. For now, anyway. It could be worse.*

Chapter Eight

Little Roy: Faunce Ridge, August 1937

When Theda and Teddy arrived, Little Roy hadn't been around children for at least a year, since the Relocation when people pulled out of Faunce Ridge. In fact, he hadn't spent a lot of time with kids since the October 1910 forest fire that burned all the towns and land along the border and took his ma and pa and twin brother, Rex. All the Rydeen family except for him.

True, him and Rex had turned twenty just before the Fire, but since they were the only offspring, their folks still treated them like they were teenagers. Little Roy always hoped that they'd meet up one day with a pair of sisters and get hitched in a double wedding. But in the meantime, there was more than enough to do on the farm, with the cows and chickens and pigs, the big garden and the fields of clover and alfalfa to hay.

Little Roy wasn't there when the fire came for his family that October. He'd gone into Baudette that day for a fiddling contest, but they were on the farm in the woods south of Baudette with no place to go but the root cellar and no river or lake close enough to jump in and wait it out. They didn't want him to go, what with the bad winds from the West and the muskeg smoke it was blowing in.

"Who knows how it'll be in Baudette," Rex warned him. "At least here we're way south of the railroad tracks, and you know how the train always kicks up sparks."

But Little Roy went anyway, catching a ride into town with the mailman. "I'll be back," he yelled at Rex. "Don't eat up all the pie!" Their mother canned pumpkin this time of year and baked.

He was just talking to make noise, like his mother would say. Deep down, he knew he shouldn't leave. It was his pride, his damn fool pride. He was the best fiddler around, everyone told him so, and he wanted to prove it by winning the contest. When they arrived in Baudette, Little Roy thanked the mailman, got off with his fiddle case on Main Street and started walking toward the school where the competition was going to be held.

He realized at once he'd made a mistake in coming. The air was smokier than back at the farm, and a strong wind blew cinders through the air. Shopkeepers were shutting their stores and families rushed past him. He stopped a boy and asked where he was going. "To the depot! A train's coming from Canada to take us over to Rainy." The town of Rainy River, Ontario, was just across the river of the same name.

Little Roy tried to think. He couldn't depend on catching the train if everyone in Baudette jammed into the cars. Water was the only thing that would keep him safe. So he cut away from the crowd and ran down to the Baudette Bay, which flowed into the Rainy. Already men and women stood knee-deep, wrapped in blankets with children and babies on their shoulders. Little Roy waded into the ice-cold water but barely had time to shiver before the wind came up even stronger, howling like a pack of wolves. Giant bundles of sparks flew over their heads, and the whistle from one of the timber mills started to blow and kept on until he thought his ears would split.

Somehow he and the others managed to stay in the water. When the blood-red sun came up, they were all safe, but Baudette was a smoldering ruin.

The National Guard arrived with tents and blankets, but all Little Roy wanted was to get back to his family. He asked everyone if they'd heard about the Rydeens, but no one had.

Finally, he went to the sheriff and talked him into driving to the farm, a good twenty miles south of Baudette. Little Roy thought he'd be jittery, but he felt a weird calm, keenly aware of everything around him: blackened grass and trees, bare foundations of farmhouses, soot that floated through the air and landed on them like dark snowflakes.

The sheriff tried to make conversation "They say a lot of folks in your neck of the woods got to Rapid River and stayed there until it was all over. Bet that's what your people did." But Little Roy knew the Rydeen farm was far south of the Rapid, certainly not close enough to walk or run there.

The closer they got, the more dread grew inside him until he felt like he'd choke on it.

As they rounded the last bend, Little Roy saw the mailbox was still standing and sighed with relief. But then the farm came into sight. Barn, chicken coop, pigsty, sheds, outhouse, all leveled. Only the plow remained, tines charred coal black. And a pit where the house should have been. Little Roy jumped down and started running toward it.

"Wait for me, son!" the sheriff yelled.

But Little Roy barely heard him, and it wouldn't have mattered anyway. He was going to find his family. He stopped short at the smoldering crater that had been the root cellar. Shards of glass glinted in the sun—the jars of canned vegetables, fruit and meat that exploded in the heat. Surely his folks must have gotten away. Surely they were going to come up the road any minute, covered with soot, tell him how they escaped. But everything was silent.

Finally, he forced himself to look straight down into the hole. And that's when he saw the three blackened forms. One tall—his pa; one shorter—his ma; and one just his size, because him and Rex came early, and they were runts and always would be, or at least that's what his pa told them, except now there'd only be one runt, which was him, and he dropped to his knees in the ashes and sobbed, fists jammed in his eyes so he couldn't have to see.

That was the last day he talked. There was nothing more to say, and even if there was, the fire had burned all the words out of him. He had no money for a gravestone, so Ma and Pa and Rex were buried in a mass grave near Baudette with all the other people who died in the fire.

Little Roy stumbled through the next years. Slept wherever he could, played his fiddle for dances to earn food money and drank all the hooch that came his way. Eventually, he heard that people were homesteading out at Faunce Ridge, south of Williams and many miles west of where his family died. He staked a claim there by the Rapid River, which flowed across the county, close as he could without getting flooded in the spring. He'd never again live in a place that wasn't next to water. Planted trees and sunflowers all around so no one could see. Played for dances at the schoolhouse and kept drinking.

Carl and Hilde Rousseau were his best friends at Faunce Ridge. Hilde brought him canned venison, chicken, vegetables. And coffee and plums and fresh-baked bread. Little Roy would try to pay her, but she'd put up her hands, shake her head and say, "Little Roy, don't you dare think about money, what with all that beautiful music you make for us."

Even so, he never imagined how much he'd miss them when the Relocation uprooted the town. When Carl and Hilde Rousseau waved their last goodbye, he choked up and had to turn around fast so they wouldn't see him cry.

They'd offered him land back of their new place north on Graceton Beach Road near Lake of the Woods. "Very deep in the forest," Carl had said. "You would never see a person unless you wanted to so much. You could build your house in those trees and then become like the wind. No one see you." Carl spoke French before English, so he talked different.

Such a kind offer that Little Roy had to think about it, least he could do. But in the end, he decided no. Hard enough to lose his folks, the farm where he grew up. And now the Rousseaus, closest thing to family he'd had since. But what if something happened to them, too? At least in Faunce Ridge he had his little place, the only other home he'd ever had, and the forest and the bog.

But then they were gone. No more smell of Hilde's rye bread. No more Carl saying things in his funny way or taking him to flush grouse. No more Hilde singing in the kitchen while he sat at their table with a cup of coffee. That's when Little Roy realized how lonely he was. Deep down, he liked to have people around. Just not too close. Thank God for Marie.

So when he heard Theda go on about Marie's garden and Teddy ask the name of trees—in that way they talked, saying *ah* for *I* and leaving off the end of words, like *mornin'* and *darlin'* and *ridin'*—he realized he was happier than he'd been in a long time. Found himself whistling again. When he woke up the next morning, he got himself right over to Marie's place to see the visitors.

"Mr. Roy," Teddy said to him over breakfast, pulling out a small notebook and a pencil and handing it to him. "I was thinking that if I ask you something, you could write the answer down here."

Little Roy hardly ever wrote. Hoped he still remembered how. But he nodded his thanks.

Marie said, "You can just call him Roy like I do. Ain't that right?"

Little Roy nodded. Truth is, he didn't care much what people called him, though he liked the way Marie said "Roy" pure and simple.

"Well, ma'am," Teddy said. "It just seems more polite to call him Mr. Roy if he doesn't mind."

Little Roy shrugged. Nobody'd ever called him Mr. Roy.

* * *

After breakfast, he showed Teddy the fire tower. On the edge of the town, but easy walking since Faunce Ridge wasn't very big—mainly houses and a schoolhouse thrown up along State Aid Road 2. The tower had stairs that zig-zagged up to a tiny room at the very top. If a fire broke out, you could climb up and see where it was headed.

"I've never been in a real fire tower," Teddy said.

Truth is, Little Roy hadn't either. The tower was just a part of Faunce Ridge, and he'd never bothered to climb it.

"Can we go up?"

Little Roy nodded, and they started up the stairs. The view shocked him. Empty houses, barns with no animals outside, a few leftover gardens with volunteer corn and tomatoes and bolted rhubarb. Ruby's store all closed up, nobody banging the screen door or sitting out on the front porch. Some big holes where people got their places up on wheels and moved them somewhere else. And everything so quiet, except for Marie's rooster with his cock-a-doodle-doo, and the wind in the trees.

"How come people left?" Teddy asked. "Did they want to?"

Little Roy shook his head. Maybe a few who were tired of trying to scratch a living out of the sandy soil, owing taxes they'd never be able to pay for the federal ditches that didn't drain that good anyway. But most folks were pretty happy at Faunce Ridge. Cheap living. No mayor or police or preacher to bother them. He remembered the goodbye party at the school, him fiddling, which was good because he could pay attention to the tunes instead of thinking about how all the dancers would soon be leaving. At one of the breaks, Carl Rousseau had thrown his arm around him and made a little rhyme the way he did: "Ah, my friend! The towns they come, the towns they go, but friendship is forever, no?" To be polite, Little Roy had nodded, but he had his doubts. Carl and Hilde's new place was a good thirty miles north. Without a car or a horse, the only way he could visit was if he walked.

"The government made them move, right?" Teddy said.

Little Roy sighed, remembering how it was in the beginning when they first got word they'd have to move.

"Hell, no," Ruby, the storekeeper and postmaster, had said. "They'll have to drag me out. And I'll yell and scream the whole time!"

But then the government took away the post office. And stopped plowing the roads in winter. Finally, they closed the school. Superintendent herself came out to talk with the parents about how important it was for their kids to get an education. So the families pulled up stakes and moved to Williams or Baudette leaving only the most stubborn folks, meaning him and Marie and the Duprees.

Teddy pointed to a collection of buildings and tents just west of Faunce, on the other side of a gravel road. They could see men walking, carrying axes and shovels. "What's that?"

Little Roy cupped his hand into a C, like he was making shadow pictures on a wall. He did it again and then a third time.

"C…C…C," Teddy said. "Oh, the C.C.C., Civilian Conservation Corp. My father says they're Reds. 'Course that's what he thinks about Roosevelt, too. Could we go visit?"

Little Roy held out his hands to say *why not?* He'd never been over to the Norris Camp CCC. Thought of it as just more government people. But if Teddy wanted to, he'd give it a try.

They scrambled down the steps and took the winding Faunce Ridge Trail to the camp. Young men who looked not much older than Teddy walked around bare-chested or wearing undershirts that showed muscled arms and chests.

"Hey, little buddy," one said to Teddy. He was tall, with brown hair bleached by the sun and freckles scattered across his nose. "Looking for a job?"

Little Roy chuckled. If the CCC hired twelve-year-old boys, Teddy was curious enough, he just might sign up.

"Your son?" the young man asked.

"This is Mr. Roy, but he doesn't talk," Teddy said.

"What's your name?"

"Teddy," the boy said. "Theodore Albert, really, but it's too long, so my mother calls me Teddy. My father says the CCC's a bunch of communists who don't want to work."

The young man laughed. "Is that what he says? Well, your pa should spend a day with us, then see what he thinks. Say, my name's Ben. Want to take a look around?"

He showed them a long, narrow washhouse with a line of covered toilets on a platform, and across from each one, a sink with soap and a towel hanging on a nail. Big shower room in the back. And just across the way, a cookhouse still warm and smelling of bacon and fried onions.

"Great chow," Ben said. "Some lady from Williams cooks for us. More food than most of us ever got at home."

"How long you been here?" Teddy asked.

Ben counted on his fingers. "About three months now. Probably stay a year, maybe more. They send most of my pay home to the folks, but I'll get a little grubstake and see what I do with it."

"And what kind of work do you do?"

The kid was sharp, Little Roy thought.

Ben smiled down at him. "Mainly plant trees," he said. "The lumberjacks clear cut a lot of the big pines. Idea is to build them up again."

As they walked back to Faunce Ridge, Teddy said, "That's a good thing, isn't it, planting trees?"

Little Roy shrugged, thinking of the empty houses on either side of them. Putting in more pine didn't seem like much of an excuse to kick all those people off their places.

But Teddy was already on to something else. "How about taking me to see the bog?"

Little Roy walked his fingers across the palm of his other hand, pointed down the road and then to himself.

"You're going to walk…" Teddy began.

Little Roy pointed at Teddy and then back at himself.

"*We're* going to walk…"

He nodded, then made the shape of a roof.

"…to a house. *Your* house?"

Then Little Roy took Teddy's hand and traced a path with an "x" at the end of the palm.

"And you're going to make something—a map?"

Little Roy nodded.

They continued down Faunce Ridge Road through the town to his house by the river. Little Roy cut through the trees and sunflowers and bramble, holding branches for Teddy so they wouldn't snap in his face. Probably the only way you could tell someone lived there was at night, by the kerosene lantern in his loft window that gave just enough light he could read *Black Watch Detective Magazine.*

They came into the clearing where Roy's place stood. Not much—half log, half board—but it had a sleeping loft and one big room downstairs with a cookstove, a table that would fit four people, though he only had two chairs, and a faded red armchair somebody'd left for him. On the stove, a pot for stew, a cast iron frying pan and a coffeepot. Above, shelves with salt and pepper, some flour, sugar and coffee, along with a few plates and cups, a little silverware and a big wooden spoon he used for everything.

His fiddle sat in a case on its own shelf, along with the rags he used to clean it.

Outside, poles held up a porch with a rocking chair where he could sit and watch the Rapid River. And beyond that, a pump with soap and a towel, and an outhouse set back a ways. Didn't really need much else. Except right now he could use something to write on. Then he remembered the notebook and pencil Teddy gave him earlier.

Sitting down at the table, he began to draw a map of Faunce Ridge that showed the bog, the CCC Camp and the narrow road that flooded in rainy times. He sketched tamarack trees, made an arrow that pointed down under them and wrote *Muskeg*.

"Mus-keg," Teddy said.

An Indian word, Little Roy's pa told him when he was a boy. He remembered that the teacher from Minneapolis didn't know what it meant, and the kids had to explain it to her. How layers of plants built up in the bog and packed together until they were like soft coal. Then homesteaders tried to burn it off, thinking they'd get rid of weed trees and scrub, plough it up and get good black soil. But the fires burrowed down into the ground, deeper and deeper, feeding on those layers. And that's where they stayed, smoldering away. In the winter, they sent up little curls of smoke through the snow. Little Roy learned not to step near them, so as not to fall in up to his waist or over his head. In spring and summer, the bog was wet but harder to read. You'd be walking along on little hills of sedge and think how nice it was that God laid out a path for you. But if you slipped or missed a solid spot, your leg could go in all the way to your hip, and you'd be stuck in something between mud and quicksand. That's why people feared the bog more than forest or water. When folks disappeared, they usually weren't found.

Sometimes Little Roy imagined all the lost people standing down there, preserved like bees in honey. Everyone said that if the Bog Witches liked you, they'd lead you out. Those who were lucky enough to find their way back swore they'd seen little dancing lights that guided their way.

Little Roy hoped that they liked him. He talked to them and left them things: blue flag irises in the spring, raspberries in the summer, bittersweet vines full of orange berries in the fall. In the winter, he stayed away. He guessed the Bog Witches had no love for people tramping around on the surface of their home with boots and snowshoes, yelling and chopping down spruce or pine.

On the map, floating above the tamaracks, he drew figures with wings and tiny human bodies, then labeled them *bogwiches*.

"Bogwi-ches," Teddy said. "Ah! Bog *Witches*."

Little Roy underlined the words and drew a circle around the entire bog. He pointed to the boy, walked his fingers across the page and shook his head, waving his finger back and forth for good measure.

"Don't go to the bog?"

Little Roy nodded.

"But you just drew it for me…"

Little Roy pointed to the boy, then back to himself, and again walked his fingers across the page to the bog.

"Don't go alone. We go together."

Little Roy inclined his head. *Yes.*

"When?"

* * *

They went the next morning, which as usual, started with breakfast at Marie's. "You've got a good guide, Teddy," she said. "Roy really knows the bog. Just don't go there alone. Things happen."

Theda's eyes got big, and she put down her fork. "Like what? Shouldn't I go, too?"

"Oh, no need to worry," said Marie. "Just things you have to learn about this place."

"But what is it exactly?" Theda said. "A swamp like in Georgia? Except we have 'gators." She looked at Marie. "You don't have those here, do you?"

"Alligators?" Marie laughed. "Now that's one critter that never made it this far north. No, what the bog has is black flies that bite you so hard you scream. And mosquitoes. But by August, most of them are gone."

Marie packed them a lunch with a jug of water, and off they went, walking west toward the CCC Camp, then north along the road that ran by the bog. Two blue herons flew overhead. Patrolling the place, Little Roy thought. He pointed to a log bridge laid over the ditch, and they crossed over. He took a few steps, looked down at his feet, placed one on a hillock, then brought the other to meet it. Shading his eyes from the sun, he repeated the process, then pointed to the boy and back to himself.

"You really have to walk that slow?" Teddy said.

Little Roy nodded. Once a person had his footing, he could go faster, as long as he was careful. He took one very slow step, then another, pushed aside purple fireweed and led the way. Sometimes he thought of it as his bog, although no one could ever really own it. He even liked the fires down below. Some people thought of them as big and angry, like Hell, but that was just foolishness. He figured the Bog Witches went down there to get warm on cold days. He pictured them flitting around the fires, just close enough to take off the chill, but not so much they singed their wings. He believed there were long tunnels that they used to fly deep into the bog and back up again. In fact, when human beings sank in and didn't come back, Little Roy figured they'd fallen down one of the tunnels. Then it was up to the Bog Witches to help them out or let them stay there.

He and Teddy made their way from one hillock to another. Little Roy stopped to show him a pitcher plant, the orange petal shaped like a big ear that attracted flies with its scent and then, once the fly landed, slowly closed over it. The last thing the fly tasted was sweet nectar, as the flower walls came together.

Too bad there wasn't a pitcher plant big enough to grab Albert whenever he came.

He pointed to a trickle of smoke coming up next to a large rock.

"So the muskeg's burning?" Teddy said.

Little Roy pulled out the map. Down in the righthand corner, he wrote *allways*. Teddy took the pencil and wrote *always* below it. Little Roy chuckled. He never was a great speller.

"Are you mad?"

He shook his head, opened his arms wide to take in all the bog they could see, then pointed to Teddy and the piece of paper.

"I don't understand. The bog is big…"

Little Roy nodded, put the map in Teddy's hand, pointed to *allways* and *always* and then to Teddy and back to himself.

"You show me the bog, and I teach you how to spell?"

They shook on it.

Chapter Nine

Hazel: Minneapolis, Spring 1923

Hazel made her way through the winter with the help of The Merry Widow crew. She was careful not to mention her job at the Woman's Hotel. Most of the girls there worked in offices or factories or as telephone operators at the Northwestern Bell Telephone Company. Hazel figured they'd be shocked at where she made her living, and she didn't want any problems. Always better not to attract attention.

Milt wrote her about the weather, the daily goings-on of the diner, the garden, which he now tended. And he often sent along notes from Theda:

March 31, 1923

Dearest Hazel,

I told you Albert wants an heir. Oh, how he wants an heir! Wish I could go downtown and buy him one!

He somehow thought he could "convert" me—brought me flowers, perfume, all kinds of things to make me feel "romantic." I told him again that's just not the way I'm made, and he stormed out of the house.

Then he came back a few days later. Remember in The Sheik, *when Rudolph Valentino kidnaps Diana? That's how it was. I didn't want to get hurt, so I decided not to fight. Just closed my eyes and pretended it wasn't happening. But he didn't like that either. Said he didn't want to make love to a dead woman. So he got rough. Which really excited him.*

I never did like Albert, but now I despise him.

Next day, he was back with apologies, more flowers, etc., etc. It's all I can do to be in the same room. I know you believe in God, Hazel, so pray that I get pregnant fast. Then maybe this will be over.

I send you a million and one kisses.

Your Theda

Hazel wanted to take the first train to Savannah, have Milt gather all his friends, grab Albert and beat him senseless. How could she stand by? How could she have her room in the Woman's Hotel—lonely, of course, but secure—when Theda wasn't safe in her own house?

April 3, 1923

Milt,

I'm sending you the note Theda wrote me. Don't know if she'd like that, but I want someone besides me to know what's happening. I miss you and her and the diner and I feel like this is all my fault. I should have turned her away that day she showed up at the H&M. I should have done a lot of things. But now it's too late.

Hazel

P.S. The big snow's melted—now it's puddles and slush. Still seems like real spring's a long way off, but Magnus says any day now we'll see pussy willows. Hope he's right.

Milt's letter came by return mail:

Hazel,

Not your fault. Remember you and me and Theda ain't cut from the same cloth as most folks. Everything's fine long as people don't pay attention to us, but once they do, it's Katy bar the door. I'll tell you this. I'm going to keep an eye on her. She comes here once, twice a month, around closing time, and we eat and talk. If Albert puts his mitts on her again, if I see a black eye, anything like that, I'll talk to the boys down at the docks. He needs a taste of his own medicine.

Love,

Milt

* * *

Spring did arrive, just as Magnus had promised. Sometime in May, a pale green mist sprouted on the bushes, then the trees. Dark green ferns uncurled upward. Purple irises bloomed near the rivulets that ran down to the Mississippi, which frothed and kicked like a new colt, still carrying chunks of ice from further north. And the air felt different—moist and with the aroma of fresh earth. Magnus had been right about the way folks here behaved in the spring. In the winter, they hurried down the streets, bundled up, heads down, on their way home or someplace warm. Now women strolled in thin dresses while Hazel still wore a sweater. For her Georgia-bred skin, the air was just too cold to take it off. But men shucked their jackets and sat on benches to take the sun during their lunch breaks. Children played hopscotch. With much hoopla, a young man wearing a bathing costume covered himself with heavy, yellow grease in front of a crowd and dove into the river. Hazel held her breath. How could he possibly survive the frigid water? But up he popped like a cork, then swam back to shore.

As the air warmed, Hazel felt her body relax to welcome it.

"Magnus," she said. "We need a garden for The Widow. I want fresh herbs and vegetables now that it's spring."

He gave her a mock frown. "Oh, you do, eh? And where would this garden be? We're on the riverbank, you know. Not much level ground."

But Hazel had already found the place, a nearby vacant lot. The men tilled up the ground for her, and Irene took her to Northrup-King & Company over on Hennepin Avenue to buy seeds: lettuce, radishes, Swiss chard, spinach, carrots, peppers, tomatoes, onions and squash. She also planted parsley, marjoram, thyme, mint, dill and verbena. And Irene talked her into planting rhubarb, which she said would be a big hit with the customers.

Once things started to come up, the crew built a fence around it and posted a sign, *Hazel's Garden,* even though she wanted it to say *Merry Widow.* It embarrassed her to have her name right out in public, but Magnus reminded her that although the speakeasy was an open secret, it wouldn't do to advertise.

"Might be the Merry Widow garden, but it ain't right to rub people's nose in it. 'Specially the cops."

And so the name remained.

Hazel bought a hat for the sun and a wooden stool so she could weed in comfort and peace. Which the garden delivered to her. As she worked, she'd think about soil, rain, earthworms and how she'd use radishes in the night's meal. She imagined Milt helping her weed or hoe, Theda asking endless questions about the ground, why she planted marigolds near the tomatoes, when the morning glories and moonflowers would come up.

And the Mississippi was always there, rolling down below all the way to New Orleans.

Chapter Ten

Theda: Faunce Ridge, September 1937

Hazel had warned Theda that fall came fast in these borderlands, and she was right. By the end of August, nights were cooler, and the birches were shading toward yellow. In the first days of September, poplar leaves turned golden, not pure dandelion yellow but with a touch of orange.

"Like a peach," she said one day when she joined Teddy and Little Roy as they walked down the Norris Camp Road on the way to the bog. "They grow them in Georgia," Theda said. "You ever have one?"

Little Roy smiled and nodded. He took out paper and pencil and wrote "can."

Theda may have had a canned peach once or twice in her life, but they were so plentiful in Georgia and so delicious fresh that she saw no reason to eat them any other way. Unless baked into a dessert, like the peach cobbler Hazel served her the first day at the H&M Diner.

Hazel. When would she see her again? She'd received a couple of letters, delivered by Sadie and François when they visited. Mainly accounts of the things she and Minnie did at the resort. Hard to believe two women could accomplish that much, even with hired help. Hazel alone planned the menus for each week, picked all the vegetables and berries, cooked three meals a day, baked bread, pies, cakes and cookies.

Farther down the road, bushes had turned bright crimson. Theda gasped.

"Sumac," Teddy said, as if he'd been surrounded by them his entire life. "And this is tamarack." He pointed to trees that looked like spruce but were turning yellow. She touched the needles, which were soft, almost silky.

Did this beautiful tree grow on Oak Island along with the sturdy evergreens she'd seen there in August? Did Hazel caress the needles, or was she used to them by now?

Little Roy pointed to a branch and rippled his fingers down from it like he was showing how rain fell. Theda didn't understand, but Teddy interpreted. He and Little Roy had established a fast and fluid system of communication. "They're the only evergreen that drops its needles."

"All right, you two," she said. "I'm going to leave you here. Go ahead and tramp all over the bog, but get back before dark." The sun went down earlier now. Theda missed the long dusk that stretched deep into the evening when they first arrived.

Sadie's car was parked outside Marie's place when Theda returned, and she and François were sitting around the table with Marie. No one was smiling. Sadie said, "Sit down." She pointed to a letter in the middle of the table. "Came yesterday from Emil Rousseau."

"Emil grew up here," Marie explained. "Came back to take pictures of it for the Resettlement Administration, the government outfit that moved everybody out. But he's a good boy. Real smart. Married Minnie's niece, Rose, that she and Hazel raised."

"We had the wedding just this past spring at the hotel," Sadie added. "Marie and Little Roy took care of the music. Anyhow him and Rose have been staying at a logging town on the Big Fork River east of here, over by International Falls. Lumberjacks are going on strike. He's taking pictures, and Rose is writing for a paper." She paused. "Then, one day, some fellow called Albert shows up."

Theda flinched. She'd been dreaming that he wouldn't come until next year. Or maybe never. That she and Teddy would get settled somewhere. Preferably with Hazel. Another story, of course.

"Says he's one of the lumber owners," Sadie went on, "And he means to do something about the strike. But that's not all. Turns out he's hired detectives to help him find his wife. Who he thinks is here in Minnesota. In fact, he'll be coming to Baudette before long. Here, I'll read the letter."

September 8, 1937

Dear Sadie,

Rose and I are in Craigville, covering the lumberjack strike that's going to break out any day. I'd strike too—the owners are getting fat, and the jacks are lucky if they get their clothes washed once a month.

But yesterday Albert Hawkins shows up. A short fellow who likes to throw his weight around, I'm sure you know the type. Says he's from Savannah, Georgia, but owns timber stands here, and he's broken strikes before and has no problem doing it again. And he's looking for his wife and kid, who ran off a couple months ago. Says that in the 1920s, before he married her, the wife, whose name is Theda, went around with someone called Hazel Goodwin.

Theda winced at the mention of Hazel's name. Sadie looked up, then went back to the letter.

And this Hazel moved to Minnesota because she got into trouble down in Savannah. But according to Albert, she's held sway over Theda and smuggled letters to her. Which his detectives found, so he figures the wife is with her. He decides to kill two birds with one stone, break the strike and find his wife and boy, too. He knows Hazel is on Oak Island, and he'll be headed there before long.

You know I'd do anything to keep Minnie and Hazel safe. They're my mothers-in-law. Already wrote them a letter they should have gotten by now.

Albert plans to stop in Baudette with his boys on his way to Oak. I bet you and François can figure out some way to slow them down. My guess is they'll go straight to your hotel—best food in town, I told him! So please warn Theda, if you know where she is.

I'll keep you posted. All our best to you both.

Emil

No one spoke for a moment. A cold knot formed in Theda's belly. So it was finally happening. Would she and Teddy ever escape Albert?

As if on cue, he and Little Roy came in from outside, smelling of muskeg smoke. Teddy looked around. "Why's everyone so serious?"

Theda sighed. "We've got some news, darlin'."

Chapter Eleven

Hazel: Minneapolis, July 1923

July in Minneapolis was, as Magnus had predicted, hot as hell. And more so in the closed-up Merry Widow. Hazel showed Magnus the boarded-up windows facing the river.

"Here's what we do," she said. "Build permanent blinds—some kind of tough wood that closes tight. Thick enough to keep out rain." *Like in the South,* she thought. The climate might be different, but you still had to move air. "Otherwise, one of these days, somebody's going to die of heatstroke, and they'll shut us down."

"How about in the winter?" he asked.

"The shutters should keep out the snow, and when it gets really cold, board up the windows again 'til summer."

Magnus lit a cigar, grabbed a cup of coffee and paced around the building. "It's a good idea," he said. "We'll try it, see how it works. Not like the Widow's a big secret anyway—no one's going to be peeking in."

In the meantime, she got a letter from Milt.

July 4, 1923

Dear Hazel,

Can't believe a year's gone by. I do my best to tend the garden and the H&M, but it ain't the same without you. And who knows when you're coming back. A year seems more than enough to me. Still a free country—that lawyer can't keep you away forever.

Theda was in the other day. She looked pretty chipper. Says Albert's traveling a lot, which she likes just fine. She's started to sew again—made curtains for the diner! They're real nice, blue gingham, perks the place up.

Well, I'm going to go watch fireworks and turn in early. Sure wish you were here.

Milt

Inside the envelope was a letter from Theda. Hazel read it once, then again and one more time, breathing in Theda's perfume.

July 2, 1923

My dearest Hazel,

Wouldn't it be sweet if we could turn time back a year? We'd be at the diner and on the Fourth we'd just stay there, not go out…but I guess I have to stop thinking of how things could have happened. It's nice at first but then it makes me really sad.

Things are better with me because Albert's on the road for business this summer. Not that he'd be here every day anyway. He likes to stay at his club, which is just GRAND as far as I'm concerned. This is an arranged marriage, pure and simple, so it's silly to pretend it's anything else.

I'm sewing! Always loved to do it—one of the maids showed me how years ago. Thank God for her and Alma—without them, I would've had to raise myself.

Father's off again, who knows where, and I think Mother is just relieved that my "situation" is resolved—at least in her eyes. Anyway, I got a sewing machine and a lot of nice fabric, and I'm sewing up a storm. Keeps my mind off things. I want to make you something nice—send me your measurements and don't say no!

Love you always,

Theda

Hazel felt relief that for now at least, Theda was out of danger—happy, even—and Milt was all right, though lonesome. *He needs to make more friends,* she thought. Maybe with her gone so long, he would. Because she had no idea when she'd be returning home. And she missed everything. Sometimes just saying the word *Savannah* could make her tear up. She knew she was lucky not to be in prison, but at least with prison, the judge said what your sentence was, and you served it until it was done.

She was waiting for some kind of sign that it was the right time to go back. Not a letter from Williams, from whom she expected nothing. Maybe for Theda to get more settled. Or Albert to move on. In the meantime, she tried to stay busy so she wouldn't think about Milt having his morning coffee alone at the kitchen table, Theda rattling around Albert's big house, trying to fill her time with sewing. She even thought about her brothers and sisters. She'd written them after she settled into the Woman's Hotel—not many details, just that she'd moved up to Minneapolis for a while, had a job and was doing fine. But no one had ever answered her, not even Mavis. Maybe they were still in shock: their Hazel, arrested in a women's speakeasy, dragged through court, picture in the newspaper. Still and all, they were her family. If she ever got back to Savannah, she'd try to talk some sense into them, make them see she was really the same old Hazel, just a little different from the one they thought they knew.

She wrote Milt about her upcoming trip to northern Minnesota with Magnus and the crew: *Wish you were coming. Magnus says the fishing is great, and they clean the fish right there on the beach and eat them with fried potatoes and coleslaw, and it's so good you never get tired of it.*

She started to write Theda that really she needn't bother to sew her anything, she was fine, plenty of clothes, but her pen stopped right on the page. Of course, she wanted a dress Theda made especially for her. Anything that she cut and touched and sewed with her own fingers. So she ran out to a Five & Dime to buy a tape measure and hurried back with it because now she yearned for that dress. Something she could wear all the time and feel Theda on her skin.

She measured smaller than she used to. Walking to and from the Merry Widow and eating her meals there was making her skinny. She'd always been an average size woman. "Just right," as Theda used to say. And she made good food at The Widow. But it was one thing to cook pretty much whatever she wanted at the tiny H&M Diner and eat it in her own kitchen with Milt or Theda, and another to grab something on the run and then turn out more food for the hungry customers who filled the speakeasy every day. Sometimes she'd get mad at them. Didn't they have any other place to eat?

About six weeks after she sent Theda her measurements—along with a letter instructing her not to go to much trouble, she was happy with any old thing, Theda knew she didn't have fancy tastes—she received a package. The clerk at the hotel desk gave it to her, and she carried it up to her room. At first, she didn't even want to open it. Wonderful just to look at it and wonder what was inside.

She sat down on the bed and undid the string, folded back the brown paper and closed her eyes before she opened it all the way. Explored with her fingers. Definitely more than one item of clothing. When she couldn't resist anymore, she opened her eyes and looked down. On top, a simple dress of heavy gray cotton with a dropped waist and long sleeves *so you won't get sunburned walking to and from work,* Theda said in the letter. Much more elegant than the house dresses women wore at home. Below that, a pale green silk robe, so soft she had to rub her cheek against it. Like Theda's skin. She would wear it every night. And finally, a dark turquoise tea dress that came down below her knees with a large bow at the waist. *For special occasions—like when we see each other next,* Theda wrote.

And in closing, *Please don't forget about me, Hazel. No matter how much time passes.*

Hazel smiled, stroking the fabric of her new clothing. Forget? Theda was inside of her, like her heart and lungs.

She went down the hall to the bathroom, blessedly empty, and ran the bathtub full of lukewarm water, the better to cool down from the July heat, leaned back and closed her eyes. When she got out, she dried off and slipped into the silk robe. It felt like a cloud, a softer skin. Her Theda robe. Maybe she'd never take it off.

Chapter Twelve

Sadie: Baudette, September 1937

Sadie was up early, out on the front porch in the willow rocker her father, Pascal Robinette, made for her so long ago. Soon dawn would break, but for now, darkness held her, and thoughts came clear and unhurried. She considered Albert Hawkins, a man she'd never met. Whose picture she'd never seen. But who she swore she'd recognize as soon as she saw him. He knew that Theda and Teddy might be on Oak Island. But he knew nothing of Faunce Ridge. At least not yet. Would his detectives sniff out the fact that a few settlers still hung on in the forest and bog country? Who'd tell them?

When Marie and Roy came into town to play music a few days after the news from Emil, Sadie'd asked how Theda was doing.

"She can't sit still since she got the news," Marie said. "Every morning she rides Butter and then mends everything she can find. Sewed wool curtains for my place and Roy's, made him a new quilt, too." She laughed. "Far as we're concerned, she can stay as long as she wants."

"Well, why can't she? If we can get rid of Albert."

"Too late to build onto my house now," Marie said, "Haymow's too cold in the winter. Some of the old houses are in pretty good shape, especially the Rousseau place, but we'd have to start to fix it up right now. Especially with Albert on the way."

"And the boy?"

"Him and Roy are out and about most days—the bog, the fire tower, the CCC Camp. Nights we have supper and then play cards." Marie chuckled. "Or charades, except Roy always wins. Anyhow, it keeps our minds off what might be coming."

* * *

Sadie opened the letter from Emil that had arrived the day before and re-read it.

Dear Sadie,

Well, things are coming to a boil here. Jacks aren't buying Albert's bill of goods, so the strike's still on. In the meantime, Albert's rubbing Rose the wrong way. His ideas about women drive her crazy. And you know she won't back down from an argument. A couple of nights ago, we're in Big Charlie's when Albert comes in. Before you know it, he and Rose are arguing back and forth. If she were a man, they'd have come to blows. As it was, I thought she might punch him. Had to drag her out of there before things got really ugly.

And just so you know, it's going to take Albert a while to get to Baudette. Someone—I hope not my wife— slashed all four tires of his brand-new truck and sugared his gas tank. So, for now, he's stuck here.

I'll keep you posted.

Best to you and François.

Emil

Sadie smiled thinking about the truck. But there was work to do, and before she started, she had to visit Joe Beaudette on his boat just down from her hotel. Story was that Baudette was named for an uncle of his, a fur trapper who'd passed through some time ago. No one seemed to know why it stuck, but it did, and finally got shortened to Baudette.

The sun would be up soon, and she was sure Joe would be, too. It was a mystery when or if he slept. All she knew was that whenever she arrived, he was there and ready to see her. She knew nothing of his history except that he'd been a fur trapper in the forests on both sides of the Rainy River. Beaver, mink, muskrat, like her own father, Pascal Robinette, who'd leave every fall to trap, then freeze his pelts. When it got warmer, he'd ship them from Rainy River or Fort Francis and return to Manitou Rapids Reserve with money for her mother. He'd be skinny and tired, like the winter beat him up, but after he ate and slept a lot, he'd get strong and start laughing again. And depart when the leaves fell. Except that the last time he never came back.

At some point, Joe must have decided he'd had enough of the trapping life. He moved into Baudette, built himself a houseboat that he anchored in the Baudette Bay where it flowed into the Rainy and earned a living by reading the cards for people and selling them potions and herbs. Sadie consulted with him whenever she came up against a big decision or a thorny problem. Most of the time, his advice was good and his concoctions worked.

She trudged down the hill to the bay. The poplars were yellow, and two or three maples blazed up crimson and orange-red. She passed the town docks where small boats rocked next to the ferry that ran back and forth several times daily from Baudette to its sister town, Rainy River, Ontario. Only the Canadian National railroad bridge linked the towns, and although a few young daredevils walked over on the trestles, most folks crossed in their own boats or on the ferry. The water was an intense blue that seemed to deepen as the fall went on.

It'd been a long time since Sadie came to Joe with anything like an emergency. She'd gotten his advice on smaller matters—the beer garden, attracting clients—but no real crisis for a long time. Not since Magnus disappeared into the bog the preceding summer.

Sadie shook her head to get rid of the memories. She had other problems. Namely *Albert Hawkins*.

How'd he talk? What'd he smoke? What was his voice like? When he got mad, did his eyes squinch up like pinholes or get so wide they took over his face? And how did he smell? Every man had his own odor, and once she picked it up, she'd feel a surge of electricity come right out of her fingers, the sign that she'd figured him out. But she was far from that, and Joe was the only one who could help her.

She pushed aside the bushes that hid his houseboat, a shack-sized wooden box weathered silver with one small chimney, a couple of windows and deer antlers fastened to the four corners. The whole thing sat on a barge with just enough room for a table and chair outside when the weather was good. From a distance, it resembled a battered cup and saucer left out in the rain. A decorated cup. Joe hung all sorts of things from the antlers: tin cans, old cooking pots, a battered porcelain doll, seagull feathers tied into bunches, a miniature chair, ribbons in various shades of red, green and blue that provided a bit of color, at least until the snow bleached them out. Sadie had no idea why Joe chose the objects, but she knew that each one meant something to him. And all of them had come to him by water.

"The river, she bring everything to me," he'd always say. It was Joe's motto, which he repeated so much that it drove her to distraction. Yet she had to admit that water often carried surprises. "Signs from *le bon dieu*," he'd tell her.

He'd touched up the painting of the beaver that covered most of the south-facing outside wall, Sadie noticed. Joe admired beavers. They worked hard, made sturdy houses and had strong, sharp teeth to cut down anything they wanted. If someone blew up their dam, they just built another one.

She stepped onto the boat, which swayed under her feet. Smoke curled out of the chimney. "Joe!" she called.

She heard noise inside, then the wooden door creaked open and Joe stood there, dressed in buckskin clothes he'd made himself. Nothing fancy, just pants and a tunic he wore over long underwear that peeked out from under the collar. Sturdy black boots. Same outfit regardless of the time of year. He was small and wiry, with black hair that had sported gray threads for as long as she'd known him but had never turned completely gray. Sun and wind had carved furrows in his face and around his eyes and cured his skin the brown of ripe hazelnuts. He smelled, as he always did, of wood smoke, tobacco and sweat.

She'd never thought to offer him a bath, and he'd never asked. She knew he washed up in the river in the warm months. François had talked to her about building him a bathhouse or sauna out back of their garden, but she knew Joe would turn it down. He didn't like to leave his boat.

"Mam'selle Sadie," he croaked.

Probably the first words he'd said in days.

"Joe, I need help."

"You come," he said.

She ducked her head to go inside. On the wall, a crate with a picture of the Virgin and a candle burning in front of her. Out of habit, she crossed herself. Not that she believed everything of the Catholic Church, but she liked what came with it: incense, music, the sign of the cross, which she made for good luck, like throwing salt over her shoulder. What she believed was that God not only listened to what she had to say but also sent her messages. Sort of like Joe Beaudette. She sat down at the small wooden table he'd dragged in from outside. In the middle, another candle and a bottle of whiskey.

"God, I could use a drink," she said, surprising herself since it was still morning. Joe fetched glasses and filled hers, then poured himself a shot, taking great care as if he were serving from a silver tea set in a big hotel in Winnipeg.

He lifted it. "To the *mystères* of the world."

Sadie raised her glass.

"And to the water. She bring everything to me."

She sat back and waited. Joe was moving into his time of seeing.

He stared off. Minutes passed. Sadie sipped the whiskey and savored the burning, which woke her up and reminded her of the trouble headed their way but also soothed her. Finally, Joe reached for his stained, ragged deck of cards and laid out four: a Jack of Diamonds, an eight of Clubs, a Queen of Spades and a seven of Spades. Gazed at them, then closed his eyes. Silence, except for waves lapping at the boat and Joe's long, even breaths. The man had a gift. In fact, Sadie didn't think he even needed cards, but they kept his hands occupied while he waited for messages.

"Mam'selle Sadie."

She started out of her reverie. "Yeah."

He pointed to the Queen of Spades. "I never see this card for you before." He tapped it. "She protect others, she help them."

Sadie looked at the calm face of the Queen of Spades. Not a care in the world. "What else?"

He shook his head as if shooing away a mosquito. "*Aussi,* this queen, she have much power. She must *faire attention,* be careful with her powers."

Sadie rolled her eyes. She'd need all the power she could lay her hands on in the coming days and weeks, and being careful with it was the least of her worries.

But Joe had moved on. "The eight of clubs, the seven of spades. They try to trap you. Maybe hurt you."

Albert and whoever was riding shotgun with him? That wasn't really a surprise. "How about the Jack of Diamonds?"

Joe grunted. "That jack, he a surprise. I cannot tell you who he is. He come from right here. Someone you see but not see."

"Should I watch out for him, too?"

He rubbed his forehead and was quiet. "No," he said finally. "Whoever is this jack, he help you."

Sadie hated not knowing. All her life she'd made it her business to see things before other people did and ready herself for them. "It's not enough, Joe," she said. "I need more."

He nodded. "*Oui.* You wait."

And he went to a tiny cupboard, so small it seemed made for a child. His back was to Sadie, but she could hear him muttering in French and caught a few words, *dieu,* more than any. Good. If God was a good luck charm, she needed as many of Him as she could get, a whole clinking bracelet. He pulled out one drawer, then another, until it seemed he'd opened and closed them all. Then grunted and turned around. In his hands a tiny buckskin bag.

Always plenty of buckskin at Manitou. Kept her warm and dry, but as a girl, she sometimes longed for wool or silk, something that didn't have the smell of an animal. But now, she treasured the only buckskin she had—her mother's moccasins which she wore when she needed comfort.

"What's in it?" she said.

Joe sat down. "I show you." He loosened the strings and poured tiny greenish-brown leaves that looked like dried parsley onto the table.

She looked down at it. "What the hell do I do with this?"

"You make tea. The eight of clubs, the seven of spades, they relax very much. Then you see."

"Goddamnit, Joe, nobody drinks tea except little old ladies. Coffee, whiskey, beer. Not tea."

Sometimes she wondered if he was getting old people's disease. God knows how many years he'd been around. Probably didn't even know himself. And what did he eat? Fish, berries, venison, not a hell of a lot more.

As if he were reading her thoughts, Joe said, "Do I ever fail you, Mam'selle Sadie?"

She folded her arms. "Not usually, but…"

"If you do not like the tea, then you tell François to bake. *Un gateau.* A special cake for the seven of spades and the eight of clubs."

Well, that was more like it. François could work wonders with the oven. "But what does it do?"

Joe rocked in his chair. "Different with each person. You see."

"Okay," she said. She knew she wouldn't get anything more out of him. "But you're sure it'll help me?"

"Ah, *oui.* It help much." He smiled, then sobered. "But you, Mam'selle Sadie, you do not eat this cake. *D'accord?*"

Sadie nodded, "*D'accord.*"

* * *

"Is Albert here yet?" she asked when François met her at the hotel door.

He shook his head. "No. I think that with fixing the tires and the tank of gas, maybe he arrive tomorrow."

"Saturday," she said. Little Roy and Marie were coming to play for the weekly dance, the main event in Baudette on a Saturday night. If Albert and his friends got to town, she was all but certain they'd show up.

"The more, the merrier," she said. "Look. I have something for you."

Chapter Thirteen

Hazel: Oak Island, July 1923

You couldn't see across Lake of the Woods, and the waves were high the day Hazel, Magnus and the others made the long trip from the mainland to Oak Island. Good thing she had a strong stomach. Finally, Oak Island came into view through the spray of the boat cutting through water. Hazel's excitement built as they approached. For once, she wasn't thinking about Theda—although she'd packed the green silk robe—or Milt or the H&M because she was watching indigo waves crashing on rocks piled up on shore. Just behind, bristly green spruce and pine. And beyond the trees a low building and cabins that seemed to grow out of the earth. The air smelled of fresh water and wood smoke.

As they walked up the path to the Island Haven Resort lodge, they passed a large garden with beans so high they made her think of Jack and the Beanstalk. She stopped to admire the corn, dill, squash and tomatoes, the raspberry bushes heavy with fruit.

"Days are really long up here in the summer," Magnus said, as if guessing her thoughts. "So the plants grow big."

As the only woman in the group, she had a cabin all to herself: a twin bed with a patchwork quilt, a small wooden table and chair and a kerosene lamp. Lake of the Woods sighed as it rolled in and out, lulling her into a long sleep. When she woke up, she brewed coffee on the tiny kerosene stove and went outside to a large rock warmed by the sun. She sipped it, lit a cigarette and closed her eyes. A breeze off the lake blew her hair. And those waves. She could listen to them all day.

Footsteps roused her, and she opened her eyes to see Minnie McGregor, the resort owner, with a young girl maybe eleven years old. The girl had strawberry blond braids with lots of flyaway strands and a skinned knee. *Like me when I was a kid,* Hazel thought. The day before, when they'd checked into the resort, Minnie had been dressed in a black jacket and trousers with a crisp white shirt; long, dark hair pulled back into a bun. Today it was loose around her shoulders. A handsome woman, Hazel thought, almost beautiful when she smiled.

"We came to say hello," Minnie said. "This is my niece, Rose—my great-niece, actually. By the way, Magnus took everyone else out fishing. Said he thought you'd like to sleep."

"He was right," Hazel replied, grinning. "Don't think I've ever slept so well in my life." She offered her hand. "I'm Hazel Goodwin. Never been so far north. This is beautiful country."

Minnie's brown eyes sparkled. "Yes, it is."

Her fingers were strong when they shook hands.

The girl shaded her eyes. "You can call me Rosie, if you like. That's Aunt Minnie's name for me. Would you like to see one of my stories?"

"I'd love to," Hazel said.

Minnie laughed. "Rosie!" Then to Hazel, "She doesn't see many women except for me. I think she gets tired of being around men."

* * *

For the rest of her time on Oak Island, Hazel ate supper with Magnus and the others, then visited with Minnie and Rose until bedtime. "I let Rosie stay up later in the summer," Minnie said. "Who can sleep when it's still light out at ten o'clock?" They played cards and talked. Rose would read from her latest story, most of them featuring a young girl who could swim forever, had superpowers and performed daring feats—rescuing fishermen who'd swamped their boat, building bonfires on distant islands to light the way for those who'd gotten lost on the endless lake.

After Rose went to bed, Minnie would bring out homemade raspberry cordial, potent stuff with a sweet-tart taste. One night after a second glass, she began to compose limericks.

"There once was a man from Nantucket," she began, sending Hazel into gales of laughter.

"Then what?"

"Depends on who's listening," Minnie said. Her cheeks were pink, and her arms and hands, tanned by the sun, looked golden under the hanging lamp.

"This is swell," Hazel said. A puny word for how being on the island made her feel. Peaceful, yet looking forward to the next day's adventures. *But this is not real life,* she scolded herself. *You're on vacation. No work, no responsibilities.*

"You know you can always come back," Minnie said. "I'd like that, and so would Rose."

* * *

When the boat arrived to pick up the Merry Widow crew, Rose and Minnie came down to the dock to see them off. Rose hugged Hazel hard around the waist. "Promise you'll be back soon."

"Rosie," Minnie said. "She'll come when she can. It's a long way from Minneapolis." She smiled at Hazel. "You're always welcome."

Hazel thought she heard Minnie stress *always*. She nodded, suddenly shy.

On the way back to the mainland, Magnus apologized for leaving Hazel to herself. "I didn't want to drag you out to fish every day. Hope you weren't sitting around twiddling your thumbs."

"Oh, no," she said, remembering the smell of lake water, the long twilights.

"Think you'd like to come again?"

"Yes," she said. "I most certainly would."

Chapter Fourteen

Sadie: Baudette, September 1937

Sadie could hardly wipe the smile off her face. Not that she was trying. Hotel Pascal sparkled. François had a fire going in the big fireplace in the lobby, and for once, the smoke was going where it should—straight up and out the chimney. He'd found red sumac and yellow leaves to decorate the place as well as Sadie's favorite, bittersweet with orange berries glowing on their vines. As usual, on a Saturday, they'd moved the chairs and sofa around the fireplace to turn the rest of the room into a dance floor.

Behind the long wooden bar, bottles of whiskey, all legal since 1933. Sadie sighed, remembering the money she used to rake in on bootleg, which they sold in bottles with phony bonded labels the local newspaper printed up in exchange for a small cut. But at least now, she didn't have to be looking over her shoulder for damn G-men.

All afternoon long, François had simmered venison with onions, garlic and bacon. Later he'd add carrots, potatoes and sell bowls of it to the hungry dancers. And coffee in case anyone wanted to sober up.

They never ate fancy, even before the Crash, but they ate good. Venison was free, and most of the rest was out of the garden or from barter. Hard to get ground coffee anymore, but François could always find roasted beans in wooden barrels at one of the grocery stores in Baudette. Smelled so wonderful when you lifted off the cover, you had to close your eyes for the pure pleasure of it. He'd grind it up and trade it to Marie for hazelnuts that grew wild at Faunce Ridge. Which he'd roasted and salted for tonight and set out with bowls of popcorn for people to nibble on.

Marie and Little Roy arrived in the afternoon and now were running through their numbers. Little Roy tuned his fiddle, eyes half-closed, as Marie plunked piano keys. She was no virtuoso like Violeta, the sad girl from Winnipeg Sadie used to have at the hotel before the Crash, who'd play all night, pale hands rippling over the keys, songs filled with longing. But Sadie was glad to have Marie's serviceable skills and strong alto.

She waited until they were done warming up. "Listen, we may have company tonight." And she explained that Albert might arrive. She was certain she'd know him when she saw him, and so would they. "A little man with lots of money who thinks his shit don't stink. He figures they're up at Oak Island with Hazel. We're the only ones in the know. So no matter what he says or does, not a word."

"Why I wouldn't so much as tell him my name," Marie said.

Sadie looked at Little Roy. He'd changed since she first met him. For one thing, she hadn't seen him drunk since The Relocation. She recalled how he used to drain bottles of hooch at the dances in Faunce Ridge, then prop himself up against the wall and play his fiddle until he slid to the floor and passed out. After which the men would carry him home, lay him on his bed and cover him with quilts the women made for him. But now Faunce Ridge was a ghost town, and him and Marie were all that was left of it if you didn't count Theda and Teddy and the DuPrees. Sadie noticed that the fiddler stood straighter, his green eyes clear, no longer bloodshot. Teaching Teddy the woods and the bog must agree with him.

He pointed to the bottles lining the shelves behind the bar and shook his head.

Even if Albert didn't show up, they'd have themselves one hell of a party.

* * *

People started to arrive. Women commented on how pretty the lobby looked. Like a fall harvest ball, they said. Nice to have something special before winter set in. The men drank whiskey, smoked and emptied the popcorn bowls, which François kept filling.

Theda had sewn Sadie a dark green wool dress. "The least I can do after you've helped us so much," she said. It was fitted with a slightly flared skirt to her mid-calf, and it brought out the color of her skin, the deep brown of her eyes. It looked good on her, Sadie reflected, and was a serious dress that a woman in Winnipeg might wear in an office. On her feet, strapped shoes with a good heel. She would tower over Albert Hawkins.

* * *

After an hour or so, Sadie'd all but forgotten about Albert. She was doing what she did best—running a party where she could keep an eye on everything and everyone and still enjoy herself. The smell of venison stew drifted from the kitchen, and fire warmed the room as Little Roy and Marie played song after song. Dancers twirled around the lobby, and François worked the bar when he wasn't in the kitchen.

She could tell he was in a good mood because he let his black and white cat, *Vache,* perch on the end, her favorite spot. Sadie personally didn't care for cats, but François had a soft spot for animals, especially lost ones. When Sadie protested, he'd said, "She came to us." And she had, meowing her way through a rainstorm the year before up to the door of Hotel Pascal where she planted herself, dripping water, in front of the door.

"I still think it's mean for you to call her *vache,* François. She's not a cow."

"*Alors,* she is black and white like a Holstein cow, no?"

Sadie turned her attention to Little Roy. He was finishing a waltz, eyes closed, filling the notes with a warmth Sadie had never heard from his fiddle. Maybe music was like another country for him, like the floating dock at Manitou Rapids Reserve was for her, where if she shut her eyes, she could be with her father, hear his crackling laugh.

Marie stepped forward. "We're going to take a rest now," she told the crowd. "Eat something, come back." Little Roy put down his fiddle. The dancers moved into clumps, murmuring and clinking glasses.

Then the big front door opened, a gust of cool wind blew in and there stood a short, stocky fellow flanked by two men. One of them looked like he'd just stepped off the cover of a detective magazine. Compact, hard-muscled, cold eyes, dressed in a suit and fedora, with an overcoat that Sadie supposed hid a weapon. Like a cop or detective or just plain thug—pretty much the same thing anyway. The other man seemed less stiff than his partner. His suit was rumpled, and Sadie thought she saw a bit of a belly under his jacket. Taller than his companion, with a crooked tie and a hat that appeared to have grease stains, he had brown, measured eyes that didn't show much. The short man between them was dressed more casually, in wool pants and a flannel shirt, but she could tell he was in charge. Broad chest, legs planted wide like a banty rooster. Neither he nor the two men moved, which irritated her but made her want to laugh. The big entrance.

Her guests turned to look. Dressed up for an evening out, men in white shirts and dark pants; women in good dresses and high heels, everyone clean and smelling of soap. She felt suddenly protective of them as she walked firm but unhurried to the door.

"Come on in, but for God's sake, close the door—it's windy out there." She smiled and offered her hand, which she knew women didn't usually do, which was why she did it. "Sadie Robinette," she said. "Welcome to the Hotel Pascal. Can I take your coats?"

The short man put out his hand. "Pleased to meet you," he said. "Albert Hawkins. We're just passing through."

"Well, you come to the right place. Plenty of liquor and food, and a room if you want."

Albert stepped into the lobby, the two men following, as everyone watched. "Keep eating and drinking, folks," Sadie said. "We got some more people for the party, that's all. This here is Albert and..."

"Gus and Cal," Albert said.

Sadie wondered if those were their real names. It didn't matter, but she couldn't resist asking, "Which is which?"

"This is Cal," Albert said, pointing at the hard-eyed man, who made a tiny nod.

"And I'm Gus," said the taller one that Sadie already found more likable. She bestowed a smile on him for acting like a regular person. Albert, she was pleased to note, scowled. *Don't fraternize,* she thought. Well, maybe Gus could think for himself.

"Take your hats?" she said.

"Sure," said Gus.

Cal shook his head.

"I bet you boys haven't had supper."

François was serving fragrant bowls of stew to the dancers. Gus and Cal stayed silent, but their eyes followed the food. And she could tell that Albert, the one she was really watching, was hungry because his pupils got big, like men's do when they want food or sex.

"Sure," he said. "We'll have some. Smells damn good."

Sadie led them to a table, brought three whiskies, though they hadn't asked for them, and a bowl of hazelnuts. "Be right back," she said.

In the kitchen, Marie and Little Roy were eating and laughing. Roy got up and did an imitation of Cal. He grabbed his hat, lowered it so it almost covered his eyes and swaggered around the table, hands in pockets, so he looked like a tiny gangster.

"Careful," Sadie said. "I think they might stay." She sniffed the air. Sweet, like burnt sugar. "What's that?"

"François says he's making a plum cake," Marie said.

Sadie brought bowls of stew to the men and lingered at the table. "Where you coming from?" she asked.

"Here and there," Albert said. "Taking a tour of your beautiful state. Thought we'd do some fishing, and people told us this was the place to do it."

"Fishing, eh?" Sadie said. "Depends on where you go. Lake is dangerous. Lots of folks swamp their boats—some come back, some don't. If a wind whips up, you can get in trouble fast. You'll need lots of clothes. It gets cold on the water this time of year."

Actually, it would be swell if they went out on the lake—way out—and a storm came up and sank their boat. A nice, clean end to their troublemaking.

"Or we might hunt," Albert said. "Deer, grouse, duck. Lots of woods around here, they say."

Sadie laughed. "Yup. Nothing but woods and water and bog in this country." She didn't mention that the bog was everywhere, beneath many of the forests. They'd find out soon enough. "Well," she said. "Let me know if you need anything. The music'll start back up in a bit."

She went back to the kitchen. Couldn't be too eager. They'd smell it. And speaking of smells, the plum whatever-it-was made her mouth water. "François, I hope you made a lot of that. Everybody'll want some."

"I know," he said, with a little smile. "I make two pans. One for our new guests, one for everyone else." He didn't have to say more. A small glow started in her belly, like hot coffee with whiskey.

Marie and Little Roy took their places and started to play again. Dancers filled the floor, blurring into a swirl of color.

Albert ordered a bottle of whiskey for the table, and she was happy to oblige. "If there's a tune you'd like to hear, ask. They probably know it."

"How about The Wabash Cannonball?"

"Ah," Marie said. "One of our favorites." She stood beside Little Roy and sang as the notes tumbled out of his fiddle: *Oh, listen to the rhythm, to the rumble and the roar...*

People started to schottische and two-step.

Albert held out a hand to Sadie. "Shall we take a turn?"

"Why not?" she said.

He was a good dancer, strong, on the beat and a confident leader. She'd learned a thing or two up in Winnipeg all those years ago. Be alert and follow well. Don't just melt into the man's arms. Use the closeness to pick up clues. Make sure you know more about him than he does about you. Albert had well-developed muscles and hands that were slightly callused. Not the hands of a laborer, but a man who did some physical work, even if not for a living.

She closed her eyes just for a second to try to get his smell. Cigarettes, of course, definitely not roll-your-own, and whiskey. Some cologne she couldn't identify, just a hair too sweet. To hide his hard edges? It didn't suit him. And underneath, the faint scent of mothballs. Not as strong as the hated Père Clément back at Manitou Rapids, who smelled like he rubbed his body with them every morning, but present. Like on clothing dragged back from the dead. It nauseated her, but she focused back to the conversation.

"Done much hunting?" she said.

"Mainly birds," he said. "And some wild boar. They're all over the Georgia hills."

"Georgia, huh? I could tell you weren't from around here. First time this far north?"

He nodded.

"Well, we hope you'll like it up here in God's country," Sadie said. "Great hunting. That's where our meat comes from. Everybody knows how to use a gun, even the young ones. We get deer, partridge, grouse."

Little Roy reached the part of the song when he leaned back and let the music fly. Everyone stopped dancing to watch and listen, Albert and Sadie too. "Best fiddler in these parts," she whispered. "Too bad he can't talk. Had a big shock a while back, and ever since…"

Albert seemed to follow every note. "That's damn fine fiddling," he said. "Maybe I could talk him into coming to Georgia, playing for dances around Savannah."

"Never happen," she said. "He wouldn't leave."

"Why not? Winter's coming. It's a whole lot warmer down there. He might get used to it."

Sadie laughed. "Not Little Roy. He'd rather hole up in his shack than anywhere in the world."

"All by himself?"

"Pretty much. A little town, just a few people."

She immediately regretted saying even that much. She had to figure that everything Albert said was designed to milk information out of her.

Little Roy ended with a flourish and sank against the wall, looking exhausted. Sadie marveled at the way he put his whole self into that fiddle. Like it was part of his body, and they got tired together. People clapped. He bowed, fiddle in one hand, just as François emerged from the kitchen. "There is dessert," he said. "A cake of plums that I make today."

"You eat good here." Albert sounded surprised.

"Saturday night we like to put on the dog," Sadie said.

She went into the kitchen with François. "For our guests first."

He pointed to the smaller pan cooling beside the stove. "She is the good one." He cut three large pieces. The plums had bled into the cake and formed a little syrup in each bowl, which he crowned with whipped cream, courtesy of Marie's cows. "I think they like it very much."

Sadie brought the dessert to Albert's table. "Specialty of the house," she said. "Want some coffee to go with that?"

They tucked into the cake. Gus ate greedily and patted his belly. Cal poked at it, had a bite, and then looked shocked like he'd never tasted anything so good. Albert watched them and took a forkful. As the cake hit his tongue, she thought she heard him moan. Men were simple, she thought. Their belly or their balls. She'd try the cake herself, but from the regular pan, not the one for the men.

* * *

Back in the kitchen, the baked plum scent filled the room, cut with something else she couldn't put her finger on. François sat at the table with a cup of coffee.

"Aren't you going to have some?" Sadie asked.

He shook his head. "Maybe tomorrow. For now, I pay attention."

She felt a tickle of alarm. "Wait. You made two cakes, right? One for us and one for them?"

"*Oui*," he said, with a rare smile that made his green eyes glow. "And we enjoy it. But they enjoy it more."

Sadie sat down and savored the plum cake and just-whipped cream. "Um, um, um," she murmured. She was not one to go crazy over food, but this was special, even for François, who was a magician in the kitchen. It was tender, just sweet enough and a little tart.

Then she heard the bark of male laughter. She got up and pushed the swinging door. Hard-faced Cal sprawled in his chair, laughing like a crazy man. Gus had his head down, doing the same, except not so loud. His back shook, and his fist pounded the table like he'd heard such a good joke he couldn't quite believe it.

Albert watched them. "Ain't that something?" he said. "I've known these fellows a long time. They never relax. Like little tin soldiers. Bless their hearts, they need to have some fun now and then."

Was this the same Albert that walked into her hotel?

"Well, they sure are doing that," Sadie replied. "Can I get you all anything?"

"More of that cake. Best thing I ever had."

"Coming up," she said. "You staying the night, I'm guessing?"

Albert nodded. "A room for me and one with twin beds for the boys here."

"Come on over to the desk, and we'll take care of it," Sadie said.

He strolled after her, swaying to the music. "How much?" he asked as he filled out the guestbook.

"Two fifty for your room." Sadie upped the price by fifty cents. "And three for the double." He surprised her by paying without argument. Rich people usually wanted to talk you down. She handed him the keys. "Be right back with more cake and coffee."

The men demolished their second helpings. Gus and Cal somehow managed to stop laughing long enough to eat every crumb, and Gus even picked up the bowl and licked it. Sadie tried not to laugh.

"Now, now," said Albert. "Manners."

But he didn't sound upset. His eyes closed halfway, and his head dipped. Eventually, he'd start awake, but it took longer and longer each time. Finally, he sagged back in the chair and began to snore.

"Hey, Albert." Sadie tried to rouse him, but he was out.

Little Roy and Marie had started to play again, and although the dancers glanced at the newcomers from time to time, for the most part, they ignored them. Anyone who lived along the border, Sadie reflected, especially Baudette, was used to people coming and going. Some trying to get as far away from civilization as possible. Others on their way to or from Canada. A few who couldn't seem to find a place in the outside world. Those were the ones who tended to stay, joining the collection of souls perched on the banks of the Rainy River. Whether they were straitlaced, criminals of one kind or another or just plain different, they found a home here, since in a place so far from everything, you either got along or you didn't survive.

She went into the kitchen for François. "Let's get Albert up to a room." She led the way back into the lobby, where Albert slept on. Gus and Cal were face down on the table, empty bowls beside them, shaking with laughter that now sounded like hiccups.

François picked Albert up by the shoulders. Sadie took his feet. They carried him through the kitchen to the hall and up the back stairs

Sadie never told guests about. They put him to bed in the room farthest from the front of the hotel, removed the loaded revolver from his jacket and closed the door.

Sadie took out her keys. "Lock him in?"

François shook his head. "It is not necessary. I think tomorrow he will still be a lamb. Then we see."

Hotel Pascal had a safe, but Sadie didn't trust it. Easy to find, easy to crack. She believed in hiding things where you should see them but never did. Her place was the bottom of the wood barrel in the hallway behind the kitchen. She removed the bullets, then nestled the revolver into its new home beneath a layer of straw.

"What do we do with Gus and Cal?"

François looked thoughtful. "They should go far away. Where they know nobody and nobody know them. Where Albert does not think to look."

"The bottom of the river?" Sadie said.

She was only half-joking. But the problem with making people disappear that way was, sooner or later, someone came looking for them. At least most of the time.

François shook his head. "No, they must go farther. Much farther. Perhaps they would like to take a trip. On the train."

"What are you talking about?" she said. The Canadian National passenger train that dipped into Lake of the Woods County on its way northwest to Winnipeg had come through earlier in the afternoon.

"Many people now, they ride the rails," he said. "Maybe these two boys also."

Sadie chuckled. "I'll get the car."

It wasn't that hard to transfer Gus and Cal to the back seat. They were loose-bodied and still laughing but growing quieter. As François guided them, one arm over the shoulders of each, he began to sing a French lullaby. The notes melted into the darkness as they bundled the men into the soft upholstery. Sadie had packed up the rest of the plum cake made especially for them.

"What now?" she said, sliding behind the wheel.

"Now," François replied. "We wait for them to sleep."

"What if they don't?"

He showed her a thermos. "I save some of what Joe give you and make a tea. We have them drink now, warm them up."

Sadie got out of the car and opened the back door. "Boys, boys," she said. "Have something hot. It's cool out there." Gus and Cal slumped together, giggling, eyes half-closed. She held the cup to their lips, first one, then the other. "Drink. Just a little. That's it."

It smelled like licorice, nothing like the dried green leaves Joe had given her. Maybe the stuff really was magic.

They waited. The two men leaned against the seat. Soon they were snoring.

It was past midnight, and the Baudette streets were empty of people. Sadie turned onto Main and drove the few blocks to the depot.

"No," said François. "The station, she is too public. There are lights."

So she took a right just before the depot, drove a few blocks and turned again, so they were next to the tracks but protected by darkness and trees.

"I hope you got a good plan," she said, turning off the car.

"I do," François said, humming the lullaby again.

Gus and Cal remained sound asleep. Sadie covered them with their coats. She wanted them to go far away, but they might as well be warm on the journey. That way, too, they were less likely to wake up.

Finally, François said, "Now we take them out."

They carried first Cal, then Gus and laid them beside the tracks. "Jesus God, they're heavy," Sadie said. She removed their guns. Cal also had brass knuckles and a blackjack. She took them, too. "SOBs came prepared."

Sadie heard the whistle, then saw the white light of the engine as it started across the bridge from Rainy River into Baudette. Then it came into view, pulling a long line of freight cars. Chug-chug-chug, as it slowly came to a stop at the Baudette Depot just west of their car. Directly in front of them, a closed-up boxcar.

"Now what?" she hissed.

"You wait."

He sprinted down the line, then ran back. "An open car," he said. "Empty. They will have it all to themselves."

It was two cars down but seemed like miles as they carried first one, then the other of the men and slid them into the boxcar and far back enough that they were out of sight.

"God help me, I feel sorry for the poor bastards," Sadie said. "Especially Gus. He was all right."

"I brought blankets," François replied. "I am not so heartless." They covered Gus and Cal, put the sack of plum cake beside them and waited by the tracks. "We make sure the train leaves," François said.

After it did, they got back into the car and returned to Hotel Pascal, where Marie and Little Roy still played and the dancers waltzed and two-stepped.

The strangers had come. The strangers had gone. No one asked any questions or seemed to care.

Chapter Fifteen

Hazel: Minneapolis, August 1923–August 1924

When she returned to the Merry Widow from Lake of the Woods, Hazel realized that her world had enlarged. Although she had managed to burrow herself into some kind of home in Minneapolis, the trip to Oak Island left her longing for fresh air and pine trees, things she didn't even know were important to her. And she often thought of Minnie and Rose. She didn't miss them the way she missed Theda and Milt and Savannah itself, but she looked forward to seeing them again.

She harvested her garden and used the produce to cook and bake well into the fall: stuffed acorn squash, bread pudding with raspberries, fried potatoes and onions sautéed with greens—no one had tried collards before, so she didn't announce anything, just cooked them up.

"Boy, this is good, Hazel," Irene told her after eating a plateful on an afternoon break. "Can I have the recipe?"

"Don't really have one," Hazel replied, "But I'll make them again, and then I'll teach you."

"Good," said Magnus, joining the conversation. "Half the customers these days come by for your food, not the booze. Hope you ain't going anywhere soon."

Hazel shook her head. "I like it here."

And she did like it, the way she would like a cozy train station with deep chairs and lots of windows, that she knew nonetheless wouldn't be a permanent home. The Woman's Hotel was modest but well-run, and the manager gave her a discount as a long-term tenant who always paid on time. She enjoyed having someone else change the linens, put out the towels and clean the room. It was a sanctuary where she could think, read and respond to the letters from Savannah. And cry when she felt like it without anyone asking her what was wrong and if they could help.

November 14, 1923

Dear Hazel,

Well, here we are coming up on Thanksgiving, and the customers are wanting their sweet potato pie. Luckily the cook I hired bakes, too—not like you, of course, but she's turned out some pretty tasty stuff. And I met a fellow, George, down at the docks. We hit it off, and now he comes over to eat, and we spend evenings playing checkers and cards and such. Nice to have a little company. Guess I didn't realize how lonesome I'd got. (Don't want to make you feel bad—not your fault you're so far away.) Anyhow, I think you'd like George. He's funny, and he makes me laugh, just like you always did.

Theda came in, too. Albert's back in town. 'Course she didn't tell me all about it—that's girl talk—but I can tell by those shadows she gets under her eyes that she's not happy. Poor thing. She gave me a letter for you, which I put in the envelope.

Yours,

Milt

Muskeg

Hazel closed her eyes and said a little prayer before she unfolded Theda's letter. She didn't know if she could bear hearing what her girl was going through.

November 12, 1923

Dearest Hazel,

Thank God I can write to you. Albert returned from his travels. And now there's just one thing on his mind—getting me in a family way.

At least he doesn't live with me on a full-time basis, but he's a regular visitor. I'll spare you the details except to say I'm not fighting him off. That would only make things worse. I go somewhere with you in my mind—far away—and try to stay there. He probably doesn't even notice, and I don't care if he does. My duty is to breed, and let's hope to God it's a boy, because I don't think Albert would regard a girl as a true heir. I try to joke about it, think of myself as a thoroughbred mare whose owner is determined to carry on the bloodlines. But it's not funny.

I send you kisses and all my love. Please write soon—your letters keep me hoping for a life beyond all this.

Your own,

Theda

Hazel wished she could take care of Albert herself, or better yet, have him beaten by professionals from head to toe. She fantasized about all the ways to deal with him in Minnesota's cold climate, should he make his way north. Maroon him on an ice floe in the Mississippi. Lead a mob of angry women to chase him down, take his clothes and leave him in the snow. It made her chuckle, but then she'd get angry with herself for letting him poison her mind.

Winter inched by the way it did, with a thaw, then more snow and ice, until finally, it was spring.

And in June, she got another letter from Theda writing her directly at the Woman's Hotel.

May 31, 1924

Dear Hazel,

Well, I'm finally pregnant—to Albert's great joy and my relief. You can't imagine how much I just want to get it over with. I'm about two months along, meaning that, according to the doctor, I'll deliver in late December or early January. I wanted a midwife. I hate having a male doctor examine my private parts. But that's an argument I lost, for now anyway. Only poor or colored women still use midwives! Horrors! We mustn't have that!!! But Alma gave me the name of a midwife she knows who I'll consult on my own, just to make sure the doctor's advice is sound. I really don't know what I'd do without her... especially since I've been sick as hell, and of course, Mother is completely useless when it comes to anything practical. Alma's got me eating soup and crackers and tea when my stomach is upset. She says the nausea will soon pass. Which just goes to show that blood doesn't make family—my two closest people until this baby arrives are Alma and you.

It's very odd to think that a little being is growing inside me. Even though it's Albert who impregnated me, the creature is half mine, and I wonder if he (or she) will have black hair like mine? Blue eyes? Then, when I realize for the umpteenth time that this baby is the result of what can only be called a violation, I fear what I'm carrying. Let's hope it's not a monster...

It's going on two years, Hazel, but my feelings for you are unchanged.

Yours,

Theda

The letter was unsettling. Hazel pictured Theda in a darkened house all alone with her swelling belly. If Hazel really loved Theda, wouldn't she return to Savannah, damn the consequences, to comfort and take care of her? But what about after the baby came? Would Theda continue to be Albert's prisoner?

Six weeks later, Milt wrote:

July 15, 1924

Dear Hazel,

Doesn't seem possible that it's been two years. I don't care for the Fourth anymore—just brings back bad memories. Hope you had a nice one—suppose the Merry Widow is open no matter what. For me, it's just a day I close the diner.

Theda came by a few days ago. Guess you know she's going to have a baby. Makes all kinds of jokes about it—says it might be a crocodile or a bear—but her eyes look scared. What a rough time that poor kid has had, even with all her family's money. You and me were never rich, but we could do what we wanted, at least after we got married and moved away from our folks.

George helps me clean up after closing, and it's nice to have someone to talk to, but no matter what, I still miss you, Hazel. Do you think about when you might be coming home? Maybe once Theda has her baby, they'll be a little easier on her. It'd be swell to see the little fellow around here. Or the little girl.

Milt

Hazel folded up Milt's letter and went for a long walk along the Mississippi in the morning before the heat rose up. She stopped at the Merry Widow garden, where tomatoes were starting to ripen and squash grew fatter by the day, and walked the rows, straightening sticks and pulling weeds. Gardening made her happy, but the news from Savannah did not. If she was to be truthful, she didn't want Theda to have a baby.

A child changed everything. Hazel didn't dislike kids—she'd always enjoyed her nieces and nephews, especially when they got old enough for her to talk to them. And she'd really taken a shine to Rose back at Oak Island. But Theda, with a child, would no longer be the carefree girl Hazel knew. How could she be? Her own mother grew more stooped and tired year by year from the endless births, cooking and housework.

Before Theda got pregnant, Hazel had been dreaming that she'd go back home, maybe at the three-year mark, and she, Milt and Theda—and George, why not?—would all live together in a big house. Two levels, one for the boys, one for her and Theda. Sell the diner, maybe start a new one. Or a bakery. They'd figure it out. Except there was never a child in Hazel's dream. She had no idea what to do with an infant, how to take care of it, how to talk to it.

But the worst thing was that Theda would be obsessed with the baby. That's how new mothers were. Hazel had seen her sisters with their newborns. And women who came into the diner with brand new babies. All of them head over heels with the tiny critters, like it was just the two of them in the world.

And, of course, that was normal. But she knew there'd be no room for her with Theda unless she dove into raising the child with her. Which she had no desire to do. *What's wrong with me?* she thought. But there it was: she wanted Theda all to herself, and she couldn't lie and pretend it wasn't so.

She couldn't bear to tell Theda what she was thinking, so she held off on answering the letter. Maybe her mood would pass. Maybe she'd figure her way out of it. In the meantime, she tended the garden and invented recipes. And finally wrote a letter to Minnie and Rose. Although that, too, plagued her with doubts. Was she playing both ends against the middle, hoping that if things didn't work out with Theda, she'd still—maybe—have Oak Island and Minnie and Rose? For the first time, Hazel didn't trust herself, wasn't even sure she knew this new Hazel.

August 10, 1924

Dear Minnie & Rose,

Well, I sure would've liked to go back to the island to see you all this summer, but I guess I'll have to wait. Magnus never gives me any time off! Actually, that's not true—he's a swell boss, but I'll need to save some money so I can go next summer. How is everything there? Is "my" rock still where it was? You two are real lucky to live in such a beautiful, peaceful spot. Rose, are you still writing stories? Send me one!

Hazel

She struggled with how to sign it. Not "love." She considered "warmly" but thought it sounded too familiar. So, in the end, she just signed her name. Hazel. Good old Hazel, who wasn't sure of much of anything at the moment except that she cooked at the Widow, was married, one way or another, to Milt Goodwin but longed for Theda Alexander. Or was it Theda Hawkins now? And was scared as hell about the baby Theda was carrying and the changes it'd bring.

All she knew was that the Mississippi still ran deep and fast. And that Lake of the Woods lay blue and endless to the north. Those things she could count on.

Chapter Sixteen

Sadie: Baudette, September 1937

Albert slept through most of Sunday. In the afternoon, Sadie brought him a tray of food. "Don't even think about getting up," she said. To her surprise, he did not argue. He ate some soup and bread, rolled over and went back to sleep. Sadie thanked God for this blessing—her personal God, who knew how to clean fish, shoot a gun and keep a secret. She prayed that Albert would sleep until Monday. He did.

Monday morning, he came downstairs to the kitchen. He looked like hell—red eyes, beard stubble, wrinkled clothes—and was back to his ornery self. "What'd you do with Gus and Cal?"

"Geez, Albert," Sadie said. "I ain't done nothing with them. They were two happy boys, I can tell you that. After you went up to bed, they took off. Probably looking for women. Haven't seen them since."

François busied himself at the stove, back to them.

"How about some breakfast?" she said. "You go on out to the dining room and I'll fix you right up. Maybe even join you if you promise not to go on and on about what you think I done."

"I know one thing." Albert's face got very red. "My gun's gone. And Gus and Cal sure as hell didn't take it, so that just leaves you and what's-his-face over there."

"Well, now," said Sadie. "Maybe they thought they should keep it for you 'til you woke up again. We'll ask them when they get back. You just calm down, and we'll get you a cup of coffee and a little something to put in your belly."

A vein throbbed in Albert's temple. One day, she thought, he'd get so worked up that he'd drop right over. "Keep your goddamn coffee," he said. "There's got to be someplace in this godforsaken town I can eat without getting rolled like a bum on the street."

He grabbed his coat from the rack in the lobby and slammed the door on his way out.

* * *

All that day, long before Albert got back to the hotel, Sadie got news of his journey through town. No secrets in Baudette, especially not when a strange man with a southern accent was storming around. People stopped in to have coffee and give reports.

"Oh, ya, I saw him," said Henrietta, owner of the notions store on Main Street. "Comes charging in, wants to know if we've seen anyone called Theda—like that movie star, Theda Bara. And of course, nobody's ever heard of her. Says this Theda likes to sew, and she's his wife, and she's got his son. Then he starts asking about Hazel Goodwin. Well, we all know Miss Hazel and Miss Minnie, though they're not in town that much, so of course, no one says a word. Think he scared some of the ladies, though. It's one thing when he goes on and on about someone we don't know, but when it's one of our own.... Why God saw fit to send him here, I'll never know, but there he is, crazy as a hoot owl—"

Sadie jumped in. "Did he say where he was going after that?"

Henrietta put down her cup. "Let me see...'course he was running in and out of every place on Main Street, but before he left my place, he scooched down to talk to little May Olson. He asked how she was, and she said fine and then he says, 'Who knows everything in this town?' and she was so scared she hid behind her mommy's skirts, and Edna didn't like that one bit. She said, 'You stay away from my little girl.' I said it was time for him to leave. So he did, but then on the way out, May speaks up and she says, 'Joe Beaudette knows everything in our town.' So he might be on his way to see him."

Sadie leaped to her feet. "François!" she yelled. "We got to get down to Joe's right now."

"I heard," said François, standing in the doorway to the kitchen. "Let us go."

Sadie grabbed her pistol from behind the bar, just in case. She figured François already had his. With Henrietta gaping after them, they ran down the hill and along the path that led to Joe's houseboat.

"Shhhh…" François warned Sadie, who was crashing through the bushes. "Remember, Joe has taken care of himself very well all these years."

She slowed down and moved as quietly as she could. They paused in the final cover of brush and looked. There was Joe Beaudette's boat, Joe sitting across from Albert at the tiny table on the deck. It was a splendid September day. Sun shone on them, and the water sparkled as it lapped against the boat. Joe picked up a card.

"Why would he read the cards for Albert?" Sadie whispered.

"Because he requested," said François and shushed her again.

She could only make out words here and there. "My wife…son…" from Albert. And from Joe, the only thing she was certain she heard was "water." She knew Joe could see things. She also knew he could be as mysterious as a locked box. What was he telling Albert? Would he lie to him? Tell him part of the truth? And which part did he know? If only she could hear more clearly. The breeze carried away the voices, and seagull cries interrupted them.

After a while, Albert got up, gave Joe some money, climbed off the houseboat and began to walk up the hill. Feeling like she was playing hide and seek, Sadie crept over to the boat, François behind her. She placed her finger over her lips to stop Joe's customary "Mam'selle Sadie" and motioned for him to go inside. She and François followed.

"All right, Joe," she said. "Tell us what happened. What did he want?"

He shrugged. "He look for his wife and son. I tell him I do not know where they are. I think he not believe me."

"You read the cards for him," Sadie said.

Joe got the faraway look in his eyes that she knew so well. But did she also see a twinkle? Hard to tell in the low light inside the houseboat. "Sometimes the cards, they are quiet. I tell him the water bring him everything. That is the truth. Now or later, the water bring everything to all of us."

François nudged Sadie. "Joe has told us much. Let us go home and let him rest."

"Not yet. Joe, where's he going? Did he tell you?"

"No. But he want many things. His wife. His son. Two boys, he call them Cal and Gus."

She and François may have made a mistake, drugging the two men and putting them on a boxcar. Not that they didn't deserve it. Not that it wasn't the most fun she'd had for years. But after all, if they were trained detectives, at some point they'd wake up, figure out what happened and find their way back to Baudette. She hadn't wanted to think about any of that the night of the plum cake. She'd felt filled with wind like a sail, as if she could fly over the land and spit at everyone who'd ever hurt her.

Sometimes, she reflected, hatred of bullies clouded her reason, made her want to get even with all of them, no matter what the cost or the risk.

Goddamn you, Alain, she thought.

He still bubbled up in her nightmares, even though she hadn't seen him since the 1920s and would never lay eyes on him again. Not in this world, anyway. His hold on her began minutes after she'd gotten off the train from Rainy River to Winnipeg, clutching her one suitcase. After she'd managed to get money for the fare from the loathsome Père Clément, who presided over the church at the Manitou Reserve. After her father disappeared and her mother, Fleur died not long after of influenza and, Sadie always believed, heartbreak.

There he was on the platform like he'd been waiting for her. Alain, too handsome to be real, with his dark hair, creamy skin and dancer's stride. First, he took her out to eat. Then he helped her get a room in a boardinghouse and in the next few days, a job as a shop girl.

The girls she worked with sighed over her dashing boyfriend, but her boss, an older woman, warned her. "Something's not right about him," she told Sadie. "How does he make his money? How can he afford to take you out every night?"

But the young Sadie, hungry for touch and warmth, didn't know or care.

After a month or so, Alain said she should quit her job. "I'll take care of you," he said. "Why should you slave away for nothing?"

He bought her dresses to wear when they went out. Shoes to match.

"Marry me, *ma belle*," he said one night.

She wanted to invite her friends, the girls from the boardinghouse, but he said no. "Just we two." In fact, she was to keep it secret. "The girls will be jealous," he said. "Tell them nothing. They will find out soon enough."

Alain gave her some money to buy a wedding dress and told her to go to the shop alone. The girls at the dress store wanted to know where her mother was, her friends. "Surely you want someone with you," one of them said. "Your wedding dress. Imagine! What if you choose the wrong one and regret it the rest of your life? We'll help you, of course, we're here to serve you, make sure you are happy. But just the same…"

All Sadie wanted was to get away as fast as she could. Chose something white, tried it on in a flash, paid for it with Alain's money and fled as soon as they'd wrapped it. But on the day of the wedding, she dressed carefully. Alain must find her perfect.

She assumed they'd be married in a church, but he took her to a house where a priest in a white robe greeted them. He wore no cross around his neck, no rosary. Of course, Sadie reminded herself, everything was different in Winnipeg. Père Clément, back at the Reserve church, wore a rosary and so many clanking chains that you could hear him coming, a never-ending source of laughter to the children.

This priest didn't ask for rings, and Alain never showed her one, but he pronounced them man and wife. Alain kissed her so long and so passionately, right in front of the priest, that her cheeks burned with embarrassment. He took her to a fine hotel that night and taught her things about her body she'd never even dreamed of. They spent the weekend, drank Champagne, ate roast quail. She felt deliciously giddy, like when she'd twirl and twirl as a child back at the Reserve.

After the weekend, Alain told her he had friends he wanted her to meet. She should dress up in her beautiful things and look very pretty. They went to a restaurant to eat and drink wine, and she got woozy. Next thing she knew, she awoke in a hotel room nothing like the one she and

Alain had stayed in. On an iron bedstead, a thin mattress barely covered springs that poked at her back. Her clothes and her underwear lay ripped on the floor, and her body ached, especially down there. She was alone. When Alain came in, she sighed with relief. But it was a different Alain.

"Get up and clean yourself," he said. "You've got work to do."

At this distance of so many years, Sadie could see the con, realize how old and tired it was, predictable as the harsh winters at Manitou. She became one of Alain's girls. He "married" many of them—teenagers like her—and kept them separated, so they wouldn't plot against him. But he needn't have bothered, as far as Sadie was concerned. All she wanted was out. She even considered returning to the Reserve—but she knew that her fate there was linked to Père Clément, with his halitosis, mothballs and uncut fingernails.

In the meantime, she was Alain's property: the virgin he'd discovered and schooled in the most sophisticated ways of love. He rented her out for an hour at a time or, if the price was high enough, an entire night. But he was always there afterward to collect her and the money, and she did nothing, went nowhere without his permission.

And there was the discipline. She was spoiled, he said, and had to learn. He never disturbed her face, although he threatened to scar it with acid if she tried to leave. After the beatings, he would clean and bandage her wounds, singing as he did so. She might never have escaped if she hadn't met François. It wasn't that she wanted or needed another man. The idea of that and of sex itself repulsed her.

François was a waiter in one of the restaurants Alain took her on a regular basis to meet clients. He liked François, efficient and discreet, often knowing what his customers wanted before they knew themselves. Sadie sensed he was different from the men at the table. Once she met his green eyes and saw what looked like real concern. Sometimes she saw him in the kitchen on her way to the bathroom. One night he took her arm and pulled her into an alcove. "You are in trouble, yes?"

She nodded. His voice had a distinct French accent. Probably *québécois*. Maybe from Saint Boniface, the French quarter of Winnipeg.

"I watch. I will follow, see where he takes you."

"What's your name?"

"François," he answered. "And you are Sadie."
"Yes." She had never been more grateful to hear someone say it.

*　*　*

It helped that Alain liked François so much he talked openly around him. And that François, in subtle and often unspoken ways, let Alain know he was trustworthy. It was François who would usher men to their table, then incline his head to Alain. Who would bring more Champagne, make sure Alain's steak was exactly the way he wanted it, seared enough to keep the blood inside fresh and just warm. And it was also François who, if ordered to bring Sadie a drink, prepared it himself with little or no alcohol, who learned all the hotels where Alain took her, who found out where she lived between customers.

Finally, Alain came to trust him so much that he allowed him to accompany Sadie to her assignations. "He becomes too sure," François said. "Lazy. You wait. It will not be long now."

One frigid January night, Alain instructed François to take Sadie to the hotel where a customer expected her, collect the money and bring her back afterward. They left but huddled in a nearby café, waiting for Alain to fall asleep. He'd taken to consuming a bottle of wine and smoking a pipe of opium before he went to bed. The combination ensured that he slept soundly and long.

When they returned, tiptoeing into the room, Alain snored in his four-poster bed with soft quilts, windows covered with thick, red velvet curtains. As they approached, he stirred for a second, then rolled over on his side. There were many feather pillows. Sadie took one of them, placed it over his head and pushed down, using all her strength to keep it there. She thanked God for her childhood of gathering and chopping wood, pounding cranberries, dressing deer and washing clothes on a rough board.

"I help," François said.

"No." Sadie didn't even turn her head.

But she hadn't counted on Alain's will to survive. He jerked and thrashed and finally got free, leaped to his feet, grabbed her by the neck and squeezed. She was starting to pass out when François pried him off her. But Alain fought with a strength she hadn't known he possessed. He knocked François to the floor and sent the pistol flying.

That was when she discovered her power.

Vision still disturbed, spots floating before her eyes, she wrested the loaded .45 always tucked into Alain's belt and fired at his face, then pushed it hard into his chest and pulled the trigger again. The discharge was hollow and muffled by his body, which collapsed on top of her. She turned her head away as his blood oozed into her dress. François pulled him off, carried him to the bed and fluffed the pillows, covering him up as if he were still asleep.

Then dream-like flashes: Sadie in the bathroom, watching red mix with the water washing down the drain. Her face in the mirror, white and at least ten years older. A musky sweet odor near the bed. Wine? Opium? Blood? Whenever she smelled anything like it in later years, her stomach lurched and she felt fingers clutch her neck.

They left that night, her and François, walking arm in arm like lovers to the train station where they bought one-way tickets to Baudette. Sadie had the money she'd recovered from Alain—hers, after all—to get them started in a new life.

* * *

But here she was, with other bullies, in 1937. Did time go around in circles, like trains in a roundhouse?

"If Gus and Cal are on their way back," she asked herself. "How would they let Albert know?"

She had hoped that somehow they'd end up so far away they couldn't possibly return in time to do Albert's bad deeds. But she knew that the Canadian National on which she and François had loaded them did not continue all the way to California or even North Dakota. It crossed into Baudette from Rainy River, then chugged west along the American side of the border for about thirty miles to avoid Lake of the Woods until it reached Warroad and then crossed back into Manitoba on its way to Winnipeg.

Maybe the immigration agents would find Gus and Cal. Or the railroad bulls in Winnipeg. In any event, the way back to Baudette was by train, and the telegraph office was at the depot.

She answered her own question. "Telegram. Of course."

The fellow in the depot was new and barely grown. Sixteen at most, with bright red hair, freckles and hazel eyes. Someday he might be handsome. But at the moment, he was awkward and looked like he should still be in short pants.

She approached the telegraph window and leaned against it. "Horace," she said, dropping her voice into a husky register. "How are you today?"

He blushed up to the roots of his hair. "Um, fine, Miss Robinette."

"Oh, call me Sadie, Horace. You know I've got a guest over at the hotel name of Albert Hawkins, a gentleman from the South. Have you met him yet?"

Horace shook his head.

"Well, he's expecting a telegram, and he asked if I'd pick it up for him. I don't suppose you've seen it."

"Um…I might have. S'pose I should check."

He turned quickly and walked just out of her sight, enough time, she supposed, for him to think about what he was going to do. She winked at François. Finally, he returned to the window. "There's a telegram, but you know I'm supposed to wait 'til he comes for it. That's the rules."

"Why, of course, Horace, but he's waiting for this, so I want to make sure he gets it as fast as he can." She paused, then whispered, "He's the kind of man who gets angry when things don't happen right away. Do you know what I mean?"

Horace nodded, looking down.

"Besides, I don't want to take the telegram. I just want to see what it says so I can tell him. He can pick it up any old time."

Sadie wondered if anyone had ever asked the boy to do something like this. She'd said enough. Neither she nor François moved. Luckily no one else was in the depot. She felt sorry for Horace and didn't want to get him into trouble. But they were in a small town, not a city. People found things out one way or another. Secrets were for places like Winnipeg or Minneapolis. She was just getting to the truth a little faster than usual.

"Wait a minute," Horace said.

He got up again and came back with something he placed just out of her sight, except that she caught a glimpse of the telltale yellow paper. "Well, if I looked at it by mistake it might say something like this," the boy said in a soft, fast voice. "Railroad bulls found us in Winnipeg. Stop. On our way Baudette. Stop. Arrive Tuesday night."

"Thank you, Horace," Sadie said. She slid a quarter across the counter. "I do appreciate good service."

He took the quarter but didn't look at her. "I should go back to work. Bye, Miss Robinette."

"Sadie," she said over her shoulder as they walked away.

Chapter Seventeen

Hazel: Minneapolis, January–March 1925

New Year's Day in Minneapolis was warm compared to the freezing week before it. A high of twenty degrees! Hazel walked to the Merry Widow with no scarf around her head. *God help me, I'm getting as crazy as the people who live here,* she thought.

She'd been waiting for news from Milt or Theda about the baby, who must have been born by now. But then again, maybe not. Her mother always said the first child took its time, and the rest could hardly wait to get out and into the world. Finally, she received a letter:

January 20, 1925

Dear Hazel,

I am a mother. How strange to write those words…

He was born on January 3, just a little over two weeks ago. His full name is Theodore Albert Hawkins, but I call him Teddy. He's got lots of dark hair like me. Can't really tell with the eyes yet—they seem to change day by day.

I want to be a good mother to this little boy, raise him to be an honorable man, not obsessed with money and power and status like his father. Albert's got his heir now, and I told him I'd fulfilled my part of the bargain and expected him to leave me alone in that way from here on out. He has other women—thank God!—who keep him occupied and away from me. So far, it's working pretty well. He visits on Sundays, brings little gifts for Teddy and me. We eat lunch and then he leaves.

When I made this pact with my family and Williams, I insisted on getting my inheritance. Used my only bargaining chip: I'd disgrace the family even more by contacting the papers, talking to reporters, telling them it was true that I liked girls, etc. Of course, they still could have packed me off to a hospital—but I knew that the one thing they prized above all else was avoiding scandal. Holding on to their precious standing in Savannah. So Father paid up, gave his permission for me to set up a bank account, and the money's sitting safely for when I need it. Besides him, you're the only one who knows.

Because, Hazel, there are two people I love in this world: Teddy is one, and you are the other. I know you'll meet him someday, I'm just not sure when. For now, I am going to raise this little creature and dream of you—us—sometime, somewhere in the future. And hope. That's all I can do at the moment. He's tiny, of course, but when I hold him, it's like having a loaf of warm bread in my arms. And when I think of you, that warmth is in my heart.

Always remember that I love you.

Your Theda

It felt like a goodbye letter, although Hazel knew it wasn't. Maybe so long for now? But how long? How many more months or years could she perch in this northern city living in a hotel, spending her days and most of her nights with the ragtag Merry Widow crew? It wasn't a bad way to live, but it would never feel permanent. And truth be told, she didn't want it to be. Minneapolis was pleasant enough, but it would never be her home.

Nor would it be much better to go back to Savannah now. Maybe she could lay low, cook at the diner and let Milt run the place. But what then? George was now a steady presence in Milt's life. She certainly wasn't jealous of him— Milt needed a companion, and she was glad he'd found one. But where would she fit? Hazel and Milt would always be linked by their years together, their secrets and the marriage that still protected them both. And she knew he missed her, as she missed him and the warmth of his company. But if George had moved in, could the three of them live comfortably in the same house?

And how would she manage to see Theda? Visiting her was out of the question. Theda would have to come to the diner. Except that now with the baby, Theda wouldn't be able to have long visits or stay overnight. And would the charges be renewed once people found out that Hazel was back in town? Williams, Theda's family and the court still had the power to turn their lives upside down. Even though Theda had turned "respectable" with her arranged marriage and now a child, Hazel knew that the same legal system that had separated them could take children away from a so-called unfit mother. And next to a prostitute or a common criminal, who was more unfit than a mother who preferred women to men?

Hazel would turn twenty-nine this year, and for the first time since she'd left Savannah, she felt truly alone. Which the Minnesota winter with its short days only made worse. She cooked, walked a lot and slept more. *Animals hibernate*, she thought. *Why not me?*

She heard from Milt:

February 5, 1925

Dear Hazel,

Well, Theda came around to show me the new baby. Cute little fellow. Takes after her, I think. She didn't say a word about Albert. Don't think he's around much. But does she ever love that little guy! Suppose she won't be going anywhere now for a while.

Got so cold here the other day, George and me made a fire out back and roasted potatoes for supper! You would have cooked up a lot more things to go along with it, but we sure had fun. 'Course our cold won't last for long, nothing like the cold up there, but it made me think of you. Stay warm!

Milt

Theda was settled, and so was Milt, Hazel thought. Only she continued to be blown about, clutching her memories as the Minnesota winds howled from the northwest. She drew more into herself, became quieter.

Magnus was the first to notice the change in her mood. He put a hand on her shoulder one morning later in February when she was making coffee. None of the crew had arrived yet. "Hazel," he said. "You still cook like an angel, so the customers don't notice anything different. But I know you're having a rough time. Can tell by your eyes. What's wrong?"

She sighed. "Guess I feel like the wayfaring stranger."

"The wayfaring what?"

She sang a few bars: *I am a poor wayfaring stranger, traveling through this world of woe…*

"Damn, that's a sad song," Magnus said. "Here, let's sit down and talk."

They huddled around the kitchen table with their coffee as the sun edged up and slanted light through the blinds of the now unboarded windows of the Widow. They closed the shutters only when deep cold blew into the city. Hazel told Magnus about Theda's baby and Milt's new companion. "Going on three years now since I left, and I'm just not sure where I belong anymore."

"Well, as long as I'm running the Widow, you got a place," he said. "Hope you know that."

"I do, and I'm thankful. It's just that—"

"You ain't sure you want to stay here forever."

Hazel nodded. "And you're a swell boss, Magnus, nothing to do with you…"

He got up to refill their cups. "Listen. I been making more money since you come here, and you deserve a break. How about this summer you go back up to Oak Island? You really liked it there. I'd give you a month off with full pay. After the Fourth, when things quiet down a little."

Weight lifted from her shoulders. "Really?"

"People got to have something to look forward to," Magnus said.

Hazel had hardly dared think of the island lately, afraid to put too much stock in something that might change from one day to the next. Like in Savannah. But that night, just before falling asleep, Hazel imagined Oak Island as a lighthouse shining in the dark.

In late March, she got a letter from Minnie with a note from Rose:

Dear Hazel,

Well, winter will be over soon. We're getting ready for the thaw and a new season on the island. Saw some crows the other day—seems they always come back too soon! But it's a sign that spring's coming. Rosie and me pop popcorn at night and play checkers or cards. We both said it would be nice to see you. It was good when you were here.

How are things in the city? Is it exciting? Can't say I envy you living there, tho. I like the quiet and the stars and Northern Lights at night.

When do you think you might come for a visit?

Minnie

Stars and northern lights. Hazel imagined the huge sky aglow, throwing light all over the lake and the island. What a sight it must be.

Rose wrote:

Dear Hazel,

I sent you a story! You can tell me what you think about it when you come to see us. Or write me a letter. When ARE you coming? I've got lots of things to show you! I could even teach you to swim if the water's warm enough.

Rose

Hazel smiled. She got such a kick out of Rose, always bubbling over, like a bottle of shaken-up root beer. She took out a pen and paper, looked out the window of the Woman's Hotel at the March snow, crusted and dirty and worn out just like her, and started to write:

Dear Minnie and Rose,

Thank you for the letters. It's really nice to hear from you folks in the winter. Well, guess what? Magnus gave me a whole month off this summer, after the Fourth, to go up and visit you all. 'Course it'll take me a bit to get there, and I hope that's not too long to stay…sure don't want to be a nuisance!

Best,

Hazel

Chapter Eighteen

Hazel: Oak Island, September 1937

Hazel and Minnie had barely rested since receiving Sadie's telegram that Albert and his detectives had been in Baudette and were most likely on their way to Oak Island. By day they tended to their guests—not as numerous as in the summer but still a steady stream. By night, they talked and planned. Hazel wanted to see Albert, look into the eyes of the man who'd done such unspeakable things to Theda. She felt full of energy, like she'd drunk a whole pot of coffee.

"Wouldn't it be fun to keep him in the minnow tank?" she said one night. "Like a big fish, except tied down. Just his head out. And we'd keep throwing leeches in there to suck his blood." She chuckled.

It was fun to imagine torturing Albert. She had other fantasies: Dropping him off on an uninhabited island and leaving him there to see if he'd survive. Staking him, coated with honey, to an anthill teeming with hungry insects.

Minnie shook her head. "I know it's fun to cook up these schemes, but I think you're getting carried away. What about us? You and me and the resort. *Our* life. Doesn't that matter anymore?" She got up. "I'm going to bed."

"Aw, come on, Minnie," Hazel said to her retreating back with the dark braid hanging down.

The truth was that plotting vengeance on Albert made Hazel feel young. Powerful. And that was a wonderful feeling, because she held

Albert responsible for pretty much everything bad that had happened in her life: The years away from Savannah. The loss of Milt and her beloved H&M. And Theda. Maybe Albert didn't cut the deal with the court, but he kept Theda like a prisoner and made sure she was tied to him with a child. The other culprits, Robert John Williams, Esquire, the Savannah judge and Theda's family were all far away. But Albert was right here, in her territory. Or would be soon.

"He needs to pay," Hazel muttered. "First one through the door gets a baseball bat from me."

She had a Louisville Slugger, supposedly in case fishermen wanted to play some ball after a day on the lake, but really for herself. She'd loved playing baseball with her brothers when she was a girl, and she had a good swing. Which she'd been practicing on the sly. She loved to feel the smooth wood in her hands, the muscle in her arm. But maybe Minnie was right. Maybe she was still stuck back in 1922 when the Savannah cops bashed in the door of the speakeasy. Maybe the bat was her very own billy club.

* * *

Two days later, with no guests at the resort, Minnie had given the dock boy and the Conley girls the day off. Hazel was weeding the garden, one of the few things that calmed her these days, when a boat pulled up at the dock with four men in it. One man hopped out to tie up while the other three sat motionless. She recognized the man as a guide from a mainland resort whose owners didn't approve of her and Minnie and made no secret of it. Which was unusual. In this part of the world, life was too harsh to quarrel with your neighbors about how they lived their lives. Cooperation was the best defense against blizzards, -40 degree temperatures and the changing moods of the massive lake.

It had to be Albert and the detectives.

Hazel stood up and walked down to the dock. Her hair was tied back, and she was wearing the gray cotton dress Theda had made for her all those years ago. A bit threadbare by now, but still sturdy and a comfort to her skin.

The first of the three men to step out of the boat wore a flannel shirt, dark pants and boots, all of them well-made and expensive-looking. He was short and stocky, with dark brown hair threaded with gray and brown eyes that looked both intelligent and unfriendly.

Hazel had a pretty good idea who it was. "I'm Hazel Goodwin," she said.

"I know." He didn't offer a hand, and neither did she. "At last we meet."

"So you're Albert." She looked past him at the two men. "I see you brought friends." One of them was shorter than Albert but tougher looking, dressed in a suit and a fedora. She wondered if he'd gotten cold on the trip across the lake. The other was tall, with a hat that dipped over his eyes. Neither of them spoke.

"Business associates." He smirked.

Hazel was not intimidated. A strange calm had settled over her as if she were watching herself and the scene from a distance. "You're looking for Theda," she said.

"*And* my boy. And we're going to find them."

Now it was Hazel's turn to smile. "Well, you go on and look for them, Albert. I'll even take you on a tour of the place. Right up here is the lodge." And without waiting for him to answer, she turned and led the way up to the porch outside the lobby, betting that the men would follow. When she reached the door, she looked back. They were coming, but slowly. They'd gathered in a little knot several yards away and seemed to be arguing. She strained her ears to hear.

"…it's a trap, boss," said the small man. "We gotta be careful. Look what Sadie Robinette did."

"Nah," said the tall man. "Sadie Robinette's a pro. She took us for chumps, and we walked right into it. This is different."

"I don't care what you think, Cal. We're going in," Albert said.

Hazel held the door for them. "After you."

"Oh, no you don't. You first," Albert replied.

"Fine." She opened the porch door and then walked into the now deserted lobby. "Dining room is through here. That's the kitchen."

"Where are the bedrooms?"

Louisville Slugger aside, Hazel knew that resistance wasn't a good idea. She was outnumbered and certainly outgunned. But the reality of having Albert in her home made her cringe. Just a few feet away was the room she shared with Minnie. The bed where they slept every night. Pictures of Rose, of Rose and Emil. Clothing. Their smells.

The tall man opened the door to their bedroom and went in. Looked under the bed and in the closet. "Nothing here."

Albert followed. "So this is where you dykes live. Let me get an eyeful."

Hazel steeled herself not to react, biting her lip so hard she almost cried out. No matter. She would not rise to Albert's bait.

Finally, the two men proceeded to the kitchen, the pantry, the root cellar. Hazel wondered where Minnie was. Probably repairing something outside. "And out here," she opened the back door for them. "You'll find the cabins. No one staying here now, and they're unlocked. And of course, there's the rest of the island, which we don't own, but people are *usually* friendly. Three miles long, one mile wide. It won't take forever."

"Pretty sure of yourself, aren't you?" Albert scowled. But they left.

Hazel stayed in the kitchen. Made a chocolate cake and frosted it, brewed a pot of coffee. Went out to gather eggs from the chicken coop. Picked the last of the raspberries. She still felt the strange tranquility but also anticipation. The men would be back at some point. She just hoped they wouldn't be forced to stay the night. Thank God for the waxing moon and the clear September sky. Any guide on Lake of the Woods had to know how to navigate with a compass and whatever light was available.

* * *

It was almost three o'clock in the afternoon when they returned. Minnie was still gone. They looked tired, with burrs and thistles clinging to their pants. Albert wore a tight-lipped frown.

"Y'all must be exhausted," Hazel said, slipping into southern talk. "How about some coffee? And I made a chocolate cake."

"If you think we're going to touch your food, you're crazy," Albert said. "Folks up here like to poison people. But yeah, we'll have coffee and some water while you're at it."

"Dunno if that's a good idea, boss," said the short man. "Who knows what she put in it."

"I'll take my chances," Albert took a seat at the kitchen table.

Hazel whistled softly as she poured three cups, fetched cream and sugar and pumped a pitcher of water. So far, so good. Although she knew the hardest part might be coming up, serenity again covered her like a warm shawl. She'd love to tell Minnie about it. Whenever she showed up.

She leaned up against the cupboards. "So no luck, eh?"

"Don't push me," Albert said. "Cal here has a real mean streak." He put his hand on the shoulder of the short man, still wearing his fedora. The tall man had taken off his hat. Albert finished the coffee, held out his cup for more and settled back in his chair. "Now you're going to tell me where my wife and kid are. And make it snappy—we're in a hurry."

"I have no idea, Albert," Hazel said. "Oh, they *were* here, Theda and Teddy." She rolled their names on her tongue. "But they were much too smart to stay on an island where they'd be sitting ducks for you and Cal and—"

"Gus," said the tall man.

Albert glared at him. "Well, they're someplace. And you know where."

"No, Albert. I don't."

"Say the word, boss," said Cal, rocking his chair forward.

"I'll handle this," Albert snarled, not even looking at him. "Gus, pat her down and tie her up."

Alarm jolted Hazel out of her calm, but she steeled herself. Gus stood up, pulled a length of rope out of his overcoat and approached her. She looked into his eyes. They weren't mean, but she couldn't read them.

"Come away from the cupboard and hold out your arms," Gus said.

She obeyed. He patted her armpits, sides, hips and down her legs. She stiffened, but he was fast and methodical, no funny stuff. "She's clean," he said, then picked up a chair. "Sit down." His voice was low and unexcited. Again she obeyed. No sense getting hurt if she didn't have to. She took her first good look at him. Tall, with long legs, wearing an overcoat that had seen better days. Gray eyes, tired and a little reddened. "Don't make a fuss," he said in a low voice that was almost a whisper. "You're better off with me than Cal."

When Gus had finished tying her up, Albert pulled his chair right in front of her. "So. Where are they?"

"I already told you I don't know."

"Of course you do. You're the one that was with her in that pervert speakeasy back in '22. Her friend. Her…"

Can't even bring himself to say it, Hazel marveled. Her heart had begun to beat fast, but some of the calm remained. "Did you come all this way to talk about that?"

"You know why I came. Tell me where Theda and my boy went."

Hazel was tired of telling him she didn't know. A lie, of course, but she felt entirely comfortable lying to Albert. "Why would you want a woman who doesn't want you? Theda's got no time for men. Never has."

He brought his face closer, brown eyes boring into her. "You think you're so damn smart," he hissed. "What do you know? She's my wife, and Teddy's my boy, and the law says they have to come with me."

"It's different up here, Albert. There's the law, and then there's what's right."

"Don't lecture me!" he said, coming in closer. "You, with your queer husband back in Savannah. You're all perverts."

The word *pervert* made her laugh as if someone had tickled her. "Albert, I swear you sound like a Baptist minister. Was your papa a preacher?"

He backhanded her, hard, striking her nose and her ear. But for the ropes, she would have fallen. A gong rang in her head and warm liquid trickled out of her nose, over her lips and down her chin. Hazel felt herself float away from the chair and up to the ceiling, from where she could see everything, including herself. Albert was breathing hard, like he'd been running. "You can beat me up," she said, "but it won't help." What could he do to her that the Savannah Police hadn't already done in 1922?

"Joe Beaudette said she was here."

She heard her voice go into a lower register. "Joe Beaudette? You'd take the word of a half-crazy fortune-teller?"

"He's too simple to lie. And he talked about water. I can put two and two together."

She almost pitied him. "Well, you and Gus and Cal searched the island, didn't you? She's not here. But the lake's a big place. And Joe Beaudette knows that."

"Bitch." His voice low and bitter. He was pathetic, a little man who'd married a woman that didn't even like him, much less love him. Who spawned a son with a mind of his own. He was like a hound barking up the tree where he'd chased a squirrel.

"You'll never get what you want," she said.

She watched his body tense. "Either you talk or we burn down your bull dyke resort and shoot you before we do it."

Gus took a step forward. "Hang on a minute," he said. "You hired me to find the wife and kid. Fine. Rough people up some—sure. But plugging women? Torching buildings? I'm not taking the fall for murder. Or arson."

Then Minnie's voice, from behind Gus, loud and clear as an ice-laden branch cracking on a winter night. "There's not going to be a fire, and no one's going to kill anybody, even though it would be a lot of fun to put a slug in you, Albert." Dressed in a black shirt and pants, hair in a long braid that fell over one shoulder, she pointed her rifle directly at Albert. "They're in the wind. We don't know where, and they sure as hell aren't on the island. But you're the one with money and detectives. Take them and your boat and whoever brought you here and go look for them."

Hazel had never been prouder of her. She descended from her perch on the ceiling back down to the chair, felt the curved wood holding her body, took in the polished barrel of Minnie's gun, Albert's silence, Gus's folded arms.

Albert locked eyes with Gus. Finally, he turned toward Minnie and the rifle. "How do we know you're not lying?" Albert said.

"You already searched the island. Do it again if you want to. But get on with it, for God's sake. We've got fishermen coming and lots to do."

"I can make her sing, boss. You know I can," Cal said.

Albert ignored him.

The sun was getting low in the sky. God, how Hazel hoped they'd be gone before dark. Albert took Gus and Cal and huddled in the corner, Gus doing most of the talking. Eventually, they came back toward the table.

"What's south of here?" Albert said.

"You mean besides water and islands?" Minnie replied. "Little towns. Pitt, Graceton, Williams, Roosevelt, Warroad and Roseau, not counting the places in between. Woods. Bogs."

"Okay," he said. "But if we don't find them, if you're setting us up, you'll see us again."

Hazel wanted to say, *You're scaring me, Albert.* Except she knew it would make things worse.

"By the way," Minnie said, voice casual. "Even if you find them, keep in mind you're not making any friends up in these parts. They won't go easy."

"We'll see about that," he said. "Come on, boys."

And they left.

The kitchen was suddenly so large that Hazel thought she could float in it if she weren't tied up. She blinked. Minnie came over, put her hand on her shoulder and started undoing the ropes. The sun was starting to set over the water. A cold breeze blew off the lake through the open window, ruffling the curtains. Hazel shivered.

"It's over," Minnie said.

"No, it's not." Hazel barely noticed the tears sliding down her cheeks.

Chapter Nineteen

Hazel: Minneapolis–Oak Island, July 1925

In mid-July of 1925, when waves of heat shimmered up from the Minneapolis sidewalks, Hazel boarded a train for Duluth, where she spent the night in a hotel near the depot. The next morning, she caught another train to International Falls, to the northwest, right on the Canadian border. She crossed to Fort Frances, Ontario, where spruce and pine trees filled in the spaces around fields and houses. The next train, a Canadian National, followed the Rainy River, an indigo ribbon between the two countries, stopping in a few tiny towns until it crossed back to the American side, into Baudette, and Hazel got off.

The Baudette depot was new and shining, built, according to the stationmaster, who loved to talk, in 1923, just two years before. "Where you going?" he asked, pushing up his hat to look at her.

"Oak Island," she said.

"Whew!" He shook his head. "Boy, you still got a long way to go! Somebody coming for you?"

"I hope so," Hazel said, looking around. But the truth was she didn't care if she had to wait. The depot smelled of fresh wood, and the floors were polished to a high sheen. She'd never traveled by herself before. At least not for pleasure. No husband, no boss, no lover, no get-out-of-town order, just her. She took in the wooden benches, the schedules posted on the wall. So quiet. Nothing like the Milwaukee Depot in Minneapolis with the deep male voice announcing trains, *now departing, train to Duluth, stopping at White Bear Lake…Hinckley, Cloquet…*

A towheaded boy who looked much too young to drive came into the depot and doffed his hat. "Are you Miss Hazel?"

"Yes, I am."

"Well, ma'am, I'm here to take you to Morris Point."

She shook her head. "Oh, there must be some mistake. I'm going to Oak Island."

The boy laughed. "No mistake, ma'am. When we get to Morris Point, a boat'll pick you up and take you there. It's way across the lake."

Hazel smiled as he picked up her suitcase. "Why, then, I'm on a real adventure!" she said.

"Yes, ma'am," the boy said, leading the way to a dusty Model T outside.

***

Many hours later, although the sun still had not set, Hazel stepped off the boat onto the dock at Oak Island. Minnie and Rose walked down from the lodge to meet her. Minnie, dark hair pulled back in a ponytail, was grinning and swinging Rose's hand. Rose broke loose and ran, then stopped—suddenly shy, Hazel concluded. She opened her arms and embraced the girl, fifteen this summer. She'd gotten taller, but her hair still smelled like sunshine and her dress like fish scales.

Minnie stepped forward. *Now what?* Hazel thought. She put out her hand. Minnie took it, then opened her arms. "Hugs all around," she said, and Rose joined in.

Hazel realized that no one had touched her in a very long time. She and Milt used to snuggle up in bed, with nightclothes on, like brother and sister. And, of course, she and Theda had always been next to each other, brushing hands, faces, shoulders. She'd never realized how comforting it was.

"Fresh walleye for supper," Minnie said.

"Hope you don't get sick of fish, Hazel," Rose chimed in. "With fried potatoes and corn on the cob. I'm starving!"

"I can't wait," Hazel said.

With every step in the cool, fresh air on the path to the lodge, her body relaxed. She'd sleep well tonight.

* * *

Hazel rose early every morning, had coffee on "her" rock, just outside the same cabin where she'd stayed on her first visit, and watched the lake. Then she'd walk the island, choosing a different path each day. Sometimes Rose came with her. She'd point out plants, flowers, blueberries, raspberries. Or she'd stay quiet, maybe planning her next story. Hazel started noticing sounds. The constant waves, of course. And the wind, which sighed as it blew through the pine trees. Songbirds. Woodpeckers. Owls who came out at night. And whippoorwills, who loved to sing after dark, meaning not until nearly eleven o'clock.

She liked to cook supper for the three of them.

"I don't want you to have to work while you're here," Minnie protested. She had duties during the day, and Hazel would often not see her until evening.

"It's not work," Hazel replied. She loved to create meals. It reminded her of cooking back at the H&M, except that she didn't have to worry about whether customers would come back or not.

Then they'd sit outside and watch the sunset—the breeze off the lake kept bugs away—and go in to play board games afterward.

* * *

Within a few days, after resting up from the long trip, it began to dawn on Hazel that she had never before felt so at peace. Not even during her first stay on the island. And she hadn't realized how much she'd craved it. The Merry Widow garden certainly soothed her, as did her walks along the Mississippi. But this time on Oak Island, she realized she'd spent the past three years running in place to forget what she'd left behind in Savannah. She'd kept getting up in the morning, walking to work, cooking, gardening, writing letters home to Milt and Theda. But now, Milt had someone to keep him company and help with the diner. And Theda had a baby.

Hazel had never thought much about peace, much less felt it seep into her. Certainly not growing up with her rambunctious siblings, their mother so scattered among them that there was little or nothing left for her tomboy daughter, who early on learned to fend for herself.

And not with Milt, their marriage a comfortable agreement to keep them both safe from people who viewed homosexuals as dangerous perverts. They were good friends, but no matter how you looked at it, they were hiding in plain sight, and that was always on her mind, in good times and bad.

And no, not even with Theda of the sapphire eyes, slender hands and restless spirit. Being with her was like being whirled in an feather eggbeater. It kept Hazel breathless, delighted and off-balance.

Oak Island was different. Hazel had always loved water, no matter where she was, and now she could see it and hear it all day, every day. Lake of the Woods smelled of fish, clamshells, seaweed and fresh water, cut at times by wood smoke. Under a clear sky, the water was bright blue. On cloudy days it turned bottle green or slate gray. She never tired of its sound, the way it crashed and rolled and sighed, especially at night when she went to sleep in what Minnie called "your cabin." Set apart from the other buildings, it was older and built to withstand cold. The logs fit tightly together, with no cracks to let in wind or snow. An oil barrel wood stove provided heat in the winter. Hazel slept under a patchwork quilt in the twin bed closest to the lake, deep sleeps in which people from every part of her life visited her dreams until she felt she had seen all of them.

"Maybe I'll stay here forever," she said to Minnie and Rose one night as they sat outside looking at the night sky, listening to the waves, watching fireflies blink on and off. She meant it as a joke—although, in the past few days, she'd dreamed of doing just that. She'd cook wonderful meals with fresh produce, fish and berries. She'd revamp the kitchen, make it bigger and more efficient. She'd bake. She'd make sure people came not only for the fishing and quiet but also for the food.

Minnie and Rose looked at each other.

"Gee, Hazel," the girl said. "Would you? Please?"

Minnie laughed. "Don't scare her away." But she put her hand over Hazel's in the most intimate gesture they'd shared up until that point and said in a quiet voice, "We'd both love to have you. For as long as you want."

Hazel felt fluttery inside. "I got to think," she said. "It's a big decision." She retired to her cabin, but she'd already made up her mind. She wrote Magnus, Milt and finally Theda:

> *Don't know what the future holds, but I'm real happy here. It's a beautiful place, and I guess I need a place to rest my soul after everything that's happened in the last three years. You take good care of that little fellow! And if you ever need somewhere to go, you always have a place with me. Wherever I am. But I'm pretty sure I'll be here on the island.*
>
> *Love,*
> *Hazel*

Chapter Twenty

Hazel: Oak Island, September 1937

After Albert, Gus and Cal left, Hazel slept for the better part of a day. Dreamed of falling into a pit filled with Spanish moss that she couldn't escape and that threatened to suffocate her. As soon as she awoke, she knew she had to go to Faunce Ridge. Whatever began when Theda walked into the H&M Diner all those years ago still lived inside her. Even though she loved Minnie. Maybe she was like a train that set off on a long journey, got sidetracked, broke down, got fixed and kept chugging along, slower now, to its destination. Just as one way or another, Albert would find Faunce Ridge, she, Hazel, had to be part of the ragtag army that would fight him, along with Little Roy, Marie, Sadie, and François.

She and Minnie talked late into the night, facing each other in bed, one lamp burning. Hazel ran her fingers through Minnie's dark hair loose on the pillow, remembered her dressed all in black, rifle aimed at Albert. "God, I'll miss you."

"Even with Theda there?" Minnie's eyes searched hers, letting Hazel's hand cup her cheek.

"Yes."

She only hoped that she would remain as steadfast once she and Theda were both at Faunce Ridge after so many years away from each other. A tender night with Minnie would help.

But Minnie rolled away and changed the subject. Sometimes her pragmatic nature got in the way of intimacy. "What I really worry about is Albert and his goons," she said. "God knows what kind of firepower they've got. Cal's a loose cannon if I ever saw one. Guy like that gets a gun, he thinks he's John Dillinger."

"Well, but there's Gus. He seems like a decent fellow. Maybe he'll ride herd on the other two. Like he did last night."

Minnie frowned. "But Albert's a rabid dog. And rabid dogs bite. Usually with no warning."

Hazel chuckled, picturing Albert on all fours, snarling. "I'll bite back!"

Minnie didn't smile. "That's what I mean. Promise me you won't start anything. Won't smart off, even if it feels good."

Hazel winced. Her sassy mouth could have gotten her into real trouble when the men were at the resort if Minnie hadn't shown up and Gus hadn't stepped in. She looked out the window at the starry sky, heard the waves lapping the shore just yards away. A lump formed in her throat.

She took Minnie's face in her hands. "I swear I'll be careful."

* * *

While Hazel was gone, Mama Conley would come over from Flag Island and take her place in the kitchen. She was a legendary cook whose large family would miss her, but who could use the extra income. "I hope it's no more than a week or two," Hazel told her. "But it could be longer."

She'd instructed the mailman to send a telegram to Sadie and François, phrasing it with as much care as possible. No sense alerting everyone who touched it:

THEY CAME STOP NO RATS HERE STOP ON MY WAY STOP.

The sun was just coming up when Hazel brought her bag down to the dock where she'd take a boat south across Lake of the Woods, then up the Rainy River into Baudette. She wore a sweater against the chill of early fall, one Rose had made for her when she was learning how to knit. The memory made her smile.

"I'd rather be swimming or writing or cleaning fish," Rose had complained at the time. "But oh no, we're to learn the 'womanly arts' or we won't get a grade in Miss Agnew's class. You can tell she grew up in a city. Probably had nothing to do but sit around and devote herself to worthless pursuits."

"Now, now," Minnie had said, meeting Hazel's eyes and shaking her head to warn her not to laugh. "Someone knit the sweaters and scarves you wear, but you don't think of them as worthless, do you?"

"Hmmm." Rose bit her lip, which she did when she was thinking something over. "No, 'course not. But that doesn't mean I have to knit them, too!"

In the end, she'd created a sweater like no other from spare skeins of wool she'd found here and there. It had a shawl collar and was long, more like a coat than a sweater, made of yarn in various shades of blue and green in no particular pattern. She presented it to Hazel one Christmas morning, told her to close her eyes while she went to her room to get it.

"All right, you can look now!" she said.

Hazel opened her eyes. She'd always been nearsighted, so when Rose held up her creation, it blurred into a woolen version of Lake of the Woods with its always-shifting shades of indigo, turquoise, bottle green and gray. "I know you still get cold up here so far from Georgia," she said. "And it's not very pretty, but it'll keep you warm."

"Those colors!" Hazel said. "Like the water!"

"You like it?" Rose's face was anxious.

"Oh, Rosie, it's beautiful!"

It became her favorite piece of clothing, along with the robe and dresses Theda had made for her.

She'd packed a few dresses, a pair of pants, two shirts and sturdy boots for walking the forest or the bog. And a coat, flannel nightgown, wool stockings, a hat and gloves. Autumn progressed fast in their part of the world, although there would be sunny days with bright blue skies when it seemed that summer had changed its mind and was coming back. But that never lasted for long. Every day, the sun would set earlier and rise later. Nights would grow thick and fat like bears preparing for winter.

What if she didn't return to Oak Island until winter? Across ice, not blue water? She had no idea how long it would take to face down Albert and his men, and even less how she and the others would do that. She wondered if they'd be chasing an invisible enemy. Still, Albert, Gus and Cal had been anything but invisible when they came to the resort. She still wore the bruise from Albert's backhand.

And the question she barely dared think: What if all the feelings for Theda came back and she plunged straight into them? What if she never saw Minnie and Oak Island again?

Minnie walked her down to the dock, where one of the Conley boys was waiting to take Hazel over to the mainland. But before they got there, she stopped and put her hands on her shoulders. "Remember what you promised," she said, dark eyes solemn.

Hazel studied the beloved face, the high cheekbones. She didn't want to cry or think of all the terrible things that could happen. So she cocked her head. "Wait, what was that again? What'd I promise?"

"Hazel."

Why did she joke about these things? "Minnie." She took her hands. "I don't know what gets into me."

"I just want you back safe and sound," Minnie said. Her eyes glistened.

Hazel started to answer that nothing was going to happen, that she was only joining forces with the others, that Albert was just a bully. But she didn't. Seeing her self-possessed Minnie on the verge of tears made her choke up. And she knew this was the most dangerous thing she'd done since she and Theda stepped into the Savannah speakeasy. Which of course, hadn't become dangerous until the cops burst in. But this time, the sensation of ropes binding her to the chair, the ringing in her ear, the blood seeping out of her nose were still fresh.

Minnie had been sleeping with a pistol under her pillow since that night. "Never going to happen again that I can't protect you," she said.

"But you did protect me," Hazel protested.

"I should've come quicker."

"You came at exactly the right minute," Hazel said.

Did she need protecting? She, Hazel Goodwin, who'd always been independent, whose head healed just fine after the Savannah cop knocked her out that night, who picked up and left her home and moved all the way up to Minneapolis. Who cooked at Magnus's speakeasy until fate led her to this island and Minnie and Rose and the lake that never ended.

But the Night of Albert, as she'd come to think of it, because Gus and Cal wouldn't have been there if not for him, robbed her of something: the Hazel she thought she was. After all, it was Minnie who rousted them with her rifle. And Gus who talked sense into the other two. Maybe it was all about luck.

And which Hazel was she now? Growing up, she took pains not to be a scaredy-cat. Not be a *girl*, meaning weak and silly, scared of bugs and snakes, afraid to get dirty or skin her knee.

But, of course, she was a girl. An older girl. Tougher than most women, maybe. Still not afraid of dirt and critters of the earth. Still ready for adventure. But she didn't have muscles like a man, and she was too damn nearsighted to aim a gun.

"Min," she said. "I couldn't stop Albert by myself, and I don't know how to shoot. I'll just be in the way out there in the woods."

Minnie's dark eyes were thoughtful. "Let's sit on the dock," she said. They walked the rest of the way down. Below them, blue water lapped at weathered gray wooden pilings. Seagulls swooped and lamented as if their mothers had abandoned them. Fish jumped here and there, splashing up in the water. To have a look at the day? Get their morning constitutional? Or were they daring the gulls to gobble them up? And was she, Hazel, doing the same thing, taking herself to the woods and bog as bait for Albert and his men?

"Look," Minnie said. "Albert's here for Theda and Teddy, and whoever gets in his way, he'll knock around. Men like that, you've got to surround, show them they're not so tough. So the more of you, the better."

They sat, heads touching. Hazel closed her eyes and listened to the waves, breathing in the aroma of the Castille soap Minnie favored. She knew leaves were falling from the trees behind them. Just as she knew the lake was cooling its way toward winter.

"When I come back," she said. "I want us to go to Savannah together. We can take the train out of Minneapolis. Time I saw my people again. Especially Milt. And time they met you."

"We'll see," Minnie said.

"What do you mean? Don't you want to go?"

She sighed. "It's not that. It's just that all kinds of things could happen between now and then. Hopefully, everything will turn out fine. But let's wait and see."

Hazel felt a chill settle over her, despite Rose's big, crazy sweater. *What if I never see Minnie again?* She pulled her to her feet, and they embraced for a long time. Hazel tried to inhale her solidity, her calm, everything about her, so she could store it inside her body. She nuzzled Minnie's ear, shy about having a passionate kiss in front of people.

Finally, she turned to the boat. Bobby, one of the older Conley boys, was at the helm. Usually he'd be working with his father. As if reading Hazel's mind, he said, "I like to get off the island now and then."

Hazel grabbed her bag and climbed in. Waved until Minnie merged with the dock, then watched the island fade into the distance.

Chapter Twenty-One

Hazel: Baudette-Faunce Ridge, September 1937

Hazel arrived at the Baudette docks in the afternoon, exhausted from bouncing on the waves and chilled by the cold wind that blew across the river and the lake. She unloaded her things from the boat and walked up the hill to Hotel Pascal. Not as cold on land as on the water, but the air was crisp, and the trees were turning. Autumn came fast in this country and winter even faster. The reverse of Savannah, where spring and summer seemed to last forever, and the cooling fall breezes took their time getting there.

Sadie met her at the door. "Got your telegram. What happened?"

"Well, they searched the resort, of course," Hazel said. "And the whole island. Albert really thought we had Theda and Teddy squirreled away someplace, so he was furious that they weren't there. Had Gus tie me up. Smacked me. Threatened to kill us and burn down the resort. I think he might have tried if Gus hadn't talked him out of it. But then Minnie showed up with her rifle, and they decided to leave."

"Lucky that was all they did," Sadie said, inspecting Hazel's purplish eye and cheek. "Come on in."

At the kitchen table, Hazel said, "I think they'll scour every single town along the border. Whether they'll figure out Faunce Ridge is even there, I don't know, but Albert's not going to give up."

Sadie nodded. "The night they were here, Albert liked Little Roy's fiddling so much he wanted to take him back to Georgia for the winter. I said that'd never happen 'cause Little Roy wouldn't leave the woods. Albert asked me how he could live there, so primitive and all, and I said something like he stays in a little town, or what used to be a town. Didn't say its name, of course."

"Albert, he is very clever," François said. "He senses things. We make a grave mistake if we think of him only as a charging bull, so mad he cannot see."

* * *

The next morning, bags packed, they set off, Sadie driving with François next to her and Hazel in the back, west on Highway 11 along the railroad tracks that ran along the border. Pitt was the first town, then Graceton. They'd been lumber villages, according to Minnie, and both still had a post office and a general store, usually in the same building.

"Whoever runs the store knows everything," Sadie said. "Sooner or later, we're going to pick up their trail."

The Graceton storekeeper nodded when they asked about strangers coming in. "Oh, ya. Man who wasn't from around here by the way he talked. Wearing clothes you could tell cost something. Wanted to know if I'd seen a woman and a boy." He laughed. "'Well sure,' I say, 'bout every day.' Then he shows me a picture. The woman was real pretty, so I would've remembered, but I never seen her or the boy, and that's what I tell him, and he leaves."

They thanked him and drove on to Williams, where they went into the Halgusson store on Main Street. The largest in town, it was high and narrow, with patterned tin ceilings and shelves that went right up to the top with pretty much everything a person could want. Ladders for the owner and his employees to scramble up, get down cans of tobacco and coffee, bolts of fabric, kerosene lanterns. Although it was only wide enough for the counter, the cooler and two aisles of goods, Halgusson's went back nearly to the other side of the block, which meant you could spend a lot of time and still not see everything it had to offer. Hazel and Minnie liked to stock up there. It was rare that they couldn't find everything on their list.

Hazel liked John Halgusson, tall and dark-haired with an olive cast to his skin. Now in September, after the long days of northern summer, he was deeply tanned. "I'm a Black Swede," he liked to say. "My father always said our people came over from Spain. Anyway, who says all Swedes got to be blond?"

When Sadie described Albert, Cal and Gus, Halgusson knew exactly who she was talking about.

"They come through all right. You just missed them."

Good, Hazel thought, and her heart beat faster. They weren't as far behind Albert as she'd feared.

"Three of 'em, just like you say. And I didn't like their look. Or their way. One bossy guy wanted to do all the talking. And two other fellows—a short guy, looks like he runs with Machine Gun Kelly. The other one taller, don't say too much. They ask me about a lady and a kid. Show me a picture. She's got dark hair, clothes right up to the minute. Boy looks a lot like her. But I never seen them before, and I told 'em so."

He leaned over the counter and lowered his voice.

"But then—the guy who's the boss asks me if I know a fiddler, name of Little Roy. And that's when I get worried. 'Cause if they're looking for Little Roy, they ain't up to no good. He keeps to himself and don't bother no one, and we all look out for him. I know he ain't got a pot to pee in, so when he comes, I give him everything half price. Or less. Figure out his bill far enough away he can't see it and lowball it so he pays something, but it don't bankrupt him. Anyhow, I scratch my head like I'm thinking, and tell the guy I might of heard of somebody like that over to Roseau, in the next county, but not here, no sir."

"And then they left?" Sadie said.

Halgusson nodded. "Glad you folks came along because otherwise, I was going to have to send somebody down to Faunce to make sure he's okay. They ain't going to find him in Roseau, but sooner or later, somebody's going to point them in the right direction."

A thrill of cold ran down Hazel's spine. Halgusson was right. Little Roy and his fiddle were well-known all along the border. Before she left Oak Island, she'd managed to find the rosary her mother gave her when she married Milt and put it into her pocket for good luck. Now she fingered the beads and said a silent prayer to protect Little Roy and all of them.

"Do not worry, my friend," François said. "We are on our way there now, as soon as we buy provisions."

They stocked up on flour, sugar, coffee, cocoa, raisins, oatmeal, kerosene, boxes of matches, packed everything into the car and went straight to State Aid 2, where they turned south to drive the twelve miles into Faunce Ridge.

Chapter Twenty-Three

Hazel: Faunce Ridge, September 1937

Hazel hadn't paid much attention to anything but Theda when she accompanied her and Teddy out to Faunce Ridge in August. So when she returned with Sadie and François over a month later, she thought for a minute they must have come to the wrong place. She saw fall bearing down on abandoned houses, barns and sheds. Weeds grew tall in spaces that looked like they'd been gardens. Huge holes here and there, where houses had stood. As if a giant dentist had come through and ripped them out like so many rotten teeth. She imagined him: legs braced, pulling for all he was worth with oversized pliers until—splat!—the house popped right out of the ground.

Before the relocation, the houses were occupied, and everyone went to the Saturday night dances. Children played stick ball, hide and seek and other games when not in school, dodging the dogs, cats and chickens who roamed the place. Faunce Ridge was alive, colorful, sometimes noisy. Now silence hung over the place, except for the birds who hadn't yet flown south.

Hazel gasped. "Sadie," she said. "Would you stop a minute?"

Sadie grumbled but brought the car to a halt. They were in front of what used to be Ruby's store and the post office, but Hazel barely recognized it. Since she'd last been in Faunce Ridge in August, a large spruce had fallen on the roof, almost but not quite collapsing the building, like a pillow cleaved by an axe. The same tree split the porch where people used to sit and drink root beer in the warm months. The American flag still flew from a teetering pole in the yard, and the jaunty Chesterfield cigarette gentleman still swayed in the breeze, rusted tin hat and eternal smile like a joke here in the woods that were rapidly growing in on him.

Sadie drove on, and Hazel sat back. Somehow, even though she knew most of the people had moved, in her mind Faunce Ridge still existed as a robust village in which everyone would join the fight against Albert and his men. But that was a dream, her way of keeping alive a past that could never return. People might have built a house, a barn, a chicken coop, kept animals, raised gardens, dug wells, proved up their homesteads, but in the end, trees and bushes would creep back and return the place to wilderness. Nothing stayed the same. Not even her and Minnie. Or her and Theda. But she resolved not to think about that now.

It was a relief to get to Marie's place, with her garden, the honey-colored horse, the bunches of drying herbs hanging from the porch roof. Like a good witch in the forest, Hazel mused.

Marie came out to meet them. "Cavalry's here," she said with a grin as they staggered up to the porch, loaded with suitcases and bags of provisions. "Looks like you're going to stay awhile. Haven't seen so many supplies since I set up house."

"For God's sake, open up, so I don't drop flour and sugar all over," Sadie said. Little Roy braced the door, and within minutes the tiny house was full to overflowing.

When she stepped into the fragrant kitchen, Hazel felt dizzy. There was Theda at the table, dark hair even more unruly, tanned skin making her blue eyes stand out. She looked beautiful and sad, like that day in the lawyer's office in Savannah. And she started when she saw Hazel.

"What happened to your face?" she said. "Albert?"

Hazel nodded. "But I'm fine. Really. He didn't do diddly squat to me." She wanted to believe that as much as she wanted to reassure Theda. "At last I got to meet the little weasel."

They embraced. Theda started to cry, first softly, then with shaking sobs. Hazel kept her eyes closed, treasuring this moment of closeness, even though she knew Sadie, François, Marie, Little Roy and Teddy were all there. She smelled Sadie's Lucky Strike, heard her blow out smoke in a noisy exhale. No one spoke.

Eventually, Theda stepped back. "I can't go through with this," she said, drying her eyes. "Albert and whoever he's hired, with their weapons and God knows what else, like we're the Barker gang or something. Anyway, Teddy and I'll just pack our things and go somewhere else. I won't put you all in harm's way. Look at Hazel's face. And that was nothing. Next time they'll use their guns…"

"Oh, we're tough southern girls, you and me," Hazel said. "If we can go up against the Savannah police, we can take on Albert."

"That was nothing. This is life and death."

Theda fell silent, and it got so quiet Hazel could hear people breathing.

Finally, François cleared his throat. "*Eh, bien.* The things that are important, are they not all death and life?"

"Maybe," Theda said. "But this time, it's because of me, and that's what I can't bear."

Hazel shook her head. "Damn it, Theda, this is how you get yourself into trouble, putting everything on your own shoulders. Back in Savannah, you let your family marry you off so the two of us wouldn't go to prison…"

"What?" Teddy's eyes got wide.

As so often happened, Sadie had the last word. "Enough crying and moaning. You're here, Theda, and that's that. Where would you go if you left?" Smoke made her voice huskier. "Canada? No place to hide unless you go all the way to Winnipeg, and you don't know a soul there. Right here in Faunce Ridge is as good a place as any to put up a fight. At least we know it—Little Roy and Marie do anyway. And one thing for sure—Albert might be after you and Teddy, but he's gunning for all of us. He and the boys could shoot us dead, throw us in the bog, leave us out for the buzzards. So it ain't just about you, and the longer we sit here jawing, the more time we waste when we should be getting ready for those sonsabitches."

Amen, Hazel thought. She kept her eyes on Theda and realized that no matter what came to pass, she was happy just to be in the same room with her.

Chapter Twenty-Four

Little Roy: Faunce Ridge, September 1937

Little Roy had plenty of ideas about how to stop the invaders. They'd start with the roads. He, François and Teddy set out with a bucket of nails, some rope and an axe.

"Let us place logs across the road," François said. "We do the hard part first."

"But we shouldn't cut down trees," Teddy said. "Ben at the CCC Camp says they're planting because there was too much clear-cutting."

François smiled. "Believe me, there is no need."

Wind blew trees down; beavers gnawed them until they fell over; dead ones rotted and sank to the ground. Little Roy scouted for fallen spruce. They took turns using the ax he'd brought to chop them off their trunks. Or the tree would pull away, wood softened by ants and time, and they'd drag it across State Aid 2.

Good thing the mailman didn't have to drive in anymore. Good thing they had plenty of food. Good thing there were almost no visitors, except for occasional hunters. Who were too resourceful to let a few downed logs get in their way. If your family needed meat, the easiest thing was to go out and bring home some venison. Or duck or grouse. But the ducks weren't flying, Little Roy knew, and it was early to flush grouse. Easier to see them once all the leaves fell. So no hunters yet.

Teddy liked placing trees across the road. "This'll stop them!" he said after each one. Little Roy tapped his shoulder to get his attention, then shook his head. He skidded his fingers across an outstretched arm to show a car going fast, then stopping.

"They'll get out..." Teddy began. "Move the tree..."

"True, *mon ami*," François said. "The logs slow Albert down, but that is all."

Little Roy nodded. Unless Albert and his men were all struck by lightning—which would be nice, except Little Roy was pretty sure God wouldn't lend a hand in that way—they would arrive, one way or another. He and François and Teddy were just buying some time, making it harder for them.

A daydream popped into his head: Albert, Cal and Gus driving on State Aid 2. They pull the first log off the road. Then another. Clear sailing for a stretch. Then something brown and furry covers the windshield. Albert sticks his head out the truck window and sees two very long legs. His eyes move up, then up some more, to the giant head and antlers of a bull moose. He honks the horn once, twice, a dozen times. The moose doesn't move. *Cal,* he yells. *Plug the goddamn beast.* So Cal does, leaning out the window like he's riding shotgun with Bonnie and Clyde. And, of course, the moose charges. Steps on the truck with one giant foot and squashes it flat. Then kicks it like a tin can to the nearby bog and boots it in with a swat of his back leg, just to show how little respect he has for them. The truck, with everyone in it, sinks slowly into the water and muskeg, finally going under with a big sucking sound. Bubbles of thick mud come to the surface. Then nothing.

He chuckled.

"What's so funny, Mr. Roy?"

Little Roy shrugged. No time to draw pictures or write it down. But he loved imagining, seeing it unroll like a moving picture before his eyes.

When it came right down to it, what they had was six grown people, plus one boy. They had guns and a bow and arrow and the advantage of knowing the woods as Albert, Gus and Cal never would. But they'd have to rely on their wits, outsmart them. Because if it came to a gunfight, the invaders would win.

"I think," said François, "Little Roy, he have many stories to tell, in his own way. When this is behind us." He reached into the bucket of nails, took a handful and began to scatter them across the road.

François could sure read folks, Little Roy thought. He grabbed some for himself, pretended they were seeds that would sprout and grow a large, angry moose with strong legs and a good kick.

Chapter Twenty-Five

Sadie: Faunce Ridge, September 1937

"Well," said Sadie. "Roads might be salted with dynamite, and that's all good if they come by car. But if I was Albert, I'd put on my boots and walk in. Or get horses." They were crowded around Marie's table after supper. They'd finished off two pots of coffee and chased it with whiskey. Not much, though. Sadie didn't want a hangover, Little Roy didn't drink anymore and François never seemed to do anything to excess.

She, François and Hazel were bunked down at the old Rousseau place—no room at Marie's—though she suspected Hazel would rather be sharing space with Theda. But there was Teddy. Not to mention Minnie back at Oak Island, but that was none of her business.

Emil Rousseau's carpenter grandfather constructed the house with built-in wooden bunk beds, benches and a table—nothing fancy but sturdy and solid. They spent a day cleaning out dust and cobwebs and brought Marie's barn cats to scare away the field mice that sought shelter this time of year. After that, with the blankets they'd brought and a good fire in the woodstove, they were about as cozy as they could be out here in the woods. Still, food and coffee were at Marie's.

Sadie looked at Hazel, face tense and drawn in the light of the kerosene lanterns hung high on the wall at either end of Marie's kitchen, and at Theda's. Each of them had taken a tiny shot of booze, she noticed, just enough to toast to victory. Some people drank more when they were nervous; some left it alone. Maybe that was the better way. Whiskey wouldn't help them beat Albert unless they poured it over him and lit a match.

Was she the only one who came up with these ideas? Her rage at Albert—and Alain and Père Clément—had burned down to a cold white flame. Her job was to feed it enough to keep it alive but not let it get out of control. The fury was bigger than Albert and came long before she ever heard his name or saw him standing in the doorway of her hotel. She knew he had plenty of money and wanted more. After all, he'd come up all the way from Georgia to stop hungry lumberjacks from getting a fair wage. Still, she suspected that money was the least of it. More than that, Albert needed to control everything and everyone around him. If he didn't, his power would dry up like morning dew. So all that he was or thought he was rode on grabbing Theda and Teddy and bringing them back to Savannah like hunting trophies. Why else would he hire detectives to make sure nothing went wrong?

"He's good on a horse, that I know. Rich folks in Savannah learn to ride from the time they're kids," said Theda.

"But Gus and Cal—who knows," Hazel said. "Gus looks like he's been sitting in a bar for the last God knows how many years. And Cal's so stiff the horse would probably spook."

Marie had been quiet until now. "We need a lookout. Highest thing is the fire tower. Roy, I'll pack up food, get you something to bed down up there."

Sadie felt she was seeing Marie for the first time. Maybe she was the real general here, the one who could sit back, not get ruffled and figure out what everyone did best. But she had her doubts about the plan. "He'd have to stay awake. And if he doesn't get some rest, he won't be any good come daylight."

Little Roy stood up, closed his eyes and lay his head on folded hands. Then he pointed to himself and shook his head.

"You don't *sleep*?" Theda said.

He put up one finger after another. One, two, three, four, five.

Marie agreed. "Roy can go five days if he has to. Seems like after The Fire, he didn't need as much rest."

Little Roy nodded and bowed as if he'd performed a trick.

Marie took him as he was, Sadie thought, and because of that, she could read him. Like an interpreter, French to English, the way she did for Joe Beaudette when he couldn't find the right word. And she got a sudden shiver, wondering what would happen to Little Roy without Marie. Who else would understand the little fiddler? Not to mention add her voice to his music.

"Okay," she said. "Little Roy's the lookout. But how does he let us know when he sees them? Tower's not far, but yelling ain't going to help."

Little Roy put two fingers in his mouth and blew. The whistle blasted through the tiny house.

"Jesus Christ!" Sadie covered her ears.

François frowned. "Yes, here it is very loud. But from the tower…?"

"Who's the fastest?" Hazel asked.

"Teddy, I suppose," Theda said. "He's the youngest, and he's always loved to run. But I won't put my child through any more danger than he's already in. Not when Albert wants to grab him."

"Mama, I won't be in any danger. Mr. Roy whistles, I get up and start ringing a cowbell. That's sure to wake everyone."

Sadie marveled at how grown-up he sounded but then remembered herself as a motherless teenager scheming how to get out of Manitou Reserve and up to Winnipeg. Things happen in life, and when they do, childhood blows away so fast you forget it was ever there.

Marie nodded. "I got plenty of cowbells. We'll try them out, see which one's loudest."

"And we all jump out of bed?" Hazel said. "Then what? I can't see far enough to shoot."

"You stay here," Marie said. "Albert, he'll expect you to be up on Oak Island. When the time's right, you surprise him."

François got up. "I have cleaned and loaded all the guns." He went to the porch and came back with a burlap gunnysack, out of which he pulled two rifles, a .22 and three pistols of different sizes. They gleamed in the low light and smelled of oil, the way guns did when they were properly cared for. Reminded Sadie of her father and how he looked after his weapons. *They give us our food and keep us safe,* he'd say. *So we treat them well.*

But this was not like going out to get a deer or flush some grouse. She stared at the weapons. The more she looked, the punier they got. A couple rifles. A .22. A few pistols. Nothing. Albert and the boys were going to pick them off like rabbits. She shook her head.

Little Roy was watching her. He went out to the porch and came back in with a bow and a quiver of arrows, which he laid on the table.

Sadie started to laugh, mean and bitter because nothing was funny. "Who the hell do we think we're kidding?" she said. "They might have machine guns. And here we are with a few guns and a goddamn bow and arrow."

"Roy can hit anything with his bow, Sadie," Marie said. "Of course, they have more guns, nothing to be done about that. But we'll outsmart them."

"And how are we going to do that?" Sadie asked.

"We keep Theda and Teddy hidden," Marie replied. "Once we know Albert's here, they go to the old Pedersen barn. It's all ready—me and Roy cleaned out the haymow, put a couple chairs up there, a little table, some blankets and water. They'll have food. It'll look like it's only us here. Roy stays hidden because that's the best way for him to take aim. François stays out of the way, too. And you, Sadie—I know what a good shot you are."

All these years, Sadie had managed to get out in the woods on a regular basis to make sure her eye was still good and her finger steady. She liked the feel of a gun in her hands. Reminded her of hunting with Pascal Robinette, and that gave her energy and made her strong.

"So you and François each get a rifle and plenty of bullets. One of you takes cover behind Ruby's store. The other stands guard near the Pedersen barn, out of sight. When they come, they'll find me. I'm the only one Albert doesn't know yet. He's seen me at the hotel but probably didn't pay much attention. Hazel lays low. I'll stay here with my house and barn and the animals."

Hazel said, "I'll go with Theda and Teddy."

"And I," said Theda, "will take one of those pistols. Growing up, we used to shoot rats down at the city dump. It's been a while, but I just bet I could plug a human rat, too."

Sadie saw a mixture of horror and admiration on Teddy's face. "You shot *rats?*"

"When this is all over, son, there'll be plenty of time to tell you all the things I did. Or at least some of them."

Marie got up. "Now, let's get some rest. We're going to need it."

François stood up, too. "Come," he said to Sadie. "She is right."

But Sadie was certain she wouldn't sleep. Not much, anyway. Caffeine and pure rage would keep her alert for days.

Chapter Twenty-Six

Little Roy: Faunce Ridge, September 1937

It wasn't quite dawn when Little Roy heard the horse noises from his perch in the fire tower. Branches cracked. Muffled hoofbeats. A couple sniffs, then a snort. He looked down and could just see the shapes of three riders, one carrying a lantern. Albert, Cal and Gus. The enemy had arrived. He got to his feet, put two fingers in his mouth and whistled as loud as he could. The horses started and neighed. Someone swore.

"You said this'd be a snap. Nothing to it. Shooting fish in a goddamn barrel." It sounded like Cal, who had a higher voice than Gus.

He whistled again, even louder. If they came after him, which he didn't think they would in the dark, he'd shinny down the back way and lose himself in the trees before they could climb the stairs. Then he heard cowbells ring. A great noise in the night. A window lit up at Marie's. The warning plan was working.

Only then, as he realized that the battle had begun, Little Roy felt a sudden wave of fatigue. He knew it wasn't just the lack of sleep, although sooner or later, that would catch up with him. It was the fear in Theda's eyes, the way Teddy, just a boy, felt he had to protect her. All the miles they'd traveled to get away from Albert. For just a minute, he wished he had a gun. Shoot all three of them, clean and simple. Put an end to all this before Teddy lost whatever was left of his childhood.

He remembered back in 1910, after The Fire, when the National Guard gave out supplies and set up tents for people to live in, how shocked he was when they called him a boy. He was twenty back then and built small, the same as before The Fire, but he would never again think of himself as young, much less a boy.

"Let's get back in the woods," said a voice he recognized as Albert's. "Sun's up soon, and they know we're here. We'll have to reconnoiter."

Little Roy didn't know what *reconnoiter* meant, but once the men were out of sight, he climbed down and got to Marie's as fast as he could.

* * *

"Roy. So glad you're here. Theda and Teddy are up in the Pedersen haymow. Hazel went along. Sadie's outside, guarding them. François is back of Ruby's store. Good view from there. So they finally drove in, eh?"

Little Roy galloped, imaginary reins in his hands.

Marie nodded. "Of course. We would of heard a car. Or truck or whatever they're driving. He's clever, Albert." She poured him a big cup of coffee. "Maybe you should go down to your place. On the road to the Pedersen's. That way, you'll see them coming."

But Little Roy had already thought this through. He shook his head. He was not going to leave Marie. He pointed at her, then at himself, hoisted an imaginary rifle. His real rifle was in the corner, and he'd have that plus his bow and arrow, which deep down he preferred.

"Roy. I don't need protecting."

He shook his head, again pointed to her, then back at him and held his two fingers together. A team, like horses or oxen. You don't split up teams.

"All right then. Go on out to the barn. Some spot where you can see them, but they can't see you. I'm going to feed the chickens, do the chores, what I always do."

Little Roy drank the coffee, then walked around the barn looking for hiding places. Nothing seemed very secure. Finally, he helped himself to a three-legged milk stool and took it into the shed attached to the barn, where Marie stored tools: a scythe, a hand plow, two pitchforks, a shovel, a hammer and saw and a bucket of nails. He positioned the stool beside the wall it shared with the barn and found a small hole that let him see in. After a while, Marie came in and sat down beside Daisy, her favorite cow, a handsome black and white Holstein with very long legs. Marie stroked her flank, whispered in her ear and positioned the bucket beneath the udder. Flexed her fingers and started to milk. Little Roy liked the rhythm, ping, ping, ping, as the liquid hit the bottom of the tin pail. Calmed him down, made him feel like things were going to be all right. He relaxed so much that he started to nod off.

Then a gunshot echoed over the barn and shed, and he jerked upright. And two more after that, closer together. Stupid tough-guy stuff. Probably Cal.

Then Albert's voice. "Might as well come out." He sounded owly like he didn't get enough sleep the night before. Being tired, Little Roy knew, would make him meaner. "If you don't, we'll go in. Or shoot some more."

Even though he couldn't see them, the men talked loudly enough that Little Roy had no trouble hearing them.

"Shoot away, Albert," Marie yelled. "Waste of bullets if you ask me. I'm not moving. You want to see me, come in here. These cows got to be milked."

Little Roy smiled. If Marie was scared, she'd never give Albert and Cal the satisfaction of showing it.

"What if it's a setup, boss?" Cal's high-pitched voice. "I'll fire through the door, see what happens. That'll change her mind." He laughed like a jittery kid.

Then a different voice that had to be Gus. "What the hell's the matter with you? Dropped on your head when you were a baby?"

"He's right," Albert said. "Nothing to be gained. Cool down."

But Albert's voice was ragged, and Little Roy guessed that whatever patience he had was wearing thin.

Cal snorted. "We'd be out of here long since if I was running the show. Just standing around in the woods, waiting…"

"You running the show? We'd be dead by now," Albert said. "Or in a beat-up boxcar somewhere in Canada. So shut up or grab your horse and get out of here."

"Horses," Cal muttered. "Whoever heard of doing a job on horseback?"

"Might help if you knew how to ride," said Gus.

"Enough! Gus, go in, see what she's doing."

Gus, still dressed in the overcoat he'd worn the night at Sadie's, went into the barn, looked at Marie and walked out again. "Milking, just like she said."

"Time to have a word with her." Albert led the way.

It was an odd sight, Little Roy thought. The three men lined up just inside the barn door like they were waiting for permission. But Marie, with her blue dress hitched up over her knees as she milked, didn't give them the satisfaction. "I'd tell you to sit down," she said. "But as you can see, there ain't really any chairs."

"We don't need chairs," Albert replied. "All we need's to catch up with my wife and son. I think you're a straight shooter, Marie, and I'm giving you a chance to tell me so's we don't have to get rough."

Marie was silent. Would she stonewall Albert?

The milk sound grew thick as the pail began to fill. Daisy's tail switched back and forth, a sign, he knew, that she was getting restless. At least once a week, the cow would step over the pasture fence and go exploring. Little Roy would have to go fetch her back from the woods, the fire tower and especially the CCC camp, where she'd wander, dropping cow pies here and there like she'd found a new pasture. Sometimes she'd let the CCC boys feed her an apple and rub her head between the ears. "Daisy's very sociable," Marie had told him. "But if she doesn't like someone, she'll kick. That's why the Halgussons got rid of her. The kids would tease her, and then when it came time to milk, she'd get even."

Finally, Marie spoke, like she'd had to think it over. "No one comes here, Albert. Just Roy and me. We go into town every now and then to get some grub, play at Sadie's, and that's it."

Little Roy could see Albert stiffen up. "Yeah. You and the fiddler at Sadie's hotel. I remember. You were playing there the other night. Then next thing I know, I'm out cold, and when I wake up, Gus and Cal are gone, and no one'll tell me a thing. You got something to do with that? You're a pretty cool customer, I wouldn't put it past you."

This time, Marie didn't even look up. "We don't get mixed up in town things."

Albert took a couple of steps until he was just behind Daisy. Little Roy shook his head. Not a good place to stand.

"Over in Roseau, they said everybody was supposed to move out of here back last summer. But you and the fiddler haven't gone anyplace. Aren't you scared the government's going to find out?"

"I don't stay up nights worrying, if that's what you mean," Marie said.

Little Roy could tell Albert didn't like that.

"What if we reported you?" he said. "Would *that* make you lose some sleep?"

Marie took her hands off Daisy, leaned back and laughed like he'd just told a good joke. Little Roy loved her laugh, a big, rolling sound like water coming to a boil. "You just go and do that, Albert. Maybe they'll send in the army. They could help with chores, give us a little rest."

Albert stepped closer. "Think it's funny, huh?"

Daisy let out a low bellow, and her tail switched faster and faster. If Albert knew anything about cattle, which Little Roy could see he didn't, he would've gotten the hell out of there.

Marie patted the cow's side. "It's all right, girl."

But it was too late. Daisy's leg whipped back so fast that all Little Roy saw was a black and white blur and smacked Albert's right shin so hard you could hear it crack. God, Little Roy loved that cow.

"My leg!" Albert shrieked, holding it and jumping on the other. "Your goddamn cow! You planned this!"

"I'll fix her, boss." It was weird how eager Cal was. Like a boy, except much more dangerous. He pulled out a black pistol.

Gus sprinted forward, grabbed Marie around the waist and dragged her kicking and screaming away from Daisy and off to the side. "Take your hands off me!" she cried. But he kept hold of her while he yelled at Cal. "Who the fuck you think you are, Dillinger? Put that thing down!"

Little Roy couldn't tell if Cal even heard him. It was like he was in another world, eyes bright, face flushed with excitement. He fired at Daisy once, twice, then again. The cow shuddered and collapsed, knocking over the bucket of milk. Blood spurted onto the yellow straw.

Little Roy felt frozen to his stool. If he moved, Cal might shoot him, too. And if Gus hadn't grabbed Marie…he tried not to imagine what would have happened.

Marie broke away, ran to Daisy, knelt beside her. Blood flowed over her hands and arms and dress and trickled into the foamy milk, turning it pink. The cow shuddered and lay still. Marie stood up and faced the men, face pale as Little Roy had ever seen it.

Albert clutched his leg. "She crippled me! Probably broke a bone! She deserved to die!"

Marie walked toward him until they were almost touching. "Well, she's dead now, isn't she?" She reached down, wet her hands in the milk and blood and wiped them on his shirt. "You happy?"

"You're crazy!" Albert screamed. "You're all crazy!"

"Just say the word," Cal said, hand on his pistol.

Gus lunged and grabbed it. "Try that again, I'll use it on you."

"Give me back my gun!"

"Shut your goddamn mouth," Gus said. "How you ever got hired is a mystery to me."

Marie raised her hand, still dripping pink. Like a priest, Little Roy thought, about to give the blessing. And in a terrible voice he'd never heard before, she said, "I curse you." She looked first at Albert, then Cal. Not at Gus, who'd stepped back and was unloading Cal's gun.

Little Roy shivered. He wouldn't want to be cursed by Marie. He'd be afraid to leave his house in the morning, too scared to do anything.

The men stood silent, Albert and Marie face to face.

Then Albert shoved a hand in his pocket, pulled out some coins and threw them into the blood-and-milk puddle. Little Roy's stomach lurched.

"Here. Buy yourself another goddamn cow."

Chapter Twenty-Seven

Little Roy: Faunce Ridge, September 1937

Little Roy vowed not to let the invaders out of his sight. God only knew what they'd get into their heads to do next. He followed them at a safe distance, sidling around abandoned buildings and hiding behind trees. Albert limped as they walked toward the old Carsten place. Daisy's last kick, in Little Roy's opinion, was the best one she'd ever landed.

Mrs. Carsten would hate to see the men prowling around the home she'd worked so hard to keep nice. The log house had been poor but cheerful, with starched white curtains in the windows and lots of flowers in and around the large garden. Now the roof sagged, and goldenrod grew tall outside, along with dill that loved the sandy soil in Faunce Ridge. If Little Roy had it to do over again, he would've planted, too. Fussed over his carrots and potatoes and peas and beans. But he was different back then, before everyone left. Just drank hooch and played the fiddle and ate whatever he could find to stay alive.

Albert pushed the door open. It stuck halfway. Little Roy shook his head. There were so many things Albert didn't understand, and one of them was what happened to empty houses. Moisture crept in. Floors buckled. Doors and window casings swelled. Every part looked out for itself, just trying to survive. Maybe one day the door would march off all by its lonesome, Little Roy thought. The windows would fly away. The roof would lift off and go somewhere it was needed.

Cal stood on the threshold. "Pee-ewwww! Smells like something died in there!"

Little Roy could not believe his ignorance. *Of course something died in there.* A skunk. Mice, for sure. Maybe a squirrel. Or something bigger. Once people left, their houses belonged to whatever animals took shelter there.

"They're not going to hole up in a dump like this, boss," Cal said, still not entering.

"We don't know 'til we look," Albert said. "They could be anywhere. And I'm sure as hell not going in with this leg."

He shoved Cal through the doorway. Gus stood back. Hard to know what he was thinking, but Little Roy had a new respect for him after he saved Marie's life back in the barn, getting her out of range of crazy Cal.

"No sign of life here," Gus said to Albert. "Cal's right about that. Let's move on."

Cal hadn't moved any farther than just inside the door. "Listen. I got a better idea." He reached into his pocket and pulled out a book of matches and a flask. "Show these fools we mean business! It's all broken down anyhow." He opened the flask and poured something on the door, then struck a match and threw it. The wood, warped and dry, caught fire.

"What a waste of whiskey," Albert said.

Little Roy prayed it would go out, that the wood would be too moist. They'd had some rain this fall, though not much. But the fire crackled and climbed toward the roof.

"It gets out of control, we'll have to run for our lives," Gus said to Albert. "And besides, people still live in this town. Maybe your wife and kid. What if they burn up?"

Albert stared at the blaze. "I don't know. Maybe it'll make them come out faster, wherever they are."

Cal laughed. "Look at it go! Think I'll light up all these dumps."

"Like hell you will," said Gus. "I got a job to go back to. I'm not letting some bonkers fire bug get me in hot water." He pulled the smaller man up by the scruff of his neck and grabbed the flask away from him. "Take your matches away, too, if you don't settle down. The Old Man told me I was going along on this caper to keep an eye on you. If I'd known how batshit crazy you really were, I would've told him to find someone else."

Cal puffed up like a little banty rooster. "Oh, yeah? He wanted me on the job 'cause you're old and washed up. Needed someone young and fast on the draw. And give me back my hooch!"

Finally, Albert turned toward them. "No more fires. Let's go to the next place."

"What about this one?" Gus pointed to the flames creeping across the roof.

Albert shrugged. "Let it burn. It's falling down anyway."

Little Roy considered organizing a bucket brigade from the Rapid River. But there weren't enough people to do it, and besides, there was no time. He sprinted right past the men into the woods toward the Pederson barn to warn Sadie.

"There's the fiddler!" Cal yelled.

"He's simple," Albert said. "Let him go."

Little Roy thanked God that Gus had Cal's gun. For now, anyway. He kept running.

Chapter Twenty-Eight

Hazel: Faunce Ridge, September 1937

Hazel, Theda and Teddy climbed the ladder into the haymow of the old Pederson barn. Plenty of hay piled up from the year before in case they had to sleep on it. Marie had packed them cornbread, hardboiled eggs and water, and Hazel had brought a deck of cards.

"Haymows feel like home now," Theda said. "I never would have dreamed of a place like this back in Savannah."

"Tell me why you like it so much," Hazel said. Theda had always amazed her, and now she was showing yet another side of herself.

"Well," Theda said, voice dropping into a dreamy register like it did when she was telling a story. "Imagine it: our two beds, a table for the lantern, another for the washstand. A little space carved out just for us. And it smells wonderful because the hay is dried sweet grass and clover. When we lie down at night, the swallows swoop in and out. Sometimes we hear owls hooting. And whippoorwills. It's so peaceful. Makes me feel safer than ever in my life." She sighed.

Hazel's eyes burned. She'd do anything to keep Theda and Teddy safe. From Albert. From all harm. But what if that meant leaving Minnie and giving up their home on the island? Sometimes at Faunce Ridge, she felt as if time had collapsed, and she and Theda were young women again, dizzy with love for each other. But fifteen years had gone by. She looked at the strands of gray in Theda's dark curls. At Teddy, who looked so much like her and was just as restless. And she saw herself, much older now than back at the H&M Diner. Life was like a wave in the ocean, she thought, that started so far out you couldn't see or hear it but kept rolling steadily toward shore, gathering strength and building so that when it landed, it knocked you off your feet before you knew what happened.

"Sometimes," she said, as if she'd been talking all along and had just taken a pause, "I'd just like to start over." She wasn't sure what she'd do different, but maybe she and Theda would be roaming free somewhere, not cooped up in a hayloft with Albert close behind.

Theda gazed at her. "I know. Me, too. But I'm not sorry for one little thing. Except maybe not getting on the train to Minneapolis with you."

Hazel's throat constricted. "How could you have? They had you like a prisoner."

"What does she mean, Mama?"

Theda kept her eyes on Hazel, but when she spoke, it was again in that dreamy voice. "Baby, Hazel and me were together all the time in Savannah. But folks thought I should have a boyfriend instead. Anyway, one Fourth of July we went out. A special night. We walked and walked 'til we came to a place I knew, where there was music and food and you could get something to drink…"

Hazel was right back there, in the sweltering air that smelled of frying shrimp, with the combo playing music she'd only heard on the radio. Jazz. Ragtime. Music that filled her with longing whenever she heard it now. And holding Theda tight in her arms, eyes closed, hoping the rest of the world would fade away by the time she opened them.

"Why'd they put you in jail?"

Theda was quiet for a second or two. "Well, darling," she said. "Drinking was illegal then. The police came. And they weren't very nice to us. You see, there are people who don't think it's right when two women like each other. They get mad when girls don't do what they want them to." She looked down at Teddy. "That's how we ended up in jail. That's why Hazel had to leave Savannah and come all the way up here. And that's how I ended up marrying your Papa."

Teddy looked deep in thought. "But if you didn't marry Papa— how would you have had me?"

"I don't know," she said, laughing and hugging him. "But I would've found a way."

Hazel sniffed. "Do you smell smoke?"

Then she heard someone climbing the steps. Sadie's head emerged from the trap door. "All right," she said. "We got to move again. Crazy Cal set fire to one of the houses. God knows what they'll do next. We're going to the fire tower. At least we'll have a view."

Hazel didn't want to leave the little space they'd made for themselves, the unhurried conversation like when they first met. Damn time. The way it sidled along like it'd last forever and then ran out, just like that. She sighed and got to her feet, put out her hand to help Theda up.

Teddy was already scrambling down the ladder.

Chapter Twenty-Nine

Theda: Faunce Ridge, September 1937

"Let's hope the fire burns itself out," Sadie said. "But even if it does, Albert and company are searching all the houses. They'll get to the barns, too."

"But why the fire tower? What if they burn that, too?" Theda felt dazed. She didn't want to leave the barn. They'd just settled in, and she and Hazel were talking the way she'd yearned to for so long, letting Teddy hear part of their story. Another place she'd thought they'd be all right, at least for a while. Would they ever be safe again?

"It's high enough up we can see them coming and watch to see if the fire spreads. I'm going up with you. Got my gun, just in case." Sadie patted her jacket pocket.

It's not in my hands, Theda murmured to herself, trying to stay calm. But Teddy *was* in her hands. Somehow she had to protect him. They followed Sadie down the haymow ladder, out of the abandoned barn and over a footpath that snaked through the woods around Faunce Ridge. "How do you know your way so well?" she asked. "You never lived here, did you?"

"No. Always liked it better in town," Sadie said. "But when Magnus moved up from the Cities in 1931, we went into the bootlegging business together, and I came out here plenty. Ofttimes we'd sit around at the still, but Magnus was so restless…" She sighed. "There were days when he just had to keep moving, so we walked these paths and talked the whole time. 'Course, he ain't around now, but I got a good memory."

"Who's Magnus?" Teddy said.

"He was my boss when I worked in Minneapolis," Hazel said. "Back in the 1920s, around the time you were born. Cooked for him at a place called The Merry Widow—"

Sadie interrupted her. "He was a good friend, kid. To both Hazel and me. I'll tell you all about him after…"

After this is all over, Theda finished the sentence in her head. *If it ever is.* Her idea of hell on earth was Albert chasing her and Teddy for the rest of her life or until she wore out and gave up. And now that he had armed detectives, anything could happen. Her belly clenched. She had to stop thinking about it, just focus on now. Teddy didn't deserve to have a mother with her head in the clouds, always worried about the future.

They followed the trail until they came to the Faunce Ridge graveyard. She hadn't been there since the day they arrived and again didn't want to step on the graves, even though Teddy had already bounded ahead.

Sadie saw her hesitate. "Think of it this way. The folks down there would be real happy to see us getting the jump on Albert. Especially now they're trying to burn the place down. They won't mind if we walk over them."

"She's right," Hazel said, grabbing Theda's hand. "Here we go."

They walked fast, threading their way among the wooden crosses and stone markers.

When they got to the fire tower, Theda looked up, then up some more. "It's so high," she said. She'd never liked heights. Savannah was in the lowlands, so she'd spent her life at sea level and loved feeling close to the ground.

"I'll show you how to do it, Mama!" Teddy was scaling the stairs. "Just keep looking up," he called back. "Not down. That's what makes you dizzy."

"All right." She put a foot on the wooden step and got to the first landing. Many more ahead. *Don't look down,* she told herself.

Teddy had arrived at the top, opening the door of the little house perched above the zigzag flight of stairs. "I'll get it all ready," he said. He'd carried up the blankets and food Marie packed for them.

She kept going, one step at a time until she was through the door. Before she knew it, Hazel was there, and Sadie was joining them in the little room with windows on all sides. "Now look," Teddy said.

Theda gazed out at the yellow poplar and birch, the red maple and the dark green of the spruces and pines, and for a minute, she forgot the danger. "Why, it's a tree house!" She'd dreamed of one when she was a girl, a little place hidden away in a spreading oak where no one could see or hear her. But tree houses were for boys, or so her mother said. She turned slowly. There was Marie's house. The tiny graveyard. And the path that led from Faunce Ridge. She took a deep breath. "It's beautiful." Then she saw the flames leaping up from the Carsten place. Fire had spread to the outbuildings, a barn and what looked like a chicken coop. "Oh, no."

"Bastards," Sadie said. "At least there's not much wind today. Maybe it won't go any farther."

There was just enough room for each of them to have a place on the floor against the wall, with blankets stacked in the middle. Hazel patted the space beside her and pulled out the cornbread and hard-boiled eggs. "Might as well eat. Keep our energy up."

Yes, Theda thought. *We're going to need it.* She knew how impatient Albert was. He must be furious, searching the abandoned houses, sheds and barns, getting cobwebs on his clothes, hay dust in his nose. He always expected things to happen fast and efficiently. He'd railed against the slow pace of Savannah, the workers he hired.

"Move to New York," she'd tell him. "Maybe that'll be fast enough for you."

He'd sneer. "You'd love that, wouldn't you?"

And yes, she would have turned cartwheels all the way through Savannah if Albert had moved away and left them alone.

Which he did in the beginning. But when Albert told her he was suing for custody, Theda realized he'd been plotting this for a long time. He knew perfectly well that she would never be his "wife" in the usual sense of the word. She'd already given him what he wanted by producing a son. And now she was in the way. Albert would have no qualms about getting her locked up in an insane asylum while he groomed Teddy to be a younger version of himself. In fact, he would take pleasure in smashing what freedom she had.

She propped a folded blanket behind her back and tried to pretend the smell of smoke was just a bonfire of dry leaves. "Don't worry, sweetheart," Hazel whispered as if guessing her thoughts, putting an arm around her. And in a funny way, Theda wasn't worried, despite all the ugliness of Albert and his machinations. Just having her love and her boy next to her in this beautiful place, if only for minutes or an hour, made her feel so peaceful that her head started to droop.

"Sleep," Hazel murmured in her ear.

And she did.

Chapter Thirty

Sadie: Faunce Ridge, September 1937

Sadie knew she wouldn't be able to sleep but was glad when Theda did, slumped against Hazel, who dozed off too. Leaving her and Teddy as lookouts. Fine with her. The kid was excited and alert, the way kids are when danger is an adventure.

As for her, the time with Alain had sharpened her senses. She knew that one way or another, she'd hear, see or smell Albert and his boys when they came. She didn't know how or when, and that set her teeth on edge. But she could wait. Her gun was loaded, oiled and ready.

She looked at Hazel and Theda. Nestled together, they looked much younger. An ease in their bodies that reminded Sadie of her and François. Were they in love like that? Because if they were, then Minnie or no Minnie, Hazel should try to make a go of it with Theda after this was all over. But Sadie didn't envy her that decision.

Sadness began to seep into her, perhaps carried on the wood smoke and pine-scented air. Would there always be men who stomped around trying to own whatever they touched, whether it was land or lumber, women or children? She'd spent much of her younger years trying to outthink, outmaneuver and outsmart men like that. Père Clément. Alain. Now Albert. How to get rid of bullies? You could kill them off, of course— quietly, no sense making a fuss or drawing attention—but no matter how many you got rid of, there'd always be more.

Finally, she dozed off, too. When she woke up, the smoke smell was stronger, the sun was lower in the sky and voices floated up from below.

Cal said, "I'm telling you, they ain't here. We went into every house, every barn, every damn shed, and nothing."

Staying out of sight, she peeked down over the edge of the window. There they were, Cal in front, running his mouth as usual. "I say torch the whole place. Teach 'em a lesson. Trying to make fools of us."

"And you think burning the town is going to help us find them?" Albert said.

"Hell," Cal answered. "We ain't gonna find 'em. Who knows where they're at by now?"

"I thought I was hiring two detectives," Albert said. "I got one man who thinks too much and a kid who thinks with his gun and his matches."

"That ain't fair, boss. I'm the one who stuck up for you when the stupid cow kicked you. Ol' Gus just got the broad out of the way and stood in the corner."

Sadie smiled. Albert was taking his licks, this time from a milk cow. Maybe he'd learn he wasn't as tough as he thought, that she and the others weren't the stupid country bumpkins he believed they were.

Albert didn't answer Cal. "What do you say, Gus?"

Sadie hadn't heard Gus's voice that often. It was lower and slower than Cal's and sounded like he'd seen a lot, slept too little and smoked too much. "I say they're here someplace. All of them. Can't just vanish."

Then silence. And cigarette smoke.

Sooner or later, they're going to look up. Then what? She thought she'd been thinking, not speaking, until Teddy turned with a question in his eyes.

"Just talking to myself, kid. Helps me think."

Gus said, "One place we haven't looked. Up in the fire tower."

"Too small," Albert said.

"They don't all have to be there."

For once, Cal was quiet. He craned his neck and stared upward. Then reached for his pistol and fired a shot that echoed into the air.

Teddy jumped. Probably never heard gunfire before, Sadie thought. She put her finger to her lips. He nodded. Cal fired again. This time she heard the bullet whistle past their hideaway. Hazel and Theda woke with a start. Sadie reached over, put her hands on theirs. "Not a word."

Gus said, "What if they're in there, you crazed hophead?"

"You on something, Cal?" Albert said. "That why you're so het up? I told you no drugs, goddamn it."

"I'm just fine, boss. But one way or another, I gotta stay awake."

"Told you," Gus said. "I shouldn't of given him back his gun."

Cal laughed. "Aw, he's just jealous I'm such a good shot."

He fired twice more.

The first bullet went through the wall just over Sadie's head and shattered the window behind her. They scrambled fast to the other wall, out of the way of the glass, and pressed themselves up against it. Then came the second shot. Hazel jerked, clutched her shoulder. "Uhhh," she muttered, face pale, blood oozing into her sweater. Her head slumped.

Before Sadie could stop her, Theda leaped to her feet and opened the door. "You monster! Hazel's hit. She could die. And Teddy's up here. You want your thug to kill him?"

Sadie covered her eyes. Now they were in it for sure—all that hiding and planning for nothing. If Sadie had to choose between Theda and Teddy for a battle partner, it wouldn't even be close. Theda was the one who couldn't keep control of herself. At least Teddy stayed quiet.

"Son of a bitch!" Albert screeched. "Cal, drop that right now or I'll have Gus take it again." Then he looked up at Theda. "This is all your fault. Stealing my son. Putting him in danger. You're going to bring him down right now, or I'll send Cal up to get him."

Theda laughed. "Danger? Oh, that's rich, you with your gangsters. Teddy's not going anywhere without me. But we are coming down. Hazel needs help."

"I ain't going anywhere," Sadie whispered. "I'll have them covered. Make sure you all stay safe."

They got Hazel to her feet, eyes half-closed, head bobbing, skin so white her red hair looked like the fire over at the Carsten place. "Keep her warm," Sadie hissed. Teddy and Theda each grabbed an arm, and they started to clamber down the long stairs.

Sadie stood in the corner, hidden by a post and the shadows of late afternoon. She was pretty sure the men couldn't see her. Besides, their eyes were on the three people coming down the stairs, moving slow and clumsy like some six-legged animal.

Chapter Thirty-One

Little Roy: Faunce Ridge, September 1937

Little Roy had watched from the woods, rifle and bow nearby, as Sadie took Hazel, Theda and Teddy up into the fire tower. Not a bad place to hide. Outsiders wouldn't know about it. And Gus was the smartest of the three men, so no surprise he figured out someone was there. But why didn't Gus stop Cal before he started shooting like a crazy man? He was fast enough to grab Marie out of the way after Cal shot up her barn and killed Daisy. And Hazel. She looked so peaked, red hair flopping over her face as Theda and Teddy dragged her down the stairs and laid her on the ground.

"Get me a coat, for God's sake, something to cover her up," Theda said. She acted like Albert wasn't even there.

Gus walked into the woods and came back, leading his horse. He slid the blanket out from under the saddle and helped Theda spread it out. Then he picked up Hazel like she didn't weigh nothing and laid her right down on top of it. Checked the bullet hole oozing blood. Theda took off her jacket and handed it to him, and Gus laid it over her. "Somebody's got to tend to her," he said. "She'll go into shock."

"Who told you to put your nose in it?" Albert said. "You're working for me, not them."

"You got what you wanted, didn't you? There they are, your wife and kid," Gus said. "I'm taking the lady back to Marie's so she can lay down. And then I'll check on Cal's fire, make sure we don't all burn to death."

"You're going to look after *her*?" Cal said in a loud, excited voice. "Thought you were with us. Some partner you turned out to be."

"Listen," Gus said, turning to look at him. "You ain't my partner, just the guy they put me on a job with."

Theda helped him drape Hazel over the saddle and cover her with the blanket. She stroked the red hair falling around her face. "Take care of her," she said. Gus nodded and led the horse away.

Good, Little Roy thought. Marie could cure anybody. But he didn't like having Gus leave, even for a little while. Because then it was down to Albert and Cal. He'd have to be real careful. All that firepower, they could blast him off this earth, straight to his family in heaven. And unlike in the early years, right after he lost them, he was not ready to go. But at least he had backup, with Sadie still in the tower.

"Son," Albert stepped forward to hug Teddy, but the boy backed away. Theda grabbed him and held on.

"The only way you're going to take my boy is to kill me, Albert. Are you ready to do that?"

"Don't tempt me, you dirty dyke. Did you really think you were going to get away with this? He's got my name, he's my kid."

Theda snorted. "Some father you are, chasing all the way up here with these… gunslingers." She pointed to Cal, who stood nearby. "What if he'd hit Teddy instead of Hazel?"

"Cal might be a little trigger-happy," Albert said. "But no one's dead."

"No one's dead," Theda repeated. "Well, not yet, anyway. Is that what you want him to learn at military school?"

Albert got red in the face. "He's going to be a man, not a mama's boy. You're not going to stand in my way. He's my son, not some sharecropper's brat, and it's time for him to take his rightful place in the world."

"I'll tell you where his place is." Theda's voice was getting louder. "And it's not learning to be a little tin soldier like his daddy, just because that's what rich folks in Savannah do with their boys."

"Ha! Don't talk to *me* about rich folks in Savannah! Your father paid your way out of every scrape you've ever gotten into."

"You mean selling me off to you so I'd look like a respectable woman? God knows I've paid for that with my own blood. And by the way, why'd you accept? You knew from the start I had no truck with men."

Albert shrugged. "Good looks, good family. Why would I give a rat's ass if you liked girls or boys? Still got pregnant, just like a regular woman. And gave me a son."

"That's the thing, Albert." Theda's voice now serious. "I never *gave* you this son. And I never will. I've raised him, he's staying with me."

Albert shook his head. "Your brain's gotten soft, being up here in Yankee land. But no judge in Savannah's going to let my boy stay with a pervert mother."

Theda stood up straight, and Little Roy could see she was taller than her husband by a good inch or so. "That's as may be, Albert, but you'll never get him back to Savannah."

"Papa," Teddy said.

"Son. This is between your mother and me."

"No. Listen."

Albert finally looked down at him. "What?"

"I'm not going back," Teddy said.

Albert shook his head. "Don't say that, son. There's a lot you don't understand—"

Teddy cut him off. "I'm staying here. Or going someplace to finish school and then maybe be a forest ranger. Something I like."

Albert stared at Teddy, then turned to Theda. "You—*cunt*," he spat.

"Call me what you want, Albert. He's a good boy, and he'll grow up to be a man with principles."

The tension in the air hung so thick that if the sky weren't clear, Little Roy would've thought it was going to storm. His ears buzzed. He looked at the two of them, toe to toe, saw Cal's hand near his pistol. And got the bow and arrow into position.

Theda raised her hand. Little Roy thought she was going to slap him, but she drew back, made a fist and hit him hard in the face, connecting with his cheek and nose. "That's for Hazel. And everything else."

Albert staggered back, just managing not to fall onto his bum leg. Cal reached for the gun, but Little Roy aimed for his shooting arm just above the elbow and let the arrow fly. Cal dropped the pistol and screamed as blood seeped into his shirtsleeve from the arrow embedded in his flesh. Maybe that would stop him from shooting and setting fire to people's places. He clasped his arm. "Goddamn son of a bitch," he said over and over, like all the other cuss words had flown right out of his head.

Albert stared at the arrow sticking out of Cal's arm. Probably woozy, Little Roy decided. Theda sure nailed him a good one. Blood dripped from his nose.

"Jesus H. Christ," Albert said. "What the hell kind of place is this, anyway? Indians in the woods?" He pulled out his gun and aimed into the trees. "Come out or I'll shoot!"

But Little Roy wasn't about to take a bullet or get caught. He took off, speeding along the paths he knew so well. Ran through bushes and under low-hanging trees until he got to the other side of Faunce Ridge and the remains of Magnus's still, half-hidden in a thicket. Caught his breath, had a swig of water, then took off for the bog. Sped by the CCC Camp, crossed the log bridge, and made his way to the big oak tree where Magnus left his belongings before taking off in his truck the summer before. Whether Magnus drove into the bog, over it or through it, he'd never know. But that tree, the way it spread out above the hillocks and water, with plenty of tamarack and brush around, Little Roy knew it would shelter him.

For now, anyway.

Chapter Thirty-Two

Sadie: Faunce Ridge, September 1937

"Help me, Boss!" Cal was really in a state, screaming so loud Sadie would've had to plug her ears not to hear. "For God's sake. What if it's a poison arrow? What if there's more of 'em?"

Sadie rolled her eyes. For a tough little detective with a fast trigger finger, Cal sure made a lot of noise when he got nicked.

Albert had been staring into the woods like he was in a trance. Finally, he went into action. "Don't move," he ordered Cal. He knelt beside him, yanked out the arrow and turned it over in his hands. "What the fuck? Thought we were in the North Woods, not the goddamn Old West."

Cal howled as the arrow came out, and the blood strengthened into a steady trickle. "Now I'm gonna bleed to death!"

Albert looked around, scowling. "Goddamn Gus, going off to save that dyke, just when I need him."

"Do something, boss!"

Sadie almost felt sorry for Cal.

When it came to the milk of human kindness, Albert's ran dry a long time ago. If he ever had any, to begin with.

"Okay, Okay." Albert turned back to Cal. "Guess we have to take off your shirt." He yanked it open, spraying buttons on the ground, then ripped it off. Sadie winced. Albert was always going to take the way that caused the most pain to others.

"You're killin' me!" Cal looked tiny and pathetic down there, barechested and shivering, skin dead white except for the blood.

Then horse hooves. Gus coming back. He cut a strange figure with his rumpled suit and hat, but he wasn't a bad rider. Interesting fellow, Sadie reflected. Albert was paying him, but Gus didn't necessarily follow his orders.

"Took your time," Albert said. "You fix him up. I got things to do."

Gus swung down from the horse, took one look at Cal's bloody shirt, tore off the back, used a canteen of water to wet it and cleaned the wound. He pulled out a flask. "This'll hurt," he said as he poured whiskey over the arrow hole. Then he made a bandage out of the clean sleeve and tied it around Cal's arm.

Cal squirmed, face all scrunched up. "Too tight. Gonna cut off my circulation, give me gangrene."

"It'll stop the bleeding," Gus said.

"I'm cold, damn it!"

"Settle down," Gus said, his voice weary as if he'd been up all night, which he probably had.

Cal shivered even harder. Shock, Sadie thought. And the cool September air as evening came on didn't help. Gus wrapped his coat around Cal. She knew he didn't like Cal, much less respect him. And yet he took care of him when he was down. Not that that made Gus any less dangerous. He was smarter than Cal, and he'd act fast without announcing what he was going to do.

She'd almost forgotten about Theda and Teddy. There they were, off to one side, still as statues. Why in God's green earth hadn't they just taken off while they had the chance? *Run, damn it,* she commanded them silently. *Get the hell out of here! What're you waiting for?* Maybe in shock themselves. Sadie would bet her hotel that neither of them had ever seen anybody shot with a gun, much less a bow and arrow.

"So," Albert said, turning back to them like nothing had happened. "Teddy comes with me, and no one else gets hurt."

"I told you, Albert. Over my cold, dead body."

He made a sound that Sadie interpreted as a laugh. "Always so dramatic. Well, if that's what you want, I'm happy to oblige. Believe me, nobody's going to miss you. Except maybe your girlfriend."

"Don't you touch my mother," Teddy yelled. He hauled off and kicked Albert in the same leg he was already limping on. Then he broke free of Theda and ran for the woods.

Good boy, Sadie thought.

Albert yowled in pain. "Kick your own father? Is that what she taught you to do? Come back right this minute!"

"Teddy!" Theda cried.

But he was gone. Kid was fast, Sadie knew. Hopefully, he'd outrun and outsmart the son of a bitch who spawned him.

"You planned this!" Albert screamed at Theda. "Something happens to him, it's on your head."

Theda didn't stop to listen. She sprinted after Teddy. Looked like she had some speed, Sadie observed. Maybe enough to stay ahead of her no-good husband.

"I'll get you! I swear I'll get you!" Albert pulled out his pistol and fired into the woods.

Dumb son of a bitch. Could hit his own kid. Even though Teddy was probably far enough away not to catch a bullet. Sadie'd had just about enough. She didn't really want to kill Albert, just put him out of business. Or scare the hell out of him. She took careful aim and shot the hat right off his head. Without it, Albert looked even shorter.

He shrieked like somebody'd goosed him. "Who the hell's up there?"

"Christ' sake," Gus said. "Go after your boy. And stop shooting wild. I'll deal with this."

And he would, Sadie thought. She'd have to be very careful.

Albert stood frozen like he couldn't make up his mind, then gimped into the woods after Theda and Teddy.

They're headed for the bog, Sadie thought.

It made sense that they'd end up there. And she'd be right behind. Opening the door of the little treehouse, she made her way down the stairs. Gus didn't even look up until she'd stepped onto the ground, where Cal lay, eyes closed, under his coat.

"Figured it must be you up there," he said.

"Bet you didn't sign on for all this."

Gus shrugged.

Sadie didn't expect an answer. Gus wasn't about to give up anything, especially not to the woman who'd slipped him a mickey and sent him for a ride on the Canadian National. But she was pretty sure he wouldn't come after her. He had to babysit Cal, and once he got him settled, he'd go looking for Albert. Or Theda and Teddy.

She walked past him and headed toward the bog. Thank God Magnus had taught her the paths, because it was getting dark, and before long, she wouldn't be able to see anything. Maybe the Bog Witches would light her way. She'd never put them to the test before. Sure would hate to find out they didn't like her enough to help her. She kept up a good, steady pace. Further she got from Gus and Cal, the better she felt.

Smoke tickled her nose. From the fire at the Carstens? Muskeg? Maybe both. A little further down the trail, she saw scarves of what looked like ground fog settling into the bushes. But fog didn't have that bittersweet muskeg smell. God help them all if the bog really started to smolder. She continued down the path she knew best, the one that would lead her to Magnus's oak tree, where he'd left his belongings just over a year ago.

Magnus wasn't one for suicide—if that's what he'd been set on, he would've come and asked her to do the job. She was certain he was setting off on another adventure—probably thought he and his truck could fly across the bog. And maybe they could. 'Course she'd never know for sure unless he came back and told her.

Through the smoke and ground fog, whatever the hell it was, she finally saw the sweeping branches of Magnus's tree. She touched it just to make sure she wasn't dreaming.

Someone coughed.

"Jesus jumping Christ! Who the hell…?"

Then someone was whistling *The Wabash Cannonball*.

"Goddamn, Little Roy, you scared the bejesus out of me!"

Maybe darkness was a rest for him. No need to act out anything when no one could see you. She'd never understood how he didn't just fall dead tired on the floor after doing charades to show what he was trying to say. Sometimes she could swear she'd seen him break a sweat.

She came in closer, so they were almost touching. "Seen anyone?"

He shook his head.

"I stayed up in the tower," she said. "Theda and Albert got into it again, and he threatened to shoot her, but Teddy kicked him and ran for the woods. With Theda right behind. I think they're headed for the bog. And I shot Albert's hat off his head. Gave him a little start."

Then came a sound she'd never heard. Little Roy was laughing, his whole body shaking. She could just see him, dimly outlined by the moon rising through smoke and fog.

She couldn't help but laugh, too, and it felt good.

"Meantime, Gus is taking care of Cal. Ask me, Cal's a yellow belly. Talks big, draws fast, but one little scratch, and he's crying like a baby."

Little Roy laughed some more.

She took out a cigarette, but he grabbed her wrist.

"Damn it, Little Roy, I'm dying for a smoke." Her nerves needed it.

He lit a match, blew it out and shook his head.

She considered. "Not that people could see anyway with all the smoke, but I s'pose you're right…" She sighed and put away the Lucky. It'd been a long time since she'd been in a place this quiet. A light wind moved the pines like back at Manitou Reserve and ruffled the oak leaves, always the last ones to drop.

Chapter Thirty-Three

Sadie: Faunce Ridge, September 1937

Sometime later, Little Roy put a hand on Sadie's arm and cupped his ear.

"I don't hear nothing. 'Cept an owl." She liked their quiet hoot deep in the woods. Like they were keeping watch.

He shook his head, put a finger to his lips.

She stood even more still, if that was possible, and listened. *Fermez les yeux,* she said to herself. *Close your eyes.* That's what Papa always said when she was a little girl, listening for something in the woods. And he was right—it sharpened her hearing. At first, all that came to her was the breeze. She kept her eyes closed, then heard a faint cry.

"Someone yelling," she whispered.

Little Roy nodded. He moved around the tree. She crept after him. Ears cocked in the smoky darkness.

Another cry. Closer? Louder? Had the wind changed direction?

Little Roy closed his eyes and put his arm out straight in front of him.

The voice called again.

He swung his arm over to his left, then grabbed Sadie's hand. Thank God, because she did not know how to navigate the bog, especially at night. Little Roy had a nice strong grip.

The cry came again, louder, and she thought she heard "Help!"

She stumbled forward. Unnerving not to be able to see where she was going. She became very aware of her feet and what was under them.

Sometimes they crunched plants and twigs, her favorite bog terrain. Solid. At least more solid than the rest of it. Then there'd be a hillock, then another, so she felt like she was walking on steppingstones. Little Roy would pause and make a splashing noise with his foot, which meant that her next steps would be slogging through muck and bog water. The splashes were fine; it was the sucking noise she dreaded, a sign the bog wanted to keep them. Muskeg smoke drifted low. Sadie liked how it smelled. Bittersweet, like the name of her favorite fall plant.

The voice grew closer. *A woman.* Had to be Theda, unless Marie was out here, but then again, she knew the bog and wouldn't get into trouble.

Now she could hear. "Help! Help!"

Little Roy pushed aside some bushes, and Sadie glimpsed the outline of a woman's torso. "Theda!" There was enough moonlight that she could just see her, curly hair clinging wet to her head, shivering so hard her teeth were chattering. And stuck in the bog nearly to her waist, with a few sumac bushes and tamarack several yards away.

Sadie'd been lucky enough never to fall into muskeg. Actually, it wasn't luck—she was afraid of the bog and rarely went there. But Theda'd been chasing her boy and probably hadn't been looking where she was going.

Little Roy knelt beside her.

"Thank God you're here," Theda said. "I went after Teddy, but he's fast. I ran and ran, then finally lost sight of him. Didn't even realize I was in the bog, but next thing I knew, my foot went in, then my leg. Tried to get out, but then the other leg went in, too. I really thought I could pull myself free, but there was nothing close enough to grab onto. Then I panicked. Started thrashing around, but I just went in deeper. I finally decided I couldn't do it by myself, so I started yelling, hoping somebody would hear me."

Little Roy coughed, pointed to himself and stretched out his hands to her.

She nodded. "Okay. Let's try."

He braced himself so he was straddling her, grabbed her wrists and pulled. Then pulled more. The bog made that horrible sucking sound, which could mean, Sadie knew, that it was taking her down or maybe, hopefully, letting her go. Either way, nothing much happened.

Muskeg

It seemed to Sadie that Little Roy worked for at least half an hour, although time was hard to gauge, but finally, the top of Theda's hips came into view. *If she could just get her butt out,* Sadie thought. Butts were heavy, and Theda's would work as a lever if it was above ground.

Little Roy kept pulling, but Theda didn't come out any further. Without letting go of her, he jerked his head toward the stand of tamaracks. What did he mean? Sadie couldn't just chop down a tree with no ax, no nothing. She stared at Theda—half in, half out. What did she need? A brace. She looked around, spotted a good-sized rock and pointed to it. Little Roy nodded.

She got down, dug her fingers into the ground, the muck, the muskeg, whatever the hell it was, until they were under the stone. Rocked it back and forth until she pried it loose, then took a breath and lifted with all her strength. The stone came up out of the earth, and she hung on as hard as she could. Fell on her back and took the rock with her, right on her belly. "Oof!" It didn't hurt so much as knocked the wind out of her.

Little Roy picked the rock off her stomach as if it weighed less than a pound, put it next to Theda and placed one of her arms on it. Then motioned for Sadie to sit down on the other side, and when she did, wrapped Theda's arm around her waist. Now that they'd braced her on both sides, Sadie got the idea. Get her anchored, then pull some more.

Theda grabbed onto her so hard Sadie almost screamed, but she bit her lip. "Okay," she said, in as calm a voice as she could manage. "We got you this far, we'll get you all the way out."

Little Roy was panting from the exertion. He took a drink of water. "Can I have some?" Theda said.

He handed her the canteen and looked just beyond them like he was thinking.

Sadie watched him. He'd rolled up his sleeves, and she could see that little or not, he had plenty of muscle in his arms. Then he raised his hands in front of him, keeping the elbows close to his body, like he was lifting up a tray, and walked behind Theda.

"You lift from behind?" Sadie said.

Little Roy nodded. He pointed to Theda's shoulders, touched his armpits, pushed out his hands and then pulled up as if he had something very heavy in his arms.

Sadie understood. "You pull her up from the back. She stays braced on the rock and me, and I'll pull as much as I can from my side."

Little Roy nodded.

Theda was pale but spoke in a calm voice. "And I'll hang on and try to push myself up."

"Give me a sign when you're ready, Roy," Sadie said.

First time she'd called him anything but Little Roy.

He placed his hands under Theda's arms. Everyone took a breath. Sadie kept Theda's arm fastened to her waist. Let her pinch, it didn't matter. She counted, "One, two, three," then tightened her grip around Theda and pulled upward as hard as she could as Little Roy pulled from behind. Theda rose a little more. At least Sadie thought so. But time was going so slow she might be imagining it. She could hear the fiddler breathing heavily, feel Theda's back soaked with sweat and mud. *Don't slip, don't let her go,* she told herself, as she pulled harder, eyes closed, the better to concentrate. *Don't stop, keep going, keep going, sweet Jesus, help me in my hour of need...*

A small circle of light shone on them. The moon? *Le bon dieu?* Bog Witches? *Keep going, Don't let go...*

They were one mass of flesh moving slowly upward. Then a hollow *plop* and Theda's butt was above ground, and Little Roy and Sadie were finally freeing her if they could just keep going, not stop, which they didn't, then her legs, then all of her. And they collapsed backward, the three of them, into the crunchy ground and cold water and muck of the bog. Sadie exhaled and felt a wave of euphoria like nothing she'd ever experienced.

Theda sobbed.

Little Roy panted like a horse that just outran the devil.

Sadie looked up at the tamarack branches, the starry sky. And the strange circle of light that stayed over them like a fisherman's lantern or a Bog Witch torch. Maybe she was imagining it, but the light felt warm, not hot like the sun, gentle as the first breezes of spring.

"Holy Mother of God," she said.

That about covered it.

Chapter Thirty-Four

Little Roy: Faunce Ridge, September 1937

Little Roy felt like he was waking from a dream. He started to wiggle his fingers, toes, arms, legs, just to make sure everything still worked. Bog muck thick with grass and weeds covered his boots, pants and shirt. The September night air was cool, but after the last pull, he felt as if he'd just gotten out of a sauna. The odd light shining on them helped, too. Bog Witches? Whatever it was, he liked the combination of warm skin and cool air. He reckoned he could lay there for a long time, just smelling the muskeg smoke that drifted over them and looking at the stars.

Sadie interrupted his thoughts. "I'm going to have that Lucky now. If someone sees me, the hell with them."

Theda's crying got softer, fading to a whimper until she lay quiet. Little Roy was just about to check on her when she spoke. "Teddy."

"We'll find him," Sadie said. "Don't worry."

How could she sound so sure, like the boy was sitting right there and all they had to do was reach out and grab him? Sadie wouldn't be looking for Teddy, and of course, neither would Theda. He, Little Roy, was the one who would tramp the bog, look under trees, check hollows, pray that Teddy hadn't stepped into a hole with no bottom. No one else knew the bog well enough. But what if he didn't find him? Or even worse, what if he fell in himself and got sucked down by the bog and disappeared? He hoped all his little gifts to the Bog Witches over the years had paid off, that they'd protect and guide him, but nothing was certain. And though he was used to doing things by himself, this one time, he wished he had company when he looked for the boy.

Eventually, he sat up, drank some water and looked around. Theda was still lying on the ground, eyes closed. It'd be good for her to sleep, stop worrying about Teddy even for a few hours. "I'll stay with her," Sadie said. "You going to leave right now, Roy?"

Well, he hadn't really had time to think about that. Be nice to have a little food first. Nothing to eat out in the bog now. No more blueberries. Cranberries not ripe yet. But they couldn't wait until morning. Not with Teddy lost, with the air getting colder and muskeg smoke making it more dangerous. And Albert bent on taking the boy away from his mother and the forest and the fire tower and all the things Little Roy knew he loved.

He decided to make some noise, just in case Teddy was in hearing range. Had another sip of water, then whistled as hard as he could. The more he blew, the more power he discovered in his belly. He whistled again. And once more.

"Jesus, Roy," said Sadie. "Hope you scare up something soon because if you keep on, you're going to bust our eardrums."

He waited for a response, listened, then listened some more. But nothing. Just a little wind moving the tamarack.

Then he spotted a light bobbing toward them. Too big for the Bog Witches, who scattered tiny splashes of brightness, like fireflies painting the darkness. He whistled again, then picked up the sound of rustling dry grasses. The light must be a lantern. He whistled one more time to let the carrier know where they were.

"Why Roy, you should talk to the Canadian National, see if they want to take you on as their new train whistle."

Marie emerged from a thicket of sumac with a kerosene lantern. He'd never been happier to see her. She looked at Theda and Sadie sprawled on the ground. "Good thing I brought provisions," she said, setting her pack on the ground and taking out two canteens of water and some venison jerky. "Thought if anyone was out here, they'd need them. I got a blanket, too, and a thermos of coffee."

Theda sat up, suddenly alert. "Hazel! How is she?"

"I made some tea to relax her, and she's sleeping. François's keeping watch. Thought I'd have to take out the bullet, but it went right through her shoulder, nice and clean. I washed it good, put on some salve I made and bandaged it up. Gus helped me. A real gentleman. If it looks worse tomorrow, the next day, we'll take her into Williams to see Doc, but I think she'll be fine. Covered her up in every blanket I had and finally got her warm."

Theda sighed. "Thank God. I was so worried."

"Quite the day," Marie went on. "I rode Butter over to the Dupree place right after Cal set the Carsten house on fire. Afraid it was going to spread, with everything so dry, so I asked Clarence Dupree to haul some water. He came back with four barrels. Hard work, but we wet down everything around the place, poured water on what we could, and finally, it burned itself out. Took the barn, all the outbuildings. Then him and his boy, Frankie, got Daisy into their wagon and hauled her away for butchering. I just got cleaned up, and there come Gus with Hazel."

Marie was the best neighbor he could ever have, Little Roy thought.

"How'd you know we were here?" Theda said.

"Well, if you weren't in the fire tower, I figured you had to be in the bog someplace. Started from Magnus's tree and went from there. Just a feeling. Say, where's Teddy?"

"Wish we knew," Sadie said and told her what had happened at the fire tower.

Marie's eyes widened. "Oh, no! We have to find him. Before Albert does."

Little Roy pointed to himself, and Marie seemed to know exactly what he meant.

"Roy, I'll go with you to look for Teddy. Theda and Sadie, you should be fine 'til morning. Here's some coffee, and me and Roy will make you up a bed of tamarack branches."

She opened the thermos and poured a cup. Little Roy sniffed the coffee steam rising into the night air. Such a wonderful smell. Maybe that was enough; maybe he didn't even need to drink it. But with the first swallow, he knew he was alive. He drank it down, then cut tamarack branches, arranged them in two layers and put the blanket on top. Good to have something to do, especially now that he was starting to cool off.

"You seen Albert?" Sadie said.

"Hasn't showed up yet," said Marie. "But François is ready if he does. How about Cal? Did that arrow do any damage?"

Sadie laughed. "Oh, yes. Wouldn't be surprised if Gus took him into Williams to get him bandaged up. Don't think we have to worry about him anymore unless he can shoot with the other hand."

"No," Marie said. "I suppose not. But there's Albert."

* * *

They left Theda and Sadie and started out, Little Roy leading. He'd always had a good sense of direction, but the bog had taught him to be extra careful. Whenever he'd found a safe trail that didn't lead to sinkholes or water, he'd mark it. Sometimes he'd tie willow branches together. Or fasten bits of cloth to a tree. Something to tell him he was going good. Of course, if a lot of rain fell, a safe path could turn into a mess. But so far, September hadn't brought much moisture, so he could still depend on his system. And with Marie's lantern, he didn't have to figure things out in the dark.

Besides, he thought, someone must be looking out for them. If not the Bog Witches, then his mother or God or all the people who had to leave this place but didn't want to, whose spirits still walked Faunce Ridge.

He kept a hold of Marie's hand. Step by step, bush by bush, the light showing them where to put their feet. He had an idea where Teddy might be. He'd always told the boy to go to the Crucifixion trees, three tamaracks that grew taller than all the others, if he got lost. He hoped Albert hadn't seen them. Or that if he did, he wouldn't know what he was looking at. The trees were on higher ground, farther into the bog, with good sitting rocks underneath.

But the lantern wouldn't help him find the trees. He scanned the sky with its stars and new moon. Nothing so far, but they were just starting into the deep bog.

They trudged on.

An owl hooted. Some folks thought they sounded like ghosts, but to him, their noise was friendly. Another good sign was a white rag tied to a tree. He'd been this way before, and hopefully, Teddy with him.

He dropped Marie's hand. Two fingers in his mouth. Took a deep breath. Blew for all he was worth for as long as he could. Probably sounded like a screech owl. Marie covered her ears.

They waited.

Another hoot. Answering him?

But then, with the little bit of moon and starlight, he spied the Crucifixion trees. He nudged Marie, pointed and grabbed her hand again. With the help of the lantern, careful walking and a few markers here and there, they stepped into a clearing with the three golden tamarack. The needles would drop soon, but for now, they glowed like they'd swallowed light. Tamarack looked delicate, almost pretty. Nothing like the scraggly jack pine, which could take wind and storms, deer munching on them, pretty much anything. But even though the tamarack faded to skeletons in the winter, they came back every spring, sprouting soft needles, turning the landscape pale green. And their branches swept low, like a lady's skirt. All the better to hide under, and Little Roy hoped and prayed that's what Teddy had done.

He saw the rocks, ideal for looking out, taking a rest, watching for hawks or blue herons. If he didn't have to find Teddy, that's what he would've done. Sit there until dawn, see the sun come up, hear the first songbirds, then make his way back to his place or Marie's. Easy. But he didn't care anymore about having things easy, didn't care if having the boy around made him work harder. Teddy wasn't his son or even his nephew, but he felt like kin, just like Marie and Theda and now Sadie, François and Hazel.

Taking a step forward, he began to examine each rock and the ground around it. No Teddy. Fear tickled his belly.

"Roy," came Marie's voice from behind the trees. "Come here."

There was Teddy. Curled up like a snail, chest rising and falling slow and peaceful, lying on boughs he must've cut for a bed. Little Roy had taught him that in the woods, aside from moss—soft, sweet-smelling but often wet—the best thing to lie down on was tamarack.

His body relaxed. The boy was found. They'd let him sleep for now, then get him back and make sure his father didn't spirit him away. He and Marie sank down on the rocks.

Little Roy had forgotten how sweet it was to sleep outside in September when the chill hadn't settled into the ground and the mosquitoes and black flies were gone. He dozed off. First thing he knew, it was morning, and Marie was opening the thermos of coffee, Teddy still asleep.

Finally, he heard rustling from behind the trees.

"'Morning," Marie called.

Little Roy got up and offered Teddy a hand.

"You came!" Then, "Where's my mom?"

"Fell into a hole," Marie said. "But Roy and Sadie pulled her out. Her and Sadie are resting by the edge of the bog. We'll go get them once we have something to eat."

Teddy's eyes widened. "Is she all right?"

Little Roy nodded.

"Just tired," Marie said.

"And what about Hazel?"

"She needs to rest a little." Marie laid down a bandana and set out venison jerky and coffee. "Breakfast."

"I'm starving!" Teddy said.

"I bet you are. Make sure you drink plenty of water, too."

She gave him the canteen, and he had a long swig, then reached for the jerky. "I figured Papa wouldn't be able to find me here," he said between bites. "Mama was chasing me, too, but I couldn't wait for her. I followed the secret trail out here to the trees. And I was pretty tired, so after a while, I laid down."

It was going to be a beautiful September day—blue sky, light breeze, yellow poplar, red sumac and golden tamaracks. Little Roy closed his eyes to memorize all of it in case things turned bad later.

Chapter Thirty-Five

Sadie: Faunce Ridge, September 1937

Sadie curled against Theda for warmth and finally dropped off. Then, just before dawn, she awoke and couldn't get back to sleep, so she lay on her back and watched the sun come up red, then pale pink as it shaded into blue. Beautiful out here, no doubt about it. But Albert was still around someplace and probably Gus with him. She was less concerned about Cal now that his shooting arm had a hole in it.

She must have dozed again because the next thing she knew, a rough masculine voice jarred her awake.

"Get the hell up." Albert stood over them.

He needed a change of clothes and looked like he hadn't slept. His eyes bloodshot, pupils tiny and darting all over. And he couldn't stop blinking. Was he hopped up on something? Or maybe the whole situation was finally getting to him. Grabbing his kid and getting rid of Theda wasn't turning out as easy as he thought. And although Albert wasn't as close to Sadie as the night they danced at the Hotel Pascal, she again picked up the scent of mothballs. What a horrible smell. Perfect for a man like him.

Gus stood to one side, face unreadable as usual. No Cal.

Theda started awake. "*You,*" she said, her voice filled with hate.

"Why don't you just give up, Albert?" Sadie said. "The kid doesn't want anything to do with you. Why do you s'pose he ran away?"

"Nobody asked you!" he screamed, face turning that reddish-purple that made him look even crazier.

She shook her head. "You're not going to win this one. There's more of us than you—and we're here 'cause we want to be, not 'cause someone hired us."

"Ha! Plenty of men for hire out there—isn't that right, Gus?"

Gus didn't reply.

"I'm not going anywhere," Albert said. "I'll stay as long as it takes. I'll make your lives a living hell…" He trailed off, lips still moving.

Gus shot a fast look at him, confirming Sadie's suspicions. Albert was coming apart. *Attention,* she told herself silently, echoing her father. *Careful.*

"Look," Gus said. "Tell us where the kid is. No one has to get hurt."

"We don't know," Theda said. "And I wouldn't tell you if I did."

Gus turned to Albert. "The fiddler's the one who knows this place. We find him, we find the kid."

And then, just over their shoulders, Sadie saw Little Roy, Marie and Teddy walking straight toward them. Not sneaking, not ducking behind bushes, just walking like they were out for their morning constitutional.

"Good morning," Marie said. She smiled as if Albert and Gus weren't there looking for the boy whose shoulder she had in a firm grip.

Albert turned slowly. Probably too tired to move fast. "Son?" he said, "What're you doing with these people? I know they're keeping you against your will."

"Against my will?" Teddy repeated. "What're you talking about?"

Albert took a step toward him. "All right, maybe you've had some fun out in the woods. But I'm here now, and I'm going to take you home. Don't you want to be back in your own house in Savannah?"

The boy shook his head. "I like it here."

At first, Albert looked blank, like he hadn't understood what Teddy said, but then his face turned ugly. "You hear that, Gus? He *likes* it here." He started to laugh. "If y'all think I'm going to let a bunch of women and a deaf and dumb fiddler take my boy, you're crazier than I thought." He pulled out a pistol and pointed it at Marie. "Let go of him," he said. "Or I'll shoot you and the simpleton with you."

Sadie was standing close enough to see the gun, and if she wasn't mistaken, it was a Smith & Wesson 19, a nasty weapon gangsters got ahold of after the cops started using it. Lot of power in that gun. She hated to see it in Albert's hand.

"Boss," Gus said. "No."

Albert ignored him. "I'm going to count to five because you're a woman. One. Two..."

"Albert." Sadie pretended she was speaking to an unruly child. "You're not *really* going to shoot Marie, are you? Right in front of your boy?"

He wheeled toward her. "Shut up! Just shut up! I don't want to hear nothing right now. Especially not from you. Lucky I didn't plug you after you slipped us a mickey at that broken-down hotel of yours."

"But you didn't plug me, did you? And you couldn't of anyway, 'cause you went and lost your guns." She shook her head and laughed. "Just couldn't keep track of them."

"Don't talk back to me! I'd just as lief shoot every damn one of you!"

"Albert," Gus said. "You ain't going to shoot anyone. Give me the gun."

"Don't come any closer!" Albert screamed. "None of you!"

He was going to bust a gasket, no doubt about it, and Sadie just hoped he wasn't aiming the Smith & Wesson at someone when it happened. Out of the corner of her eye, she saw Little Roy tense up his body like he was getting ready to jump.

What happened next looked like magic and felt like a dream when she recalled it later. The fiddler seemed to fly through the air, right onto Albert, grabbing him around the neck. Albert threw him off, but Little Roy went right back at him, and they wrestled back and forth, neither giving an inch, like a couple of drunken lumberjacks locked in a crazy dance. They were well-matched, Albert not much bigger than Little Roy and maybe as strong, but Little Roy faster and more flexible. Albert's hand still held the Smith & Wesson, but Little Roy grabbed hold of his wrist and shook it, so that Albert couldn't have fired the gun if he tried.

Then Albert pushed Little Roy forward, and they fell, Albert on top of the fiddler, pinning him to the ground, free hand gripping the pistol.

"Now you're going to pay, you mute bastard." He aimed at Little Roy's head, finger on the trigger.

But Little Roy, moving so fast he was a blur, got his hand on the gun, too, and in one motion sprang to his feet, taking Albert with him. Sadie knew that men fighting to the death could draw unnatural strength from somewhere, maybe the devil himself. Both still gripped the gun, but Little Roy jerked the weapon so that it was pointing at Albert. Then a muffled crack and Albert slumped backward, one leg sinking into the muskeg under their feet.

Little Roy staggered back, eyes wide. He looked at the gun like he was seeing it for the first time, then pitched it over the bushes and through the tamarack. Sadie didn't expect to hear it land. Hopefully, the bog would swallow it up, and they'd never have to see it again. She saw or sensed Theda run to Teddy and drag him away.

Everything was very quiet. Albert lay splayed on the ground like a crooked star that had fallen to earth. One leg in, the other stretched out in front, arms open. His hand twitched, and he mumbled something. Should she get closer, try to hear what he was saying? Bright red soaked into his white shirt. Why the hell would he wear a white shirt out here in the woods, anyway? Again Sadie smelled the accursed odor of mothballs, which clung to him even now.

Marie stood near Little Roy, who was shaking like he'd contracted a chill. She grabbed his hand. "You didn't have a choice, Roy. Couldn't let him just shoot you down."

Something like words came out of Albert's mouth. This time Sadie bent down to listen but couldn't make out anything. Poor bastard. Wrecked his life with all that pride, trying to make everything go his way. Then he made a gurgling sound, which Sadie suspected were bubbles of blood in his throat, and lay silent.

She crossed herself, not sure if she was praying for Albert or thanking God it was all over. Maybe both.

Gus took off his hat.

Chapter Thirty-Four

Little Roy: Faunce Ridge, September 1937

The voices in Little Roy's head had gone still. All he could hear was an occasional songbird and a little wind. It seemed they were all statues out under the tamarack, in the scrub brush of the bog. Maybe they'd just stay there forever, like in the Bible when the people looked back at Sodom and Gomorrah and turned into salt. Was God punishing them, too? But why, if all they did was defend their own? No one wanted Albert to die, just go away.

Still, he could've died instead of Albert. The bog might've swallowed Theda and never given her up. Cal could've shot Marie instead of Daisy. And back in 1910, if he'd stayed on the farm, not gone into Baudette for the fiddle contest, he would've been swallowed up in flames with his family and not be standing in this spot today. Twenty-seven years later, he was no closer to understanding why things happened the way they did.

Marie leaned forward to close Albert's eyes and cleared her throat. "Have to get his leg out of there," she said. "More time passes…"

She didn't have to continue. Right now, Albert was still soft as the ground that pulled him in, but that wouldn't last. As his spirit flew away, his body would harden until it was like a rock. And since Little Roy was the one who made Albert leave this earth, it was up to him to try to move him out of the bog. He looked down at Albert's face, smooth and much younger than when he was fighting for the gun. He'd need a helper, of course, maybe even a shovel, although tools didn't help much in the bog since water rushed in to fill holes. It would take some figuring, like when he and Sadie got Theda out.

Gus stepped forward as if reading his thoughts. "Least I can do," he said.

Each of them got an arm and were just starting to pull when François and Hazel came into the clearing. Sadie's face lit up like it always did when François appeared.

Hazel's sweater bulged in the shoulder where Cal's bullet went in and Marie must have bandaged her. She let out a little cry. "He's gone?"

Little Roy nodded.

She sighed. "Then my girl's finally free."

Hazel went straight to Theda and Teddy huddled together under a tree, knelt down and put her arms around both of them.

Good thing. Little Roy didn't want Teddy to see his father the way he was. François joined him and Gus as they worked to pull Albert out of his strange position. Little Roy had them take his arms and hold him steady while he pulled up from behind. Albert, or whatever was left of him, didn't move. Not even a sucking sound to show they were making progress.

"Perhaps we change places," François suggested.

He and Gus clasped Albert's torso from the back while Little Roy got into position in the front. François counted, "One, two, three," and they strained together, but the body stayed still. It was as if Albert's leg had landed in cement, anchoring him to the bog. They tried again. This time Gus counted, and they pulled even harder. Little Roy's shoulders and arms were beginning to ache. Both Gus and François were sweating. They'd taken off their jackets, and their armpits were wet.

"Look," Gus said. "This ain't working. Let's get some shovels, try to dig him out."

"I've got some in my shed," Marie said. "I'll be right back." She disappeared behind the bushes. No one could walk or run faster than Marie when she was in a hurry. It seemed that in no time, she'd returned with two shovels and a pitchfork. "You'll have to work quick," she said, although Little Roy already knew that.

No one spoke. Little Roy took his shovel and tried to dig. The edges of the hole where Albert had fallen were hard and resisted the metal blade. Things dried out in the fall, it was true, but not like this. Besides, something soft and spongy had sucked the man in, and whatever it was shouldn't be more than a foot or two down. If that.

"I'm hitting rock," Gus said. "Or at least that's what it feels like."

François's pitchfork barely penetrated the grass and sedge. "It bounce off," he muttered. "Like rubber."

Little Roy finally managed to get his blade in a couple of inches. He pushed down, then tried to pull it out, expecting to come up with a load of muck. Maybe now they'd be able to move Albert. But the shovel stuck. He motioned for the other two men to help him. All three grabbed onto the shovel, braced themselves and pulled. Still it did not budge.

"What the hell's down there?" Gus said.

"Joe Beaudette could tell us," Sadie said. "Wish I'd brought him along."

"I think," Marie said. "The bog don't want to give him up, pure and simple."

So what do we do? Little Roy thought. Leave him here with one leg in and one leg out? That wasn't right. Buzzards would come, then the wolves…

Marie had a faraway look in her eyes. "The Bog Witches want to keep him. That's why they're doing everything they can to keep you from digging him out."

"Bog witches?" Gus said. "This is a strange place for sure. But I always took you as a woman with a good head on her shoulders. No such thing as witches."

"Maybe not where you come from," Marie said.

Little Roy would never question Marie. If she thought the Bog Witches were behind this, then they must be. And it made sense. How else could Albert be stuck so good they couldn't move him, not even one little bit? How else could the shovels and pitchfork that always worked before be so useless? He looked down at Albert. He'd like it if the Bog Witches would show themselves, give them a sign. Why would they want Albert's leg? What would they do with it?

Then a shout. "What the hell's going on?"

Cal stumbled into the clearing, tripping over roots and fallen tamarack, not paying one bit of attention to the terrain. He looked awful. No shirt, bloody bandage around the right arm, bags under his eyes. He seemed even smaller, Little Roy thought. Like a kid who got into a fight.

"Gun went off," Gus said. "Albert and the fiddler were fighting for it."

Cal snorted. "Oh, yeah? Then how come the boss didn't win? He'd make two of that little runt. He murdered him! And one of *them* had to help. Look at me! Shot all to hell with a goddamn bow and arrow!"

"Nah, you got it wrong," Gus said.

"And why's he in the ground like that, all queer? How come you haven't gotten him out?"

"Tell you what," Gus said, holding out his shovel. "You give it a try."

"C'mon, you know I can't do nothing. My arm…"

"Then watch me." And Gus put the shovel to the ground, braced it with his foot and pushed. The blade didn't go in. In fact, it looked to Little Roy like it bounced right off.

"You ain't trying."

"Yes, I am," Gus said. "The ground won't move. Something strange going on, and nobody knows what. Except for her." He pointed at Marie.

"Look," Marie said, pointing to the hole where Albert's leg went in. A tiny curl of smoke threaded its way upward. Then another.

"What the fucking hell?" Cal said, backing away.

Marie yelled. "Theda, Hazel! Bring Teddy here right now. Whatever's happening, it's going fast."

"I don't want Teddy to see," Theda called back.

"Then come yourself," Marie answered.

Twists of smoke rose into the air and stuck together in clumps. They looked like bubbles that you could pop. Little Roy took the pitchfork and tried. Didn't work. They just sat there like clouds that decided to stay low to the ground and not fly up to the sky. More smoke came out of the hole. The clouds got bigger until they weren't clouds anymore but fog that covered the trees and bushes and settled all around them.

Sadie sniffed. "Smells like muskeg. But different."

"It's from the Bog Witches," Marie said. "So who knows what it is."

Theda and Hazel ran up.

"Sweet Jesus," Hazel said. "Now what?"

Little Roy looked back to where Theda and Hazel had been sitting with Teddy just a few minutes before. The smoke or fog or whatever it was had got so thick he could no longer see the trees or the boy. But the funny thing was that it didn't cover Albert. In fact, it left a space around him, so you could see him clear as anything, in that odd position but laying back like he was just resting.

"I don't understand what's happening," Theda said.

"I don't rightly know either," Marie answered. "Though I got my suspicions. All we can do is watch and see."

Cal was shaking. Too cold for him? Or was he scared by all the goings-on? "Look, Gus, this ain't right! It's another trick, don't you see? You gonna just stand there and do nothing?"

Gus shook his head. "Nothing to do. Marie here is the only one who's got some idea. And it sounds crazy, but it's all we got to go on."

"But we didn't sign on for…"

"Yeah, I know. But you can never tell what'll happen on a job."

Albert and the ground he lay on stayed clear as if an invisible wall kept the clouds out. Fog was so thick by then that Little Roy couldn't see anything beyond their little circle of folks.

"Mama! Mister Roy! Where are you?"

Teddy. Of course, he'd want to see his father.

"Right here, darlin'. Follow my voice," Theda said.

But Little Roy knew that would be hard because smoke like this, from the Bog Witches, wasn't just muskeg but something magical. He walked, one small step after another, toward where he'd heard Teddy's voice.

Which, thank God, came again. "I can't see a thing!"

Neither could Little Roy. He corrected his position based on the sound and moved forward. He'd have to depend on his ears and nose and whatever lifeline the good Lord was willing to throw him. Turned out that was his hands because he touched an arm and knew it was Teddy's.

"Mr. Roy!"

Now to get him back to the others. Little Roy had no idea how far he'd gone. Maybe a couple feet, maybe three yards, maybe more.

"This way, son!" Theda yelled, but her voice sounded a long way away.

Little Roy stood still, Teddy's hand in his. He closed his eyes to hear better, then opened them again.

And when he did, a tiny hole opened in the fog, like he was looking through a scope. Couldn't see anything around it, just a little tunnel, and at the end of it, a patch of pale blue that had to be Marie's dress. He walked Teddy toward that spot, focusing his eyes so hard they hurt. Finally they entered the pocket of clear air around Albert and joined the others.

And then, as if it'd been waiting for Teddy, the clearing around Albert began to move and reshape itself. It had opened a circle just big enough for all nine of them. Now the puffy haze closed in, creeping along the ground to border his body. No one spoke, although Little Roy heard Theda's intake of breath. Then the smoke narrowed into a line, as if someone was running a scissors around Albert. Like the gingerbread men Little Roy's mother used to bake at Christmas, except missing one leg.

"What the...?" Cal began.

The line began to shake, loosening Albert and the ground he lay on, the same ground that had resisted their shovels, the tines of a pitchfork, all their digging and muscle.

"Mama, what's happening?"

Theda, on the boy's other side, reached out for his free hand. "Wish I knew, son."

Little Roy stared intently, afraid to even blink, as Albert sank an inch or two into the ground, his outline clean and sharp, like when Little Roy cut blocks of ice from the Rapid River to store for summer.

"If anyone wants to say something, now's the time," said Marie. "He won't be here much longer."

"How do *you* know that?" Cal said, chin jutting out.

"Because she does, you ignorant little thug," Sadie said.

Cal lurched toward her, but Gus grabbed him and yanked him back. Cal couldn't help it, Little Roy considered. Something happened, he jumped.

Albert's body continued to sink into the bog. Not fast, but steady. Finally, he was about a foot down, and they had to lean in to see him.

That's when Teddy stepped closer. "Papa." His voice cracked. "You and me, we never talked much. So many things I wanted to ask you." Little Roy felt him tremble. "But no matter what, you're my pa. I just wish…" He broke off, shoulders shaking. Theda took him in her arms, stroked his head and rocked him back and forth like a baby.

We're all babies when our folks pass, Little Roy thought. *Don't matter what kind of people they were in life.*

Once Teddy stopped talking, the star cutout dropped faster until it was so far down they could barely see Albert. Then a cloud of smoke flew up from the hole and covered it. Didn't sting the eyes like muskeg smoke, but Little Roy drew back all the same, just in time to see the fog form into the shape of that lopsided star. It hovered for a bit, then disappeared into the air.

And the hole closed up like nothing had ever been there but grasses and rocks and sumac. But as they watched, a swirl of smoke rose out of the ground where the hole had been. Didn't grow, just kept curling up into the air.

Marie sighed. "That's it," she said. "Bog Witches have him now."

Cal's face was pale. "What the hell just happened?"

"You saw it," Gus said. "We all did."

"Yeah, but—it wasn't real."

"Real enough," Gus said.

"What we gonna tell the Old Man back at the agency?" Cal said. He sounded scared.

"Don't know yet," Gus said. "But I'll write the report."

The smoke thread kept coming. That would be Albert's gravestone, Little Roy reckoned. The Bog Witches would keep it going forever.

Chapter Thirty-Five

Hazel: Faunce Ridge, September 1937

Hazel's shoulder still ached where Cal shot her, but she barely noticed. She gazed at the curl of smoke. *Such a tough guy and that's all that's left of him.*

Then she looked at Teddy, standing between Theda and Little Roy, face pale, eyes fixed on where his father had been. For the first time, she let herself imagine what he must be feeling—an only child whose father had died by his own gun, right in front of him, then disappeared as if by magic. Teddy had been living an adventure, sleeping in Marie's hayloft, learning the woods and the bog with Little Roy, but now everything had changed, and one way or another, it was going to haunt him the rest of his life.

She was glad when Gus coughed, interrupting her thoughts. "Time for me and Cal to get moving. You'll probably be happy to see us go."

"You're all right, Gus," Sadie said. "But your friend…"

Cal scowled. "You mean me, say my name."

"Settle down, buddy," Gus said. "Everybody took their lumps, and now it's all over." He put his hand on Cal's shoulder and steered him toward the path.

"Hey, Gus," said Hazel. "Thanks for taking me to Marie's. And that night at the resort…"

He touched his hat, nodded, and kept walking.

Then, to Hazel's astonishment, Marie ran to catch up with him and put a hand on his arm. "Hazel ain't the only one. That day in my barn—you saved my life."

Gus smiled. *Why, he's almost handsome,* Hazel marveled. "Anytime," he said. His eyes lingered on Marie, then he turned and kept walking Cal out of the bog.

Once they were gone, Hazel felt the tension in the air drain away, as if a rainstorm had spent itself and were moving on. Of course, Cal was not as much a threat as before, but even so, his angry presence reminded her of Albert. And Gus might be an honorable man, but he was still living on Albert's dime.

"*Eh bien*, my friends, what now?" François said.

What indeed? Hazel figured he and Sadie would return to the Hotel Pascal in Baudette and resume their lives. Marie and Little Roy would hunker down in Faunce Ridge for the winter, share meals, maybe play music at the hotel on the weekends if they weren't snowbound. And who knew whether the government would ever get around to rousting them? Maybe they'd just stay in Faunce Ridge forever, along with the logging Duprees, become part of the nature preserve the CCC was building.

But Theda and Teddy. Would they return to Savannah? Hazel hoped not. Teddy had to go to school somewhere, and it would be lovely if they stayed nearby. In Baudette, Theda could design and sew clothes for people, maybe even open a dress shop. She had her own money, and by all rights should inherit Albert's fortune, but Hazel knew she'd need something to keep herself occupied. And she'd be able to see her every time she went to town.

She'd gotten used to having Theda around again, delighting in her laughter, still finding her beautiful and alluring. Her girl. Minnie would never be her *girl*. Her companion, of course. Half of a team of two. But *girl* called up hot afternoons and flapper dresses and Hazel feeling like she'd be young forever.

Theda in Baudette and Minnie on the island. As long as they never ran into each other, Hazel told herself, wouldn't there be some kind of balance? In fact, why couldn't they circulate around one another the way she and Milt and Theda did before that July 4th? Minnie would be horrified at the thought. But Minnie seemed so far away at the moment, Oak Island an entirely different world from Faunce Ridge where she and the others had held off armed men. Hazel had gotten shot, seen Albert die and then watched the bog swallow him up. After all that, how could she go back to just tending a resort, even if it was in the middle of her beautiful Lake of the Woods?

And what about Teddy? Hazel glanced at his drawn face. Even if Theda wanted to stay in the border country, Teddy might want something very different.

"Well," Marie said. "Can't say I've thought much about food lately, but it'd sure be nice to sit down together. And I don't know about all of you, but I'm more than ready to get out of the bog."

They straggled along the path back to Marie's place. Even though Hazel was exhausted, excitement simmered just under her skin, reminding her of the days in Savannah with Theda. Back at the house, they washed up at the pump with cold, iron-tinged water. Hazel soaked her whole head. It felt wonderful. A shock to her brain that cleared out her mind and made everything fresh.

Soon, the smell of toasting bread, onions and coffee floated in the cool air and made Hazel's mouth water. "You hungry?" she asked Theda.

"I guess so," she said, gazing at her with those dark blue eyes. "Though I didn't think I'd ever want to eat again."

"How's Teddy?"

Theda's face became serious. "We'll see. He just took off with Little Roy for a walk in the woods. Said he wasn't interested in food. Mute or not, Roy's more like a real father than Albert ever was."

"Or at least an uncle," Hazel said. "I'm worried about him. If I'd seen something like that as a child, I'd have nightmares the rest of my life."

"He's a strong boy," Theda replied, straightening up. "Always has been. And he barely knew Albert, really. Of course, it's been a shock, but he's going to be fine."

"Theda! How can you say such a thing? Albert was still his father. And Teddy watched him die."

"Let's not think about that right now." She threaded her arm through Hazel's. "Time for some grub."

They gathered around the table with Sadie, François and Marie. Once they were all eating, Theda's leg pressed against Hazel's. An electric current snaked through Hazel's body. It took her back to the H&M Diner, late lunch with Theda, knees touching under the kitchen table. She pressed back. She knew perfectly well she shouldn't, but God help her, the thrill of danger increased the pleasure. *Minnie's not here,* she told herself. *It's all right. Besides, wouldn't she'd want me to figure this out?*

"I sure got a good appetite, considering we just buried a man in the bog," Sadie said, helping herself to more eggs.

"*We* didn't bury him," Marie corrected her. "Bog Witches did."

"But buried he is," said François. "And I am glad." He glanced at Theda. "Especially for our friends. But also for us. We are lucky to be sitting here."

Marie looked at Theda. "You know that Roy and me'd be happy if you and Teddy stayed forever. Or as long as you want. We'll make sure you have a nice, cozy place for winter."

Theda blinked back tears.

"I love it here, and so does Teddy. If he had his way, he'd apprentice himself to Little Roy and learn everything about the woods and the bog. But one way or another, he has to finish school."

"That would be Williams or Baudette," Sadie said. "Baudette's easier because if you live in town, he could walk. Out here, you'd have to find a way to get him twelve miles to Williams and twelve miles back."

"And they could live at the hotel with us," François said. "Is that not true, Sadie?"

"But if they stay here," Marie countered, "Teddy could take Butter into Williams. We'd fix up a wagon for him."

"Yes, but it is a long way for a boy alone," said François. "Especially in a blizzard."

Hazel looked from Marie to Sadie and François and started to laugh. "Why, you're fighting over them!"

"S'pose we are," Sadie said. "Don't seem right to break up the crew after all we been through together."

Theda put her hand over her heart. "I've got a lot of thinking to do."

You're not the only one, Hazel thought.

Chapter Thirty-Six

Hazel: Faunce Ridge, September 1937

Hazel turned in early at the Rousseau place that night. Sadie and François were down at Marie's, probably drinking coffee with whiskey, smoking and talking, but she wanted only to sleep. She climbed into the built-in wooden bed, fully dressed, pulled the blankets over her and was out within minutes. She didn't hear Sadie and François come in and never woke until sun lit the room. They were still sleeping, so she got up and headed to Marie's. It was good to be alone in the cool, fresh air, to walk through a Faunce Ridge now free of Albert. She hoped Marie wasn't getting tired of feeding them, providing endless pots of coffee. Because she and Theda had unfinished business, and she had no idea how long it would take.

Theda and Teddy, both looking glum, were at the table when Hazel came in. Teddy dug into a bowl of oatmeal while Theda sipped coffee. Marie just raised her eyebrows when she saw Hazel and poured her a cup.

"Thanks, Marie," Hazel said. "Morning, y'all."

Theda nodded and smiled at Hazel. Teddy didn't reply. Theda said, "Son, it's rude not to answer when someone says good morning."

Teddy looked up, eyes exhausted and angry. "I don't care to be polite, Mama. I just want to be out in the bog where Papa died."

"But that's only going to bring bad memories. Wouldn't you rather remember the good times with your father?"

"It's his *grave*, Mama. Don't you understand? I want to sit at the last place I saw him. Even if all that's left is smoke."

He got up and left.

Marie started to clear dishes. "Roy'll take care of him. Sure as anything, that's where he's headed right now."

"What should I do?" Theda said.

Hazel had never borne a child, but she'd helped bring up Rose. "Teddy's had a big shock. He needs time."

Marie nodded. "Just let him be for now. Anyhow, the two of you got things to talk about, don't you?"

Theda met Hazel's gaze. "Yes," she said. "We do indeed."

"Well, go on, then. If you're not back by supper, I'll make sure Teddy gets some food in his belly. I'll pack up bread and cheese and a thermos of coffee for you."

Hazel felt a pang. "We've already imposed on you so much."

Marie's maple syrup-colored eyes twinkled. "Ain't really like that. Even with everything that's happened, it's nice to have company. Roy and I get lonesome out here."

* * *

She and Theda walked outside. "Where are we going?" Hazel said. She knew Theda had a plan. She always did.

"To the fire tower, of course." Theda took her hand. "Where else can we be really alone?"

The fire tower where she got shot. "There must be other places. How about the old Pederson barn?" They'd been comfortable there, at least for a little while.

"Too much hay," Theda said. "I want a floor we can sit on without coming out looking like scarecrows."

Hazel's blood was on the fire tower floor. She remembered how it had dripped onto the boards. But she tried to imagine they were young women again as they strolled through the straight poplar, some still with yellow leaves, past the birch that couldn't help being graceful no matter what, amidst the vivid green of pine, spruce and cedar. In the air, the rich scent of fallen leaves and wood smoke from Marie's stove. In her time on

Oak Island, Hazel had learned to love those smells. She closed her eyes for a second, half-expecting to hear waves crashing on a beach. But the only water nearby was the cold Rapid River. Lake of the Woods, Oak Island and Minnie were many miles north.

They walked to the edge of Faunce Ridge and the tower, which looked more than ever like a toy built by a clever child with a love for zigzag steps. Above, the little room where they'd hidden with Sadie and Teddy. Hazel touched the place where the bullet had entered her shoulder. It didn't hurt too much, and she knew it would heal, but she'd never been shot before. "Just a flesh wound," Gus and Marie had agreed as they dressed it. As if other shots entered a different way. But that didn't matter to her—what mattered was that it was *her* flesh.

"You go first," she said at the bottom of the stairs.

"That's jake with me." Theda's tone was coquettish. "After all, I'm the one who brought you here, Miss Hazel." And she mounted the steps, walking and running, then paused at a landing. "Don't be so slow!"

Hazel's legs were as solid as ever, but it felt strange not to use her right arm to steady herself. She put her left hand on the railing, feeling suddenly old. But at this moment, she was willing to follow Theda anywhere, and so she kept climbing, looking up at the tiny structure at the top.

Theda opened the door. "All ready for us!" she said as if she'd prepared it herself.

Hazel followed her inside. The wood was warmed by the sun, and the windows on every side let in the blue sky. She couldn't deny that it was cozy, with the carefully laid boards and the sloping roof. But blood still stained the floor.

"I don't know, Theda. Look." She pointed.

"Oh, honey, just pretend one of us had the curse."

But Hazel couldn't help but remember: all of them huddled, the zinging shots, then sudden pain. And before that, Albert smacking her in the resort kitchen, blood crusting under her nose.

"I won't sit there again," she said.

"All right," Theda said. "Then how about the other side?"

And Hazel obeyed. Because above all, she wanted to shut out everything but Theda and the fact that after all these years, they were finally together. But still, her eyes strayed to where a bullet had shattered the glass.

Theda sat down and patted the space beside her. "Just rest a while, darlin'. You must be so tired."

She was, despite her long sleep the night before. All the electricity that started to crackle when Theda arrived on the island was finally settling down. For a second, she longed for her bed at the resort, the big one with a quilt on top, the bed she shared with Minnie. But she put that out of her mind and used her left hand to lower herself.

Theda snuggled in next to her. "Alone at last," she said.

She was warm and soft, and Hazel's arm fit around her shoulders the way it always had. Theda leaned against her. Hazel felt a sudden urge to stretch out this time, live in it until she no longer craved it. But what if her want for Theda never went away? Could she return to Minnie, knowing she desired someone else? And if she chose Theda, how could she not yearn for Minnie, not feel she'd betrayed everything they'd built?

"Hey," Theda said, snuggling in closer. "You asleep yet?"

"What do you think?"

"When I saw you and Minnie on the island, what a great thing you had, I said, let her be. Why should I come in fifteen years later and upset the apple cart?" She paused. "Although…Hazel?"

"What?"

"It doesn't feel like fifteen years. More like five. Or less."

"I know," Hazel said. She swore that time collapsed and expanded like an accordion. And the older she got, the less she understood how it happened. Especially when it came to Theda. She felt a tremor through her fingertips.

"And I can't believe Albert's gone," Theda went on. "Except I saw it with my own eyes."

"Yes," Hazel said. "Thank God. All those years when I thought about the things he did to you…" She shuddered. "I wanted to kill him myself."

"But I'm free now." Theda's voice rose with excitement. "And I've got my own money. I can go wherever I want. Remember how we used to talk about Europe, all the cities we wanted to see? Paris, Rome, London, New York, maybe…someplace where there's girls like us and nobody cares…"

Hazel's nerves prickled her skin. *Watch out,* she warned herself. Theda was a wave that would roll right over her and sweep her away if she didn't keep her footing. "What about Teddy?" she said. "Doesn't seem like he wants to go anywhere."

"Teddy takes after me. Once he gets used to it, he'll love traveling the world. Help him forget Albert."

"For good or bad, Albert was his father," Hazel said. "He's not going to forget him anytime soon. And I don't think he wants me or anyone else to join up with you two. Have you really thought this through, Theda?"

"I've done nothing but think since you left Savannah." Theda grabbed Hazel's hands. "I've tried so hard to be unselfish. Let you go back to Minnie and your island and the resort. The new life you've made. But now, after everything that's happened… You could have died. Or me, stuck in the bog. But we didn't. Somehow we got another chance. I know Minnie's a peach. And you're comfy with her, like with an old robe. But I'm here now, and I'm begging you." She clasped Hazel's hand to her breast. "Come with me. Please. Let's make a life together. While we still can."

The words buzzed around Hazel like a swarm of bees. Tumbled away, flew back, perched on her shoulder, then took off again. But feeling Theda's warm breast under her hand connected to a place deep and low inside her, like that long-ago Fourth of July in Savannah.

"Christ, Theda," she said, her voice choked with desire and fear.

"You feel it, too, don't you?"

"Of course I do, but …"

Theda leaned back. Stripped off her blouse, revealing a lace camisole through which Hazel could see her nipples, erect and the color of cinnamon.

Hazel groaned. Closed her eyes and tried to conjure up Minnie's long, dark hair flowing over the pillow. But it didn't help. "God, baby, please don't do this," she pleaded.

But Theda peeled off the camisole. Her breasts swung free. "Well?" And then, "Don't you want me?"

Her voice shook, and Hazel couldn't bear it.

She pulled her first love toward her. Their mouths and tongues entwined as they sank to the floor. Hazel cupped Theda's breasts. How long had it been? How many times had she dreamed of this? She teased first one, then the other, with her tongue and her teeth.

Theda moaned. "Hazel, please. Please."

And Hazel dove into Theda's body, all of her swelling, straining for the exact feel of them together.

Chapter Thirty-Seven

Hazel: Faunce Ridge, September 1937

Hazel stirred awake amidst the tangled clothes and smells of her and Theda, sun low in the sky. Poplar and birch leaves drifted past the window. Theda slept, face turned toward her, lashes dark against her cheeks. Hazel felt peace, at least for the moment. No guilt. Not yet, anyway. Their coupling as foreseeable as the Minnesota autumn making way for winter. Did the falling leaves know that snow would cover them? And if they knew, would they care?

Theda, beloved Theda. Curled up in the silk and wool and cotton they'd shed. Looking at her, Hazel felt another spark of desire. She and Theda were flame and smoke. The heat, the crackle, sparks dancing, smoke rising—even the ashes that were quick to follow, still warm to the touch. What she had with Minnie was soup simmering all day on the back of the stove: chicken, carrots, potatoes, barley. A little salt and pepper. Brown bread, stewed rhubarb. Perfect for fall, the time of turning inward, getting ready for the cold, hunkering down. But was it that simple? She remembered Minnie reciting salty limericks, Minnie with her rifle aimed at Albert, Minnie's long black hair, loose or braided, flying as she sprinted to the dock to meet incoming boats.

She leaned against the wall, gathered her sweater around her, closed her eyes, then dozed off again.

The next time she awoke, the light had faded except for a smudge of sunset hanging above the trees. Theda was propped against the opposite wall, smiling at her. "I didn't want to bother you," she said. "You were sound asleep. Snoring. It was sweet."

Hazel rubbed her eyes. "Can we stay here forever?"

"Why not?" Theda said. "Too bad there's no bed, but it doesn't seem to matter, does it?"

Maybe the fire tower, blood stains and all, was a hotel for lost lovers. Who would check in for a day. A week. Maybe months. *Until they made up their minds.*

Until Hazel made up her mind. She looked around. "Dark soon."

"And just us girls. You're not scared, are you?"

Hazel laughed. "No! The owls and the whippoorwills might wake us up, but no bear is going to climb all the way up here. Least I don't think so. We'll lock the door, just in case they smell food. Little buggers are always hungry." Then she sobered up. "Do you think they'll worry? Little Roy, Teddy…"

"Marie will talk to them," Theda said. "Besides, Teddy's too mad to miss me right now. But tomorrow, if we're not back, it'll be a different story."

"So we have tonight."

"Yes."

"I don't know if that's long enough." Hazel needed to walk, feel the wind. If only she could sit by Lake of the Woods. The rhythm of its waves calmed her mind, helped her hear the inner voice that never lied. But the lake was far away. Like Oak Island and Minnie.

"It's got to be enough," Theda said.

Hazel sighed. If time were a clock with a big, stern face, she'd heave it off the ranger tower, smash it into tiny pieces. At least make it stop until she was good and ready for it to start ticking again.

"What do you want to do, Hazel?" Theda's tone was sober.

"What do I want? Be two people. One who goes off with you and another who takes a boat back to the island."

"You love it there, don't you?"

Hazel closed her eyes, heard waves crash on the beach, smelled the lake, a combination of seaweed, fish and something she couldn't identify, except that it meant fresh water. "Yes," she said. "I flat out love it." Maybe more than she loved Minnie. But it was hard to tell them apart. In her mind, Minnie rose out of the island, along with the spruce and pine and sumac, the raspberry bushes, Hazel's rock and all the things that had become part of her.

"I've never felt that way about a place," Theda said. "I could live pretty much anywhere. As long as Teddy was there. And you."

Hazel felt as if she were approaching the island in a boat, felt it pulling her. And yet she resisted. "What if," she began. "What if you moved into Baudette? Just for Teddy to finish the school year, see how you like it?"

"Would you come with me?"

"I'd visit."

"And then go back to Minnie?"

"I suppose so."

Although Hazel couldn't imagine how she'd accomplish that, how she'd look Minnie in the eye after being with Theda. She felt miserable. And then she heard the voice she'd been listening for. *You don't fool around with love. If you're lucky enough to find it.*

She, Hazel, had been very lucky. Counting Milt, she'd had three loves in her life. No, four: the island—her island—and the blue water that surrounded it.

You don't fool around with love.

"So, where does that leave us?" There was a catch in Theda's voice. "What would you do in my place? Stick around and hope for a few crumbs? Give up and leave?"

"Theda—" Hazel choked up, took a deep breath and prayed for courage. "I'll always love you. And sometimes I want to make believe it's still 1922. But it's not. I've lived on Oak Island with Minnie for twelve years. Longer than I lived with Milt. Longer than I ran the diner. I've finally made a real home. And it's not just Minnie. It's Rose—she's as much my girl as if I gave birth to her. If I left…" She paused to find the words. "If I left, I think I'd split into little pieces. Spend the rest of my life looking for myself."

She exhaled hard.

Theda sighed, rested her head in her hands.

Hazel waited.

Finally, Theda looked up. Her eyes glistened. "Then I have to go away."

Hazel could hardly speak. "Yes," she managed to say. "I'm sorry." She leaned forward until their heads touched, aware she was shaking.

"Oh, Hazel," Theda said in a soft voice. "Come here. Let's rest. God knows we both need it." She pulled Hazel down beside her. They covered up with all their clothes and snuggled together. The warmth from Theda's body gradually relaxed Hazel until the shaking stopped, and she slept.

* * *

When she woke up, something in the coolness of the air told Hazel that she was alone. The sun was up but hadn't yet warmed the wood. She sat up and leaned against the wall facing the door, half-expecting Theda to come bursting in with a new plan that would resolve everything.
But that wouldn't matter now.

What mattered was whether Minnie would take her back. *Because she'll know.* Know that Hazel and Theda had made love—joyously, holding nothing back. Know that Hazel had betrayed Minnie, if only for a night.

"I'll just tell her straight out," Hazel said aloud. "Maybe it won't be so bad."

But she had no idea if that was true. Nor could she predict what awaited her back on Oak Island. All she knew was that she had to get there as soon as possible, see what was left of her life now that Theda was gone.

And she was really gone this time. Nothing of her remained except the faintest thread of perfume, which persisted just under that of rotting leaves and wood smoke.

Hazel got up and looked around. How would she get back to the island? Theda had probably left Faunce Ridge or at least gone somewhere else for the day so as not to see Hazel. Sadie and François had a car, but Hazel had no idea if they'd waited for her. How could they know whether she'd return to Baudette with them or stay with Theda? She herself hadn't known a day ago.

Don't panic, she told herself. *There has to be a way.* There was always a way.

Marie could hitch up Butter and take Hazel into Williams. From there, she'd catch a ride—maybe with the mailman—to the nearest mainland resort where she could find a boat to take her across the lake.

She wished she could send Minnie a telegram, but maybe it was better this way. She'd show up at the dock like just another fisherman.

And if Minnie wasn't there, Hazel would go find her, wherever she was.

Acknowledgements

I owe the idea for *Muskeg* to an attendee at a St. Cloud reading of *Hand Me Down My Walking Cane* who suggested I write a sequel showcasing the first book's secondary characters: Hazel, Minnie and Little Roy. As *Muskeg* took shape, Sadie, François, Rose and Emil from *Hand Me Down My Walking Cane* joined them, along with new characters Theda, Marie, Teddy and Albert.

I developed Muskeg in Peter Geye's yearlong Novel Writing Class, 2018-2019, at the Loft Literary Center in Minneapolis. Many thanks to my classmates: Delma Bartelme, Barbara Butts-Williams, Brendan Fortune, Bree Kaiser-Powers, Linda Krug, Laska Nygaard, Bonnie Oldre, Vijay Pothapragada, Susan Sink, Jason Weidmann and Monica Wiant, as well as to teacher and coach extraordinaire Peter Geye. The novel writing group (now including Margaret Hartman and Daniele Longo) which grew out of that class has been key to my revisions.

My wonderful longtime writing group—Patricia Cumbie, Carol Dines, Alison Morse, Marcia Peck and Julia Klatt Singer—has sustained me for nearly three decades. Without their close reading, solidarity and friendship, none of my writing, including Muskeg, would be possible.

I became a fiction writer in the Hamline MFA program with the help of Judith Katz and Sheila O'Connor, who immersed me in the world of multiple point of view.

My brother, John Hagen, and my Baudette friends, Dave and Mary Marhula, did invaluable fact reads of the manuscript.

Thank you to John and LuAnn Hagen for the map of the Lake of the Woods borderland.

Ella Carlsson and Kelly Grady of Red Mood Marketing, building on Håkan Carlsson's stunning bog photographs and their own sizzling creativity, have brought *Muskeg* to visual and social media life and to the world. I am forever grateful. A special thanks to Ella for our long friendship and our years of biking, hiking and swimming adventures.

A huge thanks to Ian Leask, Calumet editor and friend, who has encouraged me through the long process of bringing *Muskeg* to fruition and talked me off the ledge many a time. And to his Calumet partner, Gary Lindberg, calm, kind voice of reason.

A shoutout to Carol Nash and the late, much-missed Norma Helsper, dear friends and swimming companions, who listened to early chapters and wanted more. Also to the San Miguel Poetry Week collective, all of whom have improved my writing over the years, especially Diana Anhalt, *amiga de tantos años,* who has read most of what I've written since the 1970s.

Finally, to LeRoy Sorenson, husband, lover, friend and *cómplice,* for unconditional support and spirited discussions about what my characters would and wouldn't do.

Author's Note: Norris Camp, located in what is now the Beltrami Island Forest, was built by the Civilian Conservations Corps (CCC) in 1935. Since then, it has served as headquarters for the Red Lake Wildlife Management Area. Beginning in 1936, the Resettlement Administration (RA) replaced the CCC in Norris Camp. Tasked with the relocation of farmers on poor land, many of whom owed back taxes to the federal government, they also performed some of the same work as the CCC: they planted trees, improved roads and built dams, recreation areas and lookout towers. Because my first novel, *Hand Me Down My Walking Cane*, dealt extensively with the RA, I decided to take the fictional liberty in *Muskeg* of keeping the CCC workers at Norris Camp in 1937 in order to showcase another Great Depression institution created by President Franklin Roosevelt's New Deal. I thank the Minnesota Department of Natural Resources, the Living New Deal, the Red Lake Wildlife Management Area and the invaluable Lake of the Woods County History (Lake of the Woods Historical Society, 1997) for the history of Norris Camp and the CCC.

About the Author

Carla Hagen's debut novel, *Hand Me Down My Walking Cane,* won the 2012 Midwest Independent Publishers Awards for literary fiction and historical fiction. Her work has appeared in anthologies such as *Voices for the Land* and *When Last on the Mountain,* as well as in journals like *Talking Stick, Saint Paul Almanac, Border Senses* and *Sing, Heavenly Muse!* She received a BA in Spanish and French at St. Cloud State University, did graduate work in Latin American Literature and Folklore at the University of Texas (UT) at Austin; and in Spanish Language and Linguistics at the National Autonomous University of Mexico (UNAM). She received a JD at the University of Minnesota, 1986, and an MFA in Writing at Hamline University, Saint Paul, 2002. She was chosen as a fiction participant in the 1999-2000 Loft Mentor Series.

In 1979-1980, funded by a Youthgrant from the National Endowment for the Humanities, she recorded oral histories and topical ballads of migrant workers in the Rio Grande Valley. She has taught English as a Second Language in Mexico; worked at Migrants in Action, St. Paul; taught Spanish at UT Austin; danced with Cross/Culture Dance Troupe, Austin, Texas; and investigated discrimination complaints for the Minnesota Human Rights Department. From 1987-1994, she worked as an Assistant Hennepin County Public Defender in Minneapolis, then as an Assistant Hennepin County Attorney from 1994-2018. She has co-hosted a weekly Latin music show with Eve MacLeish on KFAI 90.3 FM in Minneapolis from 1982-1990 and from 2006-present. The Minnesota-Canadian border, where she grew up, and Mexico, where she came of age, inform much of her work. When not writing, she swims, bicycles, hikes, travels and studies French, Arabic, Portuguese, Norwegian and Catalan. She lives in Saint Paul, Minnesota with her husband and is working on the third novel in her Minnesota-Canadian border trilogy.

Made in the USA
Middletown, DE
06 September 2022